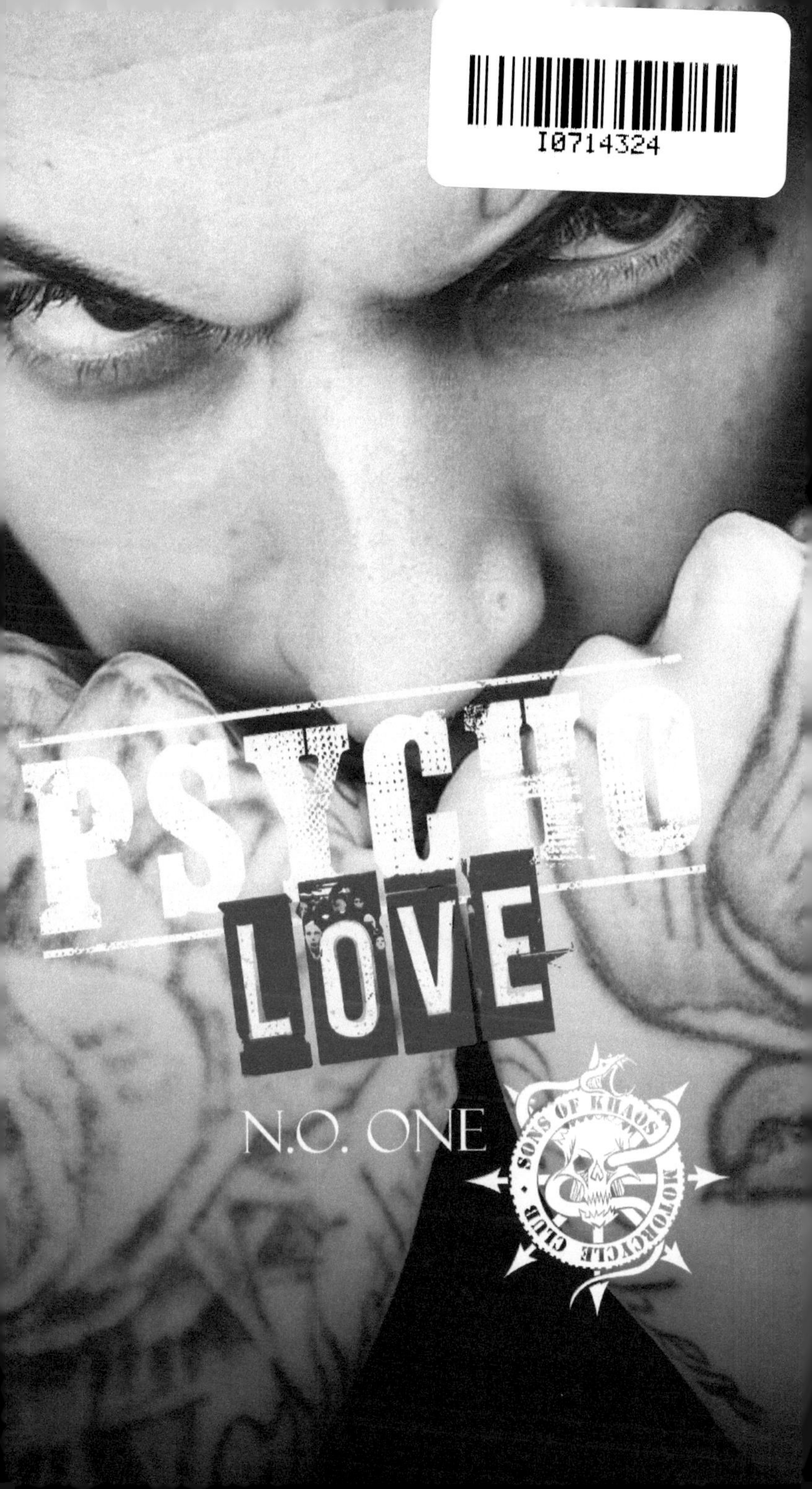
PSYCHO
LOVE
N.O. ONE
SONS OF KHAOS
MOTORCYCLE CLUB

PSYCHO LOVE

ISBN-13: 978-1-917471-13-8

DEDICATION

To you...

The sexy and brave

Courageous and strong and resilient.

The broken and glued back together whose cracks are

proof of survival.

The proud and fierce and outspoken.

The shy and acutely keen

We see you.

Warning / Foreword

We love that you've picked up our books! But please, take the warning here seriously if you in any way shape or form have triggers of any kind. This trilogy deals with a variety of subjects, sexual assault, lots of violence, death, characters you may not agree with...

We try to deal with some of the sensitive subjects in a way that isn't completely on page, but we can't guarantee that they won't affect you in some way if they are triggers for you.

If by any chance you have a specific thing you need to know about, feel free to drop us a message on social media, email us, or visit our website—details for these at the end of the book.

If you're the person who likes to check the number of times certain words appear in a book before you read it, here's a helpful word count:

Fuck - 759 (91 more than book 1! Oops...)

Dick - 42

Cock - 64

Cunt - 19 (Sorry, we'll do better next time)

Pussy - 36

For those still with us... ;)

The characters in this series will do what they need to do to get to their end goals. Please don't go into this trilogy thinking that these characters are morally gray because, at times, they are downright abysmal.

Remember, this is fiction!

So, as usual, strap in and strap on.

The main male character can be seen first off *8 years ago* in The Escort Series, but we have made sure there are few spoilers so this trilogy can be read without having to read anything else first.

Lastly, we hope you enjoy Aleko!

GLOSSARY

Sons Of Khaos

President/Prez: Griffin Michaels

Vice President/VP: Hoops (Leo Clarke)

Sergeant At Arms/Sgt at Arms: Shade (Slate Carter)

Road Captain: Crow (Lucas Minecast)

Secretary: Sledge (Rainer West)

Treasurer: Bear (Brock Levine)

Enforcer: Psycho (Aleko Kastellanos)

Members: Grinder (Diego Russet)

Boner (Felix Gray)

Axle (Rafael Rodriguez)

Diablo (Holden Diaz)

Prospects:

Python (Flint McKenna) – Deceased

Bash (Sebastian Flores)

Kincaid Ford

Jonesy (Kellan Jones)

Toxic Rebels

President: Isaac/Zac Moore

Vice President: Jake Wilson

Sergeant At Arms: Cameron Matthews

Road Captain: Booker (Benjamin Stripley)

Secretary: Jah-jah (Elijah Mountbatten)

Treasurer: Goblin (Graham Whitley)

Enforcer: Brick Earhart

SUMMARY

A quick refresh on Psycho Hate, book 1 of the Psycho Trilogy

- Psycho fucks Mackenzie in the back of a truck on her 21st birthday at a street race.

- Turns out Mackenzie is the sister of the Toxic Rebels VP (The rival MC).

- Psycho doesn't care about rivalry, he wants her. So he goes after her.

- Mackenzie has drama with her brother and her mother—who is currently in a psychiatric hospital.

- Both clubs are vying for the top spot in the street races, one that comes with a big cash prize—Cain from Toxic Rebels and Aleko from Sons of Khaos are the two main contenders.

- Rocks off is the strip club owned by Sons of Khaos where Mackenzie works very briefly.

- Trauma happens.

- Aleko is amazing.

- Don't forget about Ninja, our cute little resident rodent.

- Oh, and Bear, Grinder... all the brothers!

- Cliffy ending where some of y'all are still hating on us.

- Book 2 begins minutes after the ending of Psycho Hate - Book 1.

- There, you're all caught up. Now, as we like to say...

Strap in and strap on.
Enjoy the ride ;)

CHAPTER ONE
ALEKO

"Sir, you can't go in there!" Some five-foot-nothing little woman practically jumps over her desk to keep me from seeing my girl, but Bear catches her in flight and sits her back down with a gentle pat on her head.

"The fuck I can't." I'm barreling through the hospital, looking at the signs that point to the morgue when a security guard who looks like he's got a bigger addiction to donuts than the gym does a decent job of getting in my way.

"Personnel only." His voice is deep and would be scary as fuck if I weren't pumped full of adrenaline and grief.

"I don't give a shit if it's for the fucking president of this motherfucking country. Get out of my fucking way." The guy, bless his soul, barely has time to reach for me before I've punched him in the throat then elbowed him in the gut. The bigger they are and all that shit.

"Stay down!" I hear Bear roar just as I push through the double doors, instantly attacked by the unmistakable and overpowering scent of disinfectant, as if it could remotely mask the smell of death.

It really fucking cannot.

My head is turning left then right, looking down the perpendicular hallways as I pass them, following what feels like a fucking neon sign toward the one place I never thought I'd have to go... not for her.

My body is so fucking amped up that I'm able to ignore that piercing stab of pain in my chest, the one that has been repeatedly going at me since Mackenzie laid in my arms, motionless. Lifeless. Long enough to punch my brother in the face for not keeping his promise. Deep inside, I knew it wasn't his fault. Mac is too stubborn for her own good.

Was.

She *was* stubborn. Oh, fuck. It's like being stabbed in the chest over and over again.

"Fuuuuuck!" My cry echoes throughout the corridor, two, then three orderlies coming at us but, at this point, Bear is just playing football, tackling them away from me so I can get to my destination.

The last door on the right.

It's just feet away, but my body freezes like I've hit an invisible titanium wall. I can't move. I can't even fucking breathe at this point. It's like my brain knows that going in there will make it all real. If I walk into that cold chamber of death and she's there, I won't be able to pretend this is all a fucking nightmare. I won't be able to pretend that I'll eventually wake up and hug her warm body to mine.

"Come on, man. They're going to send more line-backer-sized motherfuckers in here, and I may be big, but I ain't that big, brother."

Swiveling my head to the side, I look at Bear, taking in his strong, reliable features. Those big brown eyes have so much soul in them, it's like he communicates his emotions without having to speak, and in that millisecond I realize he's the only reason I'm not losing my fucking mind.

Well, that's debatable.

At this point, all I want is my Cherry Pie back in my arms again, I don't care how it happens.

"Shit's gonna hit the fan if she's in there."

Slowly, Bear's head motions up and down, eyes fixed on the small windows at the top of the double doors. "Yeah. But you know, my mama used to say: These are the moments that define a man."

I frown. That sounds way too fucking airy for his mom.

"Really? I thought she was more down to earth than that."

"Nah, man. She'd tell me to grow a spine and get shit done." Ah, that's more like it.

"Grow a spine and get shit done," I repeat like a mantra until my right foot is able to cross the invisible barrier keeping me from Mackenzie.

"Yeah, brother. Let's grow a spine, then we can get shit done with a multitude of explosives." I grin but my heart is cracking from the base to the very top where my aorta pumps the blood to my entire fucking body.

"Fuck." We both burst through the doors and are greeted by a tall, lanky dude wearing a white coat and blue latex gloves.

It's impossible to tell if the sudden noise of us entering or the fact that two pissed off big dudes are suddenly at the entrance of his morgue is the reason for him jumping high enough to slam dunk a basketball. But he does, and the shock on his face would be fucking hilarious if I weren't completely anchored to the floor with my lungs unable to catch a breath.

"Shit." I almost miss Bear's curse but he's so close to me that it permeates through my haze of disbelief.

Lying there, naked save for a white sheet covering her from chest to upper thighs, is Mackenzie.

My Mackenzie.

Her skin tone is all wrong, the blue tint like a placid lake in the winter cold. Her normally blonde hair is slicked back, darker, like she's just stepped out of her shower and is sleeping off a twelve hour shift. It's all wrong. All of it. Every fucking color on her is a fucking lie.

Have her features ever been so peaceful and relaxed? Has her body ever been so... quiet?

My head is shaking no, like my mind and my heart are at war trying to convince the other of what is happening on that cold, metal table. It's all wrong. All fucking wrong. She should be lying on a big-ass bed with me covering her body and fucking her until her throat is sore from calling my name.

We should be laughing and planning our day.

We should be teaching new tricks to Ninja while I watch her giggle every time his nose tickles her skin.

We should be happy, living life the way fate had intended.

Not this.

Not *this*.

It's all fucking *wrong*.

"Dude, I don't know what you were about to do but I suggest you move away." My eyes dart up to see the guy standing by Mackenzie is holding a scalpel.

A wave of heat runs like wildfire through my veins and everything I see has a red hue at the edges, quickly filling in to the middle.

"What's your name, man?" Bear is talking, one hand on my shoulder holding me back as I try to make my way to this motherfucker who thinks he can cut into my girl.

"S-s-s-tev-v-en…"

"Well, Steven, I think you should step away before…" Bear pauses as I lean in like an animal smelling fresh blood. "Someone kills you."

"I-I-I c-c-can't. You… you shouldn't be here." Bear is full on holding me back, his big-ass arms wrapped around my chest so I don't fucking kill this guy with a goddamn knife so close to my girl. "Security will be here soon, you s-sh-sh-ould leave." Dude has balls. Not for long 'cause I'm about to rip them off, but he's got them.

"Aleko." I turn around so fucking fast at the sound of my name that I almost dislocate every joint in my body. "You can't touch him, man. You need to go." I recognize the face and I recognize the voice but my mind is refusing to add all the puzzle pieces together.

Standing there is Spencer, Mackenzie's best friend, red-rimmed eyes telling me more than I really want to know. It's then that I notice his uniform.

"You were working tonight?" I ask, like it's even relevant right now. Except, my brain can only handle information that won't send me into a fucking tailspin.

"Yes. I picked up an extra shift."

I nod like I give a fuck.

Suddenly, my need to pummel the guy who, thankfully, put the fucking scalpel down, is gone because the only thing that matters is her.

Shaking Bear off, I free myself from his hold and in three steps I'm lying across the love of my life. There's no movement, no chuckle, no rise and fall of her chest. There's nothing. No reaction except for the last shard of my heart shattering into a million pieces.

"She's not as cold as she looks." I don't know why I say this but it feels like someone should know that. That maybe *I* should know that.

"Come on, man, security is going to be here and you'll end up in jail." Bear pulls me off and in a haze of disbelief and pure, unhindered agony, I let him.

"I'll get in touch," is the last thing I hear from Spencer before we walk out of the morgue.

Without her.

Without the one person I love more than anyone or anything.

The ride back to the compound is a blur. Bear mentioned something about Vanessa calling, saying she had Ninja with her and would take care of him until I got back. It's a good thing, too, because in my state I'm not sure I'd have the mental capacity to take care of anything… least of all myself.

It's the middle of the night when we finally park the bikes in our garages, I don't bother with my ritual of wiping down Philia, it doesn't fucking matter at this point. Nothing does. No, that's not true. One thing does matter but that's going to have to wait… for now.

"Prez called an emergency meeting…" He looks at his phone then back up to me as I put my helmet on the gas tank. "In fifteen minutes." I nod before making the mistake of looking up at my brother.

"I'm gonna go take a piss, wash my hands and face. I'll be right there." We lock eyes and I'm not sure what he sees in mine but his worry is swimming in his dark irises. "Christ, I'm fine, Bear. It's not like I'm going to off myself or some shit."

I don't know what I was expecting but the clenching of his jaw is not it. Does he seriously think I'd just take a gun to my head and what? Leave Mackenzie's death unanswered? I ain't no fucking Romeo. If I meet my death, it'll be while avenging hers.

But he doesn't need to know that. Bear needs to believe that I'm fine, I'm dealing. Grieving, yes, because that's normal and I have to prove to him that I'm being reasonable.

"You sure?"

"Fuck off, Bear." I turn and walk away without giving him a backward glance. I've got fifteen minutes before he starts asking questions. Time to get moving.

While my best friend goes straight to the bar, I head to my room, veering last minute once I'm out of sight so I can jog down to the far end storage unit where our heavy artillery is locked up. Before leaving the garage, I grabbed a backpack big enough to stock up on everything I'll need for the next few hours.

My adrenaline is pumping so fast that I'm barely winded by the time I reach the storage unit, unlock it, and roll it open. There's no need to search for long; I know exactly where we hid the explosives.

Filling up my bag, I pull up my hoodie and step outside, closing up behind me and running back to where Vanessa keeps her truck. It's old enough that hotwiring it is as easy as most Khunts at the clubhouse.

The goal is to get as far as possible before anyone notices I'm gone because none of my brothers are idiots, especially not Bear. As soon as church begins and I'm not there, they'll be on their bikes and hot on my tail. Hopefully, by the time they catch up to me, the deed will be done. The rest I'll figure out later.

Once I'm on Highway 17, I push the old pickup to its limits, knowing Vanessa is going to rip me a new one if I break her baby down. I can't imagine why a piece of junk like this could have such a hold on her. It's fucking weird.

Switching off the lights once I reach the entrance of the Rebels' trailer park, I dig into my jacket pocket and pull out a sucker. The cherry flavor soothes my nerves, centers me for what I'm about to do. For her.

As I step out of the truck, I notice how quiet it is. Why aren't they out there avenging their VP's death? What the fuck is wrong with these people? Then again, they raped and beat the love of my life until only a carcass of her true self was left... then they killed her.

Karma is coming for you, assholes.

Keeping to the shadows, I trot along the side of the property until I reach the hole in the fence where I could go in and out of Mackenzie's trailer when she still lived here. At the sight of her plants, my teeth crunch down on the sucker, the memories almost bringing me to my knees, knowing all this was her way out; the poison to slowly kill them all without getting the blame for their deaths.

Fuck. I push my emotions to the side because I don't fucking have time to lose my shit. Instead, I crouch down and make my way to the center of the lot, making sure no one is around when I cross over to the trailer in the center—their clubhouse—and make quick work of placing the first explosives under the aluminum siding. Once that's over, I sprint to their Prez's trailer because that motherfucker doesn't deserve oxygen. He does, however, deserve to be blown to kingdom fucking come, and I will light a joint in celebration.

All three bombs are hooked up to my phone app, the one Python built for us a few months ago. The satisfaction I'll get watching their shitty little piece of the world blow up will be priceless.

With the last bomb in hand, I run to the entrance where a whole row of bikes are parked.

I'm taking the explosive out of my bag just as an entire cavalry of cop cars skids into the compound, headlights suddenly on as well as their lightbars dancing from one side to the other. I'm too stunned to move. Too confused as to why the fuck there are so many cops here. For me? Am I that predictable?

Probably.

"Freeze!"

I carefully place the explosive on the ground, the stick from the sucker bumping against my tongue ring as I rise to my full height and grin.

Here we go again.

CHAPTER TWO
ALEKO

Grief wears so many faces. When my parents were taken out by the Italian mafia, I was barely old enough to understand. My brother and his crew took care of me, taught me how to be ruthless, and I looked up to him more than I had our father. I wasn't naïve. I knew that, as Greek mafia, they did bad shit—*I* did bad shit—but my brother took it too far and I shot him. He deserved it. The grief came in small waves for the loss of my last blood relative, until I found the Sons of Khaos, until I discovered my love for speed was shared. Until I found a real place for myself. True brotherhood.

Then, one of my chosen brothers died. Python was a prospect, but that didn't make him any less one of us. The pain was new to me, and with nobody to blame, I know I wasn't the only one rattled by it. But I had Mackenzie, my Cherry Pie. Holding her all night in my arms was soothing in a way that can't be replicated.

Now, I've been holed up in a jail cell for two months, charged with intent to maliciously injure by use of explosives—I had planned on more than injuring the Rebel fuckers but that's irrelevant. What *is* relevant is that my Cherry is gone and I can only think of one thing worth living for.

Retribution.

I won't rest until every single Toxic Rebel is rotting in the ground, but I can't do fucking shit from where I am.

The cops showing up right at that moment had me questioning how they knew what I was planning, but it turns out I was just in the wrong place at the wrong time. They'd been tipped off anonymously with a shit load of evidence to finally put the Rebels behind bars.

A few days after my arrest, my arraignment was held, and even with the best lawyer in the world, the crap falling from the prosecution's mouth landed me here awaiting trial with a fucking ridiculous bail amount that I refused to let the club pay. Days have merged into weeks, and if it weren't for the visits I've had from my brothers, I'd be six-feet under with Mackenzie. Not that dying is the worst thing in the world; at least we'd be together. A life without her feels impossible. But Bear, especially, has kept me relatively sane. Prez was angry with me at first for trying to blow the Rebels up by myself; getting arrested and leaving the club without an Enforcer means others have had to step up, but he gets it. With everything he did to tie his old lady down, blowing shit up is like a walk in the park. At least, that's what I've heard.

The fact that he got his old lady, and mine is dead, is something he can never comprehend. As I held Mackenzie in my arms, lifeless and limp, whatever light I had inside me snuffed out. Darkness I've always known was there creeped in thicker and more somber with every foot, then yard, then mile the ambulance put between me and Mackenzie. But the final blow to my sanity came when I saw her lying frozen on the cold, hard, stainless steel table of the morgue.

I'm a broken man but, for once, I have a semi-plan. Kill every fucker who ever touched my Cherry Pie. If that takes me to the afterlife right along with her, then so be it.

The lock on my cell creaks, followed by the door swinging open before the guard, Roy, bangs on the metal.

"Lunch."

Once a day, we're allowed out of our cells for an hour—in shifts because there'd be a riot if we were all out at the same time. We get to eat lunch in a communal cafeteria. It's the only semblance of normal this place provides. They allow thirty minutes for yard time, where we literally have to walk in a giant circle. This is what they call exercise time, which I suppose I shouldn't scoff at since the same privileges aren't available at every jail.

Pushing up from my bed—if you can call it that—I walk out of my cell, glad to be free of the four walls surrounding me. Being who I am has benefits, one of which is being given a cell of my own.

Regardless of the friends the club has here, I'd kill a motherfucker without blinking if I had to share this tiny space.

Landon and Jackson catch up with me as we head toward the cafeteria, walking silently by my side. They've both been here for over a year awaiting their trials, which is lucky for me. As friends of the club, it means I have allies while I'm here. I don't know exactly what their connection is, and I haven't asked, but their presence is strangely comforting. In my broken world, they're a quiet reminder that my brothers are still with me.

We each wear matching dark green pants and shirts with a beige undershirt that itches like a motherfucker. The green sports the Rockford Beach County Jail logo, and the beige indicates which wing we're in.

Some kind of soup is served today, which tastes like watered down cabbage with a hint of onion, but I need sustenance if I'm going to survive long enough to draw Rebel blood. Hell, any blood would do right now. There are only so many exercises and movements a man can do alone in his cell to occupy his mind.

"Hey, Psycho, I heard Roy mention a new inmate was arriving today." Landon, the shorter but bulkier of the two, is the most talkative. Not that talkative is the worst thing in the world. "Heard this one's been on the run for a couple of months."

That piques my interest. Mostly, I communicate with a series of grunts and head movements because I'm consumed with a rage so deep that anything more than that feels next to impossible. These guys are loyal friends of the club, but I don't wanna get to know them. I have enough people to leave behind when I'm done here, I don't need to be adding more. However, the information Landon is giving right now causes my eyes to move quickly, glaring through my lashes at him and silently telling him to continue.

"I'll find out what dinner rotation he's on later. But I think it's one of the guys on that list of yours. Goob? Gabe? Something like that."

Yes, I have a list. One I've written out several times a day on scraps of paper before ripping them to shreds. Scratching their names down with a pencil, then destroying them afterward has become a bit of a habit.

I know exactly who Landon is talking about.

"Goblin." My voice is low, deep, my tone scratchy. The only time I really speak these days is when one of my brothers visits.

"That's the one!"

"We'll find out which section he's in a—"

Whatever Jackson is saying has turned to white noise as my gaze zones in on my target.

Goblin is already fucking here. Sitting in the corner of the cafeteria with a group of skin-heads. They're not particularly friends of my club—not at all, in fact. They're dirty fucking scum who deserve to be hung from the ceiling by their scrotums. Just like their new friend.

He's getting closer, or I'm getting closer to him, I guess, since he's still sitting down. I feel hands on my arms, attempting to get my attention, pull me back...? I don't know and I don't fucking care.

Goblin's arm is no longer in a cast from when I shattered his elbow with a baseball bat a few months ago, which just means it's going to hurt more when I break him all over again. There's even a fucking smile on his smug little fucking face as he talks, without a care in the world, to his new soon-to-be-dead friends.

Darkness invades my vision from the edges, shrouded in red as I move closer. I may as well be floating because nothing is registering. Nothing except my rage. My breaths are coming short and fast, the sounds of the cafeteria nothing but a buzz, and just as the stupid fucking prick notices me, I grab the back of his head and slam his face into his lunch bowl.

It cracks and smashes everywhere, luke-warm soup spilling all over the plastic table, and the sound that he makes as I lift his head and see a piece of the bowl sticking out of his cheek fills me with pure satisfaction. One of the skin-heads tries his luck, standing sharply and throwing a fist in my direction, but he's too fucking slow. Grabbing the first thing available, which happens to be a spoon, I block his punch and shove the spoon into his eye before returning my attention to Goblin.

"What the fu—"

My fingers are still gripping the greasy strands of his hair, and I yank it backward so he's looking up at me, stopping him mid-sentence.

"Dead man walking." It's all I can manage to say, my jaw is clenched tight, anger rolling through my body in waves.

With my free hand, I grip his wrist and smash his arm against my knee, grinning when he screams like a fucking banshee as the bone snaps, leaving his arm at a very wrong angle.

Sobs are the only thing leaving his mouth now as he tries to bring his arm into himself, but I bash it against the table a few more times before letting go. Forcefully, I yank his head up once more and throw him out of his chair.

His back meets the floor with a loud thud that makes me grin as I approach him, ready to stamp on this fucker's head and end him. Someone steps in front of me, trying and failing to block my path before I punch him and push him so he falls out of my way. Another body is in front of me, and another, hands held up in surrender, and I take a deep breath, allowing some form of clarity to focus on the wall of Jackson and Landon.

Did I mention they've stopped me from killing a few motherfuckers in this place already for simply looking at me funny?

They're right.

The red haze fades and I continue to take deep breaths to calm my trembling limbs. Adrenaline is coursing through my veins and I'm struggling to contain it, but if I ever want to get out of here, I should definitely not kill people. There are only so many officers around here that are willing to be paid off for turning a blind eye. Luckily for me, they happen to be on duty today.

"You back with us?" Jackson is first to speak, the rest of the cafeteria so silent that Goblin's blood can be heard dripping onto the cold tiles beneath us.

One edge of my mouth involuntarily creeps upward into a half grin as I narrow my eyes and nod once. Before I walk away, I hold up a finger, letting Jackson and Landon know I just need a second, I'm good. Then I slowly step to the side and glare down at Goblin, clutching his arm to his chest as blood falls down his face where the piece of bowl still protrudes.

"You won't die today. Lucky fucker. But then again, maybe you will. Who knows? Oh wait... I do." I punctuate my sentence with a sharp kick to his ribs before turning and walking away.

There are still fifteen minutes left, but I'm done here. If I can't kill the fuckhead, I sure as shit can't be in the same room as him.

The officers are conveniently not here right now, and everyone else quickly averts their eyes when I walk past, pretending their lunch is the best thing since fucking was discovered.

A few feet from my cell, Shane—another officer here at the county jail—heads in my direction.

"Today's visitor is here, room three." Shane's on our payroll, but he doesn't like it, and I have to follow procedures and be led to the room instead of being able to make my own way there.

"Forty-five minutes." He opens the door to let me in, closing and locking it behind me.

"Is that blood on your knuckles? Again?" Bear stands, all six-foot-six of his bulking frame, landing his deep brown eyes on me in amusement.

"It is." I nod, gripping Bear's wrist as he grips mine, pulling each other in for a back tap. Seeing one of my brothers brings a lightness to the dark that consumes me, even if only briefly. "Goblin's here."

"Fuck yeah." We both take a seat on opposite sides of the clinically white table in the most uncomfortable plastic seats known to mankind. "Celia called Prez this morning when they arrested him for something to do with a robbery. They'll file the same charges against him as the others they arrested at their compound that night, so he's fucked."

I can't help the low laugh that escapes. Celia Shipman is the Deputy of the Rockford Sheriff's Department, and our agreement with her has been a godsend. She keeps us informed on things we need to know, and we do what we can to keep our town safe from people who think they're worse than us.

"You could say that, yeah." The image of Goblin lying on the cold floor of the cafeteria, whimpering like a fucking dog, blood pouring from his face... it sends a pleasurable shudder up my spine.

"You didn't kill him, did you? How much clean up do we gotta do here?"

His concern is warming in the strangest of ways. I don't want to feel good, not at all. It's like I'm cheating. How am I allowed to feel things when my Cherry Pie can't? There hasn't even been a funeral. Prez said that her best friend Spencer had been seen at the churchyard with a large vase about a week after the night she...

I missed Python's funeral too...

Shaking myself free of the spiral I will no doubt continue to travel down when I'm alone in my cell, I shrug.

"Nah. Didn't kill him. Just fucked him up a bit." I know Bear can see my internal struggle. You don't become best friends with killers unless you can really know or trust them, and he knows me almost better than myself. It's like he sees something in me that I just can't anymore.

Any hope I ever had of a good life died right alongside Mackenzie.

I zone in on the package in the center of the table, at my sucker stash that's replenished with every visit—thank fuck because I need the taste, the smell, to center myself and stay on task. They're only allowed if I have the papery sticks that go soggy if I suck on them for too long and it pisses me off, but they're better than none at all. Then another wave of grief hits me, because Mackenzie will never again have the pleasure of anything, let alone a sucker.

"Okay, brother, drop the shit act. You're no good at keeping things from me and you know it." His tone is firm and he relaxes back into his chair, his thumbs casually slipping into the pockets of his jeans.

"I'm good, man. Nothing to worry about." I hold my hands out, palms up, before cracking my knuckles and linking my fingers behind my head, mirroring his laid-back posture. Inside, I'm screaming, trembling for some kind of justice, for time to be turned back, for one more second of pure happiness. All things that will never come.

But justice can't be had because we don't know which motherfucker shot the gun that killed her. And everything else is impossible.

"So, what's new? That new parts dealer working out?" Outside, I'm the picture of calm and collected.

"Yeah, Jed's stuff has been good so far. But fuck that shit. Look, the lawyer said she should have you out in a few days. They're dropping all charges. I don't know the details, but she'll probably come and see you first. All you've gotta do is keep your shit together for a while longer. Okay?"

I'm getting out.

Finally.

Someone's going to die.

The real world outside of here feels like something from a TV show, someone else's life, and like a tornado, pain twists through me at the thought of the life I could have had. The life that was ripped away from me.

I'm nodding in response, words not forming as I try to contain the wave of grief.

"Let it out, brother. Let it out. Argh!" He yells out, then, as though that wasn't the weirdest thing he's ever done, he gestures for me to do the same. "Your turn."

"Fuck off, man." I shake my head, guilt now trying to overpower the grief, because I'm being and have been a shitty friend and a shitty brother to my club.

"Why?! ARGH!" he yells out again, and with each shout, he appears lighter. He gestures again for me to have a turn.

So I do. I scream, I yell until I can barely breathe. Fuck, that actually feels good. And hello again, grief. Why is feeling good so fucking painful? I yell again, and it's louder this time, but seeped in anger. I stand, pick up the chair, and throw it across the room.

The door clicks open as the chair smashes against the wall and Shane enters, concern written all over his face.

"Fuck off." Bear and I shout out at the same time, because I do not need that cunt in here witnessing this. He holds a hand up and backs out, scowling as he slams the door closed again.

"Feel better?" Bear's beside me now, an arm across my shoulders.

"No, I feel like fucking shit."

He chuckles. "Yeah, well, shit's better than nothing, brother."

"You sure about that?" It's a serious question because I'm not positive that he's right.

"Listen, don't kill or maim anyone in the next few days and you'll be sailing free faster than Greased Lightning. Ninja misses you."

Another pang of guilt hits me. My beautiful boy has been sleeping in our suite at the compound, on my pillow.

"You mean *you* miss me, fucker."

Bear squeezes my shoulder in a kind of side-hug before walking over to the chair I threw and picking it up, placing it back beside the table.

"Yeah, I kinda do, brother. We all do."

Shane gave me a visitor request to approve for some woman I'm assuming is on Veronica Luna's team—our club lawyer—as soon as Bear left from his visit three days ago. Scarlett Green is hopefully going to be the lady that tells me I can walk the fuck out of this hellhole.

Bear gave me a lot to think about. He always fucking does, the smug shit. I probably would've taken out every motherfucker in this place given half a chance if it wasn't for the two visits a week from Bear or one of the others.

This is it though.

I follow Shane through to the visiting rooms, door number thirteen today. If I believed in superstition I'd say it was a bad omen.

He opens the door, closing and locking it behind me once I'm inside.

Some woman, all decked out in a gray suit and black heels, sits at the same white table where Bear tried to talk me down from the ledge. Her profile is hidden by a long, thick curtain of red hair as she scribbles something onto a notebook.

With a tone that clearly says, get on with it, because at this point I don't give a shit about anything, I ask, "You Veronica's messenger?"

My body reacts before my brain can even register what the fuck I'm seeing as the woman's face comes into view. Every muscle in my body freezes, even my lungs. I can't move. I can't breathe. I can't... understand.

Words spill from my mouth in a barely audible whisper but I'm not sure how I was even able to form them since my mind is a complete and total blank.

"What the actual fuck?"

CHAPTER THREE

ALEKO

"H i."

I shake my head like maybe I can get rid of this disturbing hallucination that feels as if an icepick has pierced straight through my heart. Did she just say… "Hi" to me?

"What the fuck?" I repeat my words except, this time, they're stronger, edgier, as I take a step back from what can only be proof that I'm losing my fucking mind.

"You need to calm down or else they're going to end the visit," she whisper-yells.

Is she fucking serious right now? She's scolding me?

Burying my hands in my overgrown hair, I pull on the roots, only two seconds away from ripping every strand from my scalp.

"I need to calm down, she says." I freeze and stare at her, wondering if I'm sleeping. Dreaming? Am I? Dreaming, that is. If so, why am I wasting precious time questioning it all?

"They took your tongue piercing." Shaking my head at the randomness of it all, I scoff at her words.

"Yeah, well, that's what happens when you're arrested." I fucking hate it, too. The piercing was the first thing I got done when I patched in so I've had this one for almost nine years. It's weird and disturbing not having it and when I get out, I'll have to get it pierced again since I can feel it closing up. But that's completely off topic and she fucking knows it.

With only two steps, I'm facing her again, my palms pressed against the table separating us. Closing my eyes, I inhale long and deep until the sweet, sweet scent of my babydoll invades every single molecule in my body. Cherries. My addiction, my salvation. My pain and my destruction. She's all of these things. Where only a few months ago, smelling the comfort of cherries was a balm to my soul, today, it also brings with it the memories of losing her.

"Aleko, please. Sit down." I raise a brow at the bossy edge to her voice and I swear to fuck I'm about to have a Groundhog's Day in this very visiting room with the same fucking chair flying at the same fucking wall.

"How is this possible?" I shake my head again because it is not fucking possible. "You died in my arms. You weren't breathing. You were cold and... and dead at the morgue. I fucking saw you there."

"Yeah, that wasn't supposed to happen." Narrowing my eyes at her mumbled words, I feel like I'm in some poorly written television thriller where the main character shows up completely fucking fine after being dead for months.

This is my life. This isn't some cookie cutter daytime soap opera. So I say the only thing that makes any fucking sense.

"What the actual fuck, Mackenzie?" My arms are wide open, my chest heaving and my brain on the verge of shutting down.

Blue eyes the same shade as the rolling waves on the Carolina shores dart from me to the door and back to me, pleading. She's right, if I don't calm down, Shane will come in here and put an end to this visit, and fucking hell, I can't let that happen.

Dropping my arms back down my side, I take a seat across from the love of my life. The love of my life who's supposed to be dead. Who has presumably been dead for over two months now. How am I supposed to make sense of this?

Reaching out to place her palm on the back of my hand, I jump from my seat at the spark that runs through my entire body.

Holy shit, what the fuck?

"Sorry." Pressing her ruby red lips together, she looks up through her lashes, the corners of her mouth pulling up just enough to make my blood boil.

I don't know if I should throttle her or kiss the fucking breath out of her.

"Sorry? For what, exactly, Mackenzie? What exactly are you sorry for? Because I've been slowly dying without you. I've been planning a lot of shit before putting a bullet in my own brain so I don't have to live without you. Are you sorry about that? Or is it the fact that you were able to walk away without a fucking ounce of regret? No, that can't be it." My fingers are tapping against the plastic table, faster and faster, in rhythm with the cadence of my words. "You're here, so maybe it wasn't all that easy."

"This isn't the place to talk about this, Aleko, but I heard about what happened with Gobli—"

"Fuck no. You don't say his name. His scum name does not come out of your mouth." My vision is going back to red at the thought of any of those fuckers who made this happen.

"All I'm saying is that you need to keep your head down. Don't do anything stupid that'll keep you in there for the rest of your life. Can you do that?" Holy shit, her backbone just stiffened the way it does when she's being the boss of me.

Two months ago, it would have made my dick instantly hard, but right now? I'm too confused to understand any of what's going on.

One thing I do understand is that this better not be a drive-by visit.

"Why are you here?" What I really want to know is... are you staying?

"To warn you. To..." The confidence dripping from her very pores fades away slightly as she slices her gaze to the side, unsure of herself, before hitting me with her blues again.

Fuck me, I missed her to the point of agony.

"To what?" My fingers are clutching the edge of the table as if her next words will have one of two effects. Either I snap the plastic in two or melt at her feet.

"To give you a reason to survive this."

It's then I do snap a piece of the cheap, plastic table with my death grip because how fucking dare she?

"I did have a fucking reason." Spitting out my words through clenched teeth, it hits me that I've never spoken to her in this tone. In all of our time together, she's never seen the real psycho in me, at least not directed at her. Then again, it was never warranted... until now. "A whole fucking lot of them, to be honest. Justice and retaliation just to name two."

"And now you have me."

I blink at her words, the red veil of anger dissipating just enough for me to realize that my Cherry Pie is sitting right here with me. Just inches from me, barely an arm's length away.

Then I remember what she is capable of doing and now it's my turn to steel my spine.

"I'm getting out soon. Go to the club and wait for me there." Looking over my shoulder at the door, I can see the clock on the wall. We've barely got five minutes left.

"I can't do that. No one knows I'm... here." The fear in her eyes is palpable, and I get it, but also, I don't. I don't fucking understand why she's doing all this.

"What do you want from me, Mackenzie? What am I supposed to do with all this?" Oh fuck, is she going to leave me again? Disappear from my life? I suppose knowing she's alive somewhere is at least better than thinking she's dead.

"This isn't the place but I'll explain everything next time we meet." Her eyes dart over my shoulder, no doubt checking the clock.

"When the fuck is that going to be, huh?" I won't survive losing her a second time.

"Soon." Her hand reaches out again and this time I don't jump or feel electricity. No, this time, I feel warmth and life and a love so fucking strong it can destroy buildings and sever the heads of our enemies.

Then she's up, walking away in heels so fucking high I'm surprised she isn't falling all over herself as she reaches the exit door and walks out without a backward glance.

I just sit there, dumbfounded, wondering if this was all a dream.

Or a nightmare.

Or some kind of mental breakdown.

It doesn't take Shane very long to escort me back to my cell. The heavy door with a long rectangular window and a slit for the food tray slides open, revealing the mind numbing quiet of my temporary home. Where most of the other inmates have to walk around with handcuffs to and from the visiting room, I'm offered special privileges for a hefty price.

"Bet you wish you could have conjugal visits, huh? That tight little ass must be something sweet." I'm about to redecorate my cell with Shane's brain matter when a sweet little voice echoes in my mind.

"To give you a reason to survive this."

I stop moving, my jaw clenched so tight the pain travels down my neck to every muscle in my chest.

This motherfucker is going on my list for disrespecting my woman.

The sound of the metal door slamming shut brings me back to my reality. In the span of forty-five fucking minutes, everything I thought I knew about my world has been shattered into a million tiny pieces of who I used to be.

Without a single fuck flying anywhere near me, I turn on my heel, rear my arm back, and punch the concrete wall once, twice... five times.

What. *Punch.* The. *Punch.* Fuck. *Punch.* Just. *Punch.* Happened. *Punch.*

The cell door slams open again, and when I look up all I see is Shane's mouth hanging open as he reaches for me. My first instinct is to paint his face with my blood by getting my knuckles acquainted with his nose but that same voice stops me.

"To give you a reason to survive this."

"Jesus Christ, Kastellanos. You tryin' to piss me off, today?" This asshole has no idea how close he is to meeting his maker. "Come on, you need to get to the infirmary 'cause we ain't allowed to have you bleeding like that."

I look down, and yup. My knuckles are dripping with blood. Silver lining to this mind-blowing day is less time in a cell.

We head to the nurse's station in silence as we pass door after door of prisoners awaiting their trials or doing short time for a lesser crime. Shane waits with me for the doc to come back as I lie down on the narrow examiner's bed covered in a strip of paper for hygiene.

Closing my eyes, I think back to how my world was completely turned on its axis. Again. A-fucking-gain. Two hours ago, I was planning the murder of every mother-fucker who hurt Mackenzie and set her on the path to death. Two hours ago, I was ready to die so I could be with her, in death the way we were in life.

Except, I'd be alone in death, wouldn't I? Because she's not fucking dead. Every thought of her makes my blood pressure rise and rise until I'm breathing hard again and ready for round two with my cell room wall.

"Sorry about the wait, had a little complication next door. Inmate didn't see my foot and tripped. Poor guy fell on his already broken arm. Oops."

Funny, dude doesn't sound sorry at all.

I crack open an eye, turning my head to the side to look at the doc. I'm met with familiar green or light brown eyes. I think there's a name for that color but I can't be fucked to concentrate on the appropriate vocabulary. My brows slant down and my eyes narrow at what can only be the second weirdest shit to happen to me today. Obviously, Mackenzie in the visitation room tops that list like an overachiever.

Spencer gives a subtle shake of his head, silently telling me to shut the fuck up.

"I've got it under control here, Officer." Shane nods at Spencer, who's not even pretending not to scan his body from bottom to top and back down again. It's only when he's gone that Spencer blows out a breath. "He'd be pretty if he didn't look like a hateful sack of shit." I want to grin at his jab but I remember that I'm pissed off.

"What the fuck is going on, Spence? I just saw a ghost and now you're here? I don't believe in coincidences—at least not ones this fucking obvious." I grit my teeth as he pours sterile water over my open wounds then inspects my knuckles like they hold the location of hidden pirate gold.

"I've been here for about two weeks, volunteered at Mac's request so—" Everything goes flying as I sit up, my healthy hand fisting the fabric of his scrubs.

"You've known this whole time?" My voice is so low it almost scares me and I'm the one fucking talking. Spencer though? He just places a thumb and forefinger on my wrist and pulls it away like it's covered in shit.

"First of all, I do not need prison germs on my clean clothes." I scoff, dude is brave. Or stupid. I mean, to be fair, I wouldn't hurt a hair on his head... again. Last time I did, I had to grovel like a weak fucker to get Cherry's forgiveness. "Second, she's my best friend, which trumps our barely-there acquaintance." Narrowing my eyes, I start to speak, but he just shushes me. Goddammit. "As I was saying... she asked me to keep an eye on you and what you did to Goblin was stupid and dangerous."

"Pfft, bastard got off easy if you ask me." My anger deflates as Spencer picks up all the shit I made him drop. I'd apologize, but fuck that.

Spencer doesn't react right away, just looks at me, almost dissecting me.

"I don't give a fuck about that rapist piece of shit. *Your* actions were careless. I care about Mac and she cares about you. Ergo…" Without finishing his phrase he returns to his bandaging, making sure I'm not bleeding through it. "Give me your other hand."

"All right, so you were here. What? You felt sorry for me and called her?" I'm staring at his face, scrutinizing his every tic and feature.

"Yeah, figured you were going to get yourself life in prison for murder. Let's just say, men like you are better controlled when you've got something to lose." He shrugs like he didn't just reduce me to some kind of Neanderthal. Okay, fine, he's not wrong.

"I can't believe she's alive." I freeze and he notices, looking at me as he presses gauze to my second hand. "She *is* alive, right? I didn't hallucinate her?"

The soft chuckle he lets out makes the bandage dance in his hold as he applies it to my knuckles, wrapping it around my hand four or five times before checking it like before. "She's alive but she's not living." Closing the plastic bottle of sterile water, he shakes his head as his lips drop into a frown. "She misses you, you know?"

No, I don't fucking know! is what I want to scream at him but I can tell he has something else to say to me, something important.

"She's battling her demons, and until they're gone she can't step back into life." Taking a deep breath, he puts the material away before crossing his arms and looking down at me. "She may never truly heal from what happened to her, what's *been* happening to her, but one day she's going to need you and you're gonna have to step up."

My lip curls into a snarl because now I'm pissed all over again.

"I *did* step up. I was there for her. Hell, I would have slit every one of those motherfuckers' throats for her, but whatever this"—I wave my hands all around to signify this and him and her here today—"shitshow is, I wasn't privy. She. Didn't. Trust. Me." I poke my index finger to my chest over and over again, punctuating the words that really hit home.

In that moment, I realize I'm hurt because she didn't think I could handle her problems or didn't trust me with her solutions. Not sure which it is, but neither bodes well. No doubt a shrink would have a field day with me and my need to control and protect.

"Hmmm, you're butt hurt. I get it. But see…" Uncrossing his arms, he slides his hands into his pockets and takes on a fatherly posture that truly makes me uncomfortable. "Your temper and your anger issues could have thrown her entire plan in the shitter. Also, she was protecting *you*."

I scoff. What a crock.

"I don't need protecting." I get up, ready for some solitude in my cell, but I make the mistake of looking at Spencer, who's staring pointedly at my knuckles before raising his gaze up to mine.

"Clearly."

CHAPTER FOUR
MACKENZIE

Two Months ago

Waking up on a cold, hard table with a bright light shining above me is scarier than I'd imagined, and the shouting I heard as I was coming to is heartbreaking beyond compare.

"Timed that to perfection, you lucky bitch." My best friend's voice calms some of my fraying nerves as I wonder if this was all really worth it.

"Was that him?" My throat is as dry as the Sahara, my words almost catching for more than one reason as Spencer hands me a bottle of water, nodding solemnly in response. The water is cool and soothing and I gulp down the whole thing before stopping to breathe. "Did it work?"

Spencer's brows rise and he inhales sharply through his nose before replying on the exhale, "Yeah."

"Why're you saying it like that?" Tiredness rolls through my limbs as I slowly sit up, worried something went wrong, swinging my legs around so they're dangling off the table.

"Take it easy, Mackenzie. The drugs are still going to be in your system for at least another twenty-four hours, so you might have dizzy spells over the next few days." Steve, the mortuary technician and Spencer's current boyfriend, approaches me with a stethoscope. Holding the white sheet over my naked body, I let it drop a little so he has access to my chest to check my breathing.

"Thank you for this, Steve. I know how much trouble you could get into if anyone finds out how you've helped." I flinch a little at the coldness of the metal against my skin. My thoughts are all still trying to catch up to me right now, and I'm struggling to narrow down any particular emotion other than being happy I didn't die for real.

The drug I used to fake my death can be dangerous and cause permanent side effects or even death, but it was a risk I was willing to take. Along with the pouch of blood I wore beneath my shirt to pop at the race, the drug was necessary in case someone other than Spence or Steve wanted to check my vitals.

"Why do you look like you've been crying?" I eye my best friend, noting his puffy eyes as he casually leans against one of the empty steel tables in here.

"Had to make it believable, didn't we?" He shrugs, huffing a laugh with a smile that doesn't fully reach his eyes.

Wordlessly, I glare at him, trying and failing—still—to raise one single eyebrow.

"What are you doing with your face?" That smile of his grows as Steve finishes up whatever checks he's been making, scribbling down information on his metal clipboard.

"Trying to raise my damn eyebrow. Don't change the subject, though. Talk to me, Spence."

"Don't ever try that again because you look like you're having a stroke. And I'm fine. It's all fine." He pushes off from the table, smacks his palms against his jean-clad hips, and turns to grab the duffel bag from the corner of the room.

"Fuck off with that. We've all just broken the law. A lot. So spill." I gladly take the offered black T-shirt—that I may or may not have stolen from Aleko—and jeans Spence passes to me, beginning to shimmy the clothes on so I'm no longer naked beneath a practically see-through sheet. Both of the men currently in the room may bat for the men's team, but I feel wrong for being near-naked in front of anyone other than *him*.

"You didn't see him, Mac. He's broken. In fact, several of them are. That Bear dude, I think his name is, fell to his knees when he saw what happened. And he's a big fucking dude. It all felt so real and, for a moment, before my brain kicked in as we were driving back here, I couldn't help it. I imagined life without you, how I'd feel in their shoes. It's just..." Spencer sighs, shaking his head as he pulls out my sneakers and the red wig I plan on wearing when I walk out of here. "It's fucked up, Mac. I love you, but this is beyond the realms of normal. You know that, right?"

Way to hit a girl while she's down. I don't want to picture myself in anyone else's position because I know what I'm doing is fucked and dangerous, but I've been nothing but a tool since the morning after Dad died. I haven't been given the opportunity to figure out who I am as an adult without all the bullshit.

Living in a world full of monsters has led me down this path.

Surviving those monsters is a whole other thing. It's something I'm working on.

"Yeah, I know. But I owe you fucked up things in return; all you've gotta do is ask." Winking, I slide off the table to finish pulling my jeans on. I'm a little light-headed, but leaning against the surface helps as I slide the zipper up.

"You know I will." Stepping forward, Spence holds my arms, keeping me stable when he sees me struggling, and places a soft kiss on my cheek.

It's obvious we're both aware of the gravity of this situation, but he's not pushing me and, for that, I'm thankful.

"Your death certificate is in this envelope." Steve hands me said brown envelope, thick with the paperwork needed to make this all official.

"Thanks, Steve."

Here's the thing, the attack in the trailer was the final nail in my coffin. My plan needed to change. This meant that I had to die too. The alternative was getting arrested for murdering my brother and serving my sentence before getting the money I needed to help Mom. With Jake dead and me incarcerated, she still would have been cared for by the state until I got out, and it'd probably be a damn sight better than the care she was currently receiving.

This way, Mom still gets everything she needs, I can get the money together sooner, and I'm now free to do what needs to be done.

Spencer dating the mortuary technician has certainly helped. We were struggling with how we were going to manage two bodies in one ambulance with only one EMT, without it raising suspicions, then Steve came along. It's not the smartest idea of mine to trust him with all of this, but he seems pretty smitten with Spencer, and vice versa, and it was worth the risk.

With the red wig in place as my disguise, I sit in the wheelchair Spencer is standing behind as he waits to wheel me out of here like any other patient.

"Ready for this?" His words are whispered in my ear, and I check out my new ID that's also in the brown envelope.

"Not really." He chuckles at my response, ruffling my wig with affection.

"C'mon, Scarlett. Let's do this."

Now

Walking to the bus station after visiting Aleko gives me the time to think about the consequences of my actions—something I've been avoiding for weeks now. He wasn't supposed to be at the Rebels' trailer park when the police arrived, he was supposed to be away from all the shit I caused. Not right in the fucking middle of it all, holding explosives, no less.

I shouldn't have been shocked when I found out what he did, but I was, right alongside the guilt that is still eating me alive. Aleko fucked me into my official adulthood and I haven't been able to get him off my mind since. He's pushy, and obsessive, and a crazy ass motherfucker, but he loves harder than anyone I've ever known. It's scary and all-consuming, and when it was directed at me, I felt complete in a way that I don't deserve.

All I bring is trouble, and that's not what I want for him.

However, seeing him today has made it difficult to push aside the way he makes my heart beat, the way he ties my stomach in knots, the way his voice soothes every nerve in my body. It's difficult to remember why I kept him out of the loop on this, then I picture the way he was led into the small room by the officer, hoping I was from his lawyer's office.

I'm the reason he's there. Which is the complete opposite of what was supposed to happen.

After I'd removed all the things I wanted from my storage unit, taking them to the run-down cabin Spencer's gran left him, I sent the key and a detailed note to Celia Shipman. She seemed like a good deputy sheriff when I met her, so she was the ideal option. I'm not sure anything would have been done if I'd given the same information to the station in Stonebrook Falls.

My unit held all of the drugs I'd been told to deliver to local dealers, and I made sure to conveniently leave behind some personal items of each of the Rebels—except Cameron and Booker, because they're actually mostly good guys. They just got mixed up with the bad guys is all. The note I sent gave the names and addresses of the Rebels, as well as details of what illegal weapons and drugs they're likely to be carrying, just to make the arrests easier and quicker so they didn't have to wait for prints and shit to come back.

Aleko fucked the plan by being there with explosives and got himself arrested.

It's kind of sweet though, that he was ready to blow shit up for me. Well, sweet and heart wrenching all at the same time. If I'd have just stopped and thought about what I was doing, I'd have realized I had become one of those stupid bitches that keeps secrets when everything would be all better if I had just told the truth.

Although, that's not a guarantee. At least this way Aleko isn't actually in any real danger now. Their club lawyer will get his charges dropped. I have no doubt about that.

But now he knows I'm alive and he hates me. Maybe that's for the best.

I don't know what I expected when he first walked into that room, but it wasn't hatred. My stomach flipped when his blue eyes met mine, I struggled to stay seated and not run into his arms, and every fiber of my being was screaming at me to kiss him. It was dangerous and stupid of me to visit a county jail, but when Spencer told me about what happened with Goblin, I just couldn't stay away.

The bus pulls up alongside the road in front of me and the doors open for me to enter. I pay my fare and head toward an empty middle seat, leaning back to settle in for the hour-long ride. Should've peed before I left the jail, damnit.

The journey gives me more time alone with my thoughts, which is a dangerous thing right now. The last two months are a blur of guilt, regret, freedom, revenge, and I'm afraid I'm a lot more fucked up than I ever realized. These are the years that make a person who they are, and I'm scared that I actually like who I'm becoming.

If I could turn back time, I'd probably do it all the same because I'm stubborn like that. I know the outcome of this path; another path would be a gamble that I'm glad I don't have to take.

Eventually, the bus stops for me to get off and I thank the driver politely before watching it pull away. The driver and other passengers don't need to see me heading into the forest behind me. That'd definitely be cause for suspicion.

It's muggy out today and I find myself silently wishing for some heavy rain to clear the air a little. This suit I'm wearing isn't the most comfortable thing in the world either, and the shoes? Well, I love a pair of heels, but not in the undergrowth of a forest as I make my way to Spencer's inherited cabin by the mountain.

I kick them off, picking them up before continuing my thirty-minute walk. There is a dirt road that leads to the cabin, but I was going for the whole incognito thing today so as not to draw any suspicion from anywhere.

Now that I've revealed myself to Aleko, I thought I'd feel lighter. Like, one less secret to carry and all that. But no, the hate in his eyes only fuels my own anger at the person I'm choosing to hold responsible for every-fucking-thing.

Finally stepping into the old cabin, I throw my shoes into the basket by the front door and rip my wig off, ruffling my hair to ease the building tension-headache. I grab a bottle of water from the fridge, gulping it down on my way into the tiny basement beneath the cabin.

There, I find the source of all my problems. Battered, bloody, and broken.

Unwrapping the sucker I've had in my pocket all day—because it's the only thing that brings me joy lately and is as close to Aleko as I can get—I muse on what to do as I pop it into my mouth when practically dead eyes meet mine.

"Nice to see you awake, brother."

Chapter Five
Aleko

"You sure you wanna do this?" I'm not looking at Landon when he speaks, my attention fully on Roy standing guard at the far end of the cafeteria. From the corner of my eye, I see the poor excuse for a hamburger rise to Landon's mouth before the sound of teeth sinking into a soggy bun and leather-hard patty gives me anything but an appetite.

"Yup." Shane, who takes club money to protect us but hates that he does it, joins Roy. With a quick glance my way as I answer Landon's question, I don't miss the way his head then whips around to face the entrance. I know exactly what he sees and that knowledge gets my entire body buzzing with anticipation.

"Show time, boys." Jackson, who's sitting on the other side of me, drawls out his words like he's about to entertain a room full of fans. In some ways, I guess he is.

"Yup," I repeat, leaning forward on the plastic table to allow Landon and Jackson just enough space to start their play acting. The distraction...

"Here we go." Landon barely whispers his words before Jackson grabs onto the table and topples it over. Food and plates and metal glasses go flying all over the fucking place. Landon gets the first punch in, making me cringe when I hear a pop. Pretty sure we didn't plan on actually breaking noses today. Yet, here we are.

As always, this kind of fight only gets everyone else excited. Some run for safety, others just start throwing punches left and right without really knowing why.

We were counting on this kind of mayhem. Once Shane and Roy start running for our position, I join the others on the far side of the room where the new group of inmates has just arrived for lunch.

The asshole's voice echoes in the hallway, almost making this too fucking easy. Just as he arrives, the guard leading them runs toward the commotion, leaving Goblin all too vulnerable. When he comes into view, I take half a second to appreciate my earlier work on him: the bruises, the stiff way he has to walk from the broken ribs, the limp from his now-bad knee. If I do say so myself, I did a bangin' job on him last week and now I'm ready to finish my masterpiece.

My left arm wraps around his neck as I pull him back toward my chest and keep the air from reaching his lungs.

"You touched my girl, you filthy piece of shit. For that, you get the death penalty." With my right hand, I give him four quick jabs with my shiv in four different areas around his kidneys, then I twist once, twice, before I pull it out a final time and wipe it on his thigh. "I'll see you in Hell, motherfucker."

Once he's limp in my grasp, I lower him to the floor just as whistles begin to blare all around and I step away, slowly, like I have nothing to worry about.

I don't. Our guards know what the fuck is happening and none of these assholes will rat on me. Not that anyone actually saw me doing anything in the back, their attention was on Landon and Jackson beating the shit out of each other.

Good plan.

Playing along, Roy and Shane escort my Oscar-winning friends back to their cells, and I decide that wasting food should be a crime, not killing rapists. With that newfound belief trotting in my mind, I pick up Landon's burger that he carefully placed on his chair, knowing it would be on the floor if he hadn't, and take a satisfied bite into the cardboard patty.

It's still fucking disgusting, but knowing one less scumbag inhabits this world makes it taste a whole lot better.

"Kastellanos! You got a visitor." My ears perk up at the word "visitor", my mind conjuring up images of my Cherry Pie doing unspeakable things to me. Who the fuck am I kidding? I'm pretty sure her showing up last time was a fluke brought on only by the fact I beat the shit out of Goblin. Then again, the bastard's dead and the lock-down that followed probably made the six o'clock news in Rockford so maybe, just *maybe*, she's back to rip me a new one. Then again, probably not. The risk of her being seen and recognized is too great. Besides, my lawyer was supposed to come the day I killed Goblin, but all visitors were ushered out and all inmates locked in.

Following Shane to the visitor room, I replay—for the hundredth time—both conversations I had with Mackenzie and Spencer four days ago. Not gonna lie, I was a little too distracted by the fact that my dead girlfriend was no longer dead to fully grasp what she was actually saying to me. With Spence, I wasn't much better but at least I didn't have her face—all pink skin and bright eyes—fucking with my mind.

Seeing the love of your life lying cold and soulless on a metal table in the fucking morgue, does something sinister to your brain. At least, it did with me, and no matter how many times I try to tell myself that this is cause for celebration, that image keeps coming back to haunt me.

Just as we reach the door and Shane unlocks it, I realize that it doesn't fucking matter, does it? The moment I set my eyes on Mackenzie Wilson, my fate was written in permanent ink across the fibers of my soul. The rest is white noise and I'm an expert at blocking useless shit out.

Taking a deep breath with my renewed train of thought, I realize the corners of my mouth are ticked up for the first time in months with renewed hope that maybe, just maybe, I'll be seeing my Cherry Pie again. To be fair, it's not like she's a stranger to taking risks.

That smile quickly drops when the only person in the visitation room is Veronica, our lawyer. And isn't that fucked up? I should be bouncing on my feet knowing she's here to get me out, Bear told me as much at his last visit but, of course, the only thought that crosses my mind is… where's my Cherry Pie?

"Hey." I slump down onto the plastic chair, eyeing the brown envelope sitting between us.

"I would have thought you'd be much happier to see me."

I like Veronica. She's no nonsense, smart enough to run circles around everyone I know, yet when she looks at me, that fierce glint in her eyes softens. Kind, competent, and beautiful. The triple threat. I'm convinced Bear has a bit of a crush on her, probably because, from what he's told me, she reminds him of his mother. Then again, she does bear an uncanny resemblance to that actress in *How to Get Away With Murder* and he fucking binged that show like his life depended on it.

"I just realized something..." My eyes narrow as I speak because... yeah, I see it now. I can't believe I didn't before. "You look so much like—"

"Boy, let me give you some advice." Oh, shit. I'm about to get a tongue lashing and I don't even know why. "Do not, in all your white boy glory, start a conversation with a Black woman saying she looks like another Black woman." As she pauses, for effect I'm guessing because she's a lawyer and excellent at her job, I try to back pedal but quickly realize I just need to shut my mouth. "It's a slippery slope that says we all look alike. Don't do it. Regardless of color, no woman wants to be compared to another woman, no matter how amazing. And yes, Viola Davis is my universal twin but still... don't do it."

I just got schooled.

Leaning back in my chair, I flash her a cocky grin, giving her a heads up that I'm about to be annoying. "Does this apply to Black men, too?"

The way her face goes completely blank has my mouth drying up and making it impossible to swallow my saliva.

"That awkward bit of racism went straight into misogyny. What's next, Aleko? Homophobia?" My mouth drops open. What the fuck?

"You're gay?" I don't know why the fuck I say that. Like, seriously, shut your fucking mouth, dude.

"And we have the trifecta." Shaking her head at what I'm guessing is a dumbfounded expression on my face, she changes the subject, thank fuck. "Now, stop talking and listen... for once."

Raising my hands in surrender, I say nothing just as instructed by the one person whose job it is to gain my freedom.

"The paperwork has been filed. Now, it's only a matter of it going through the proper chain of command. You can expect to walk out in the next few hours.

Our goodbyes are succinct but no less thankful on my part. As soon as she leaves, I'm escorted back to my cell where I wait long enough for my clean shaven face to have a prominent five o'clock shadow.

"You're free to go, Kastellanos." I bet it physically hurt Shane to say that to me. I don't give a fuck, he's paid very well to keep us safe.

"I'd say I'm gonna miss you but we both know it's bull-shit." All I get in return is a grunt.

Shane never did have a good sense of humor. Flashing him a grin that promises more than he can comprehend, I let the memory of him disrespecting Mackenzie wash over me.

"I'll see ya on the other side, Shane."

"Not if I can help it."

I don't respond to his snark but I know one thing, he won't be able to help a damn thing when it comes to his fate.

It takes another hour to get all the paperwork signed and my shit given back to me in a brown envelope. Well, except for the tongue bar that was placed in a plastic baggie. When I step out of that fucking hell hole, I freeze and lean my head back in the late afternoon sun, soaking up some good old vitamin D.

"You're looking mighty pale for a Greek god, brother." Before I can lower my head, my smile is automatic.

"You're looking ugly as ever." When my eyes land on Bear, there's a deep, calming feeling that soothes all my aches.

"You wish." With that, he wraps his huge arms around my shoulders and squeezes hard, like he too needs to make sure this moment is real. "Missed you, brother. Don't ever fucking do that again, ya hear?"

"Not planning on it, man." Stepping back at the words, Bear scans my face, starting with my eyes, my mouth, my eyes again.

"What aren't you telling me?" How the fuck does he do that?

I start walking when I see half the fucking club waiting in the parking lot just a couple of yards away. Holy fuck... the doors to the white van open and my baby girl, Philia, is being pushed out slow and easy.

"The fuck you talking about?" I can't look at him because Bear can snuff out a lie better than any modern tech at the FBI or CIA and it doesn't take a genius to know that Mackenzie, as she made it very clear, did not go to the club and wait for me.

"You're lucky I don't want to stick around this place longer than I have to, but you'll spill. I'll make sure of it." I shrug at what feels like some twisted threat knowing that I'll have to tell him eventually, but at the same time, this is Mackenzie's secret, not mine.

Prez is the first to greet me as he stands tall and unmoving, features completely closed off. Pretty sure I'm about to get my ass handed to me.

"That stunt you pulled was reckless and fucking stupid. I don't give a fuck what the reason is, the next time you step out of order, you'll be riding alone." My mouth dry, I try to swallow my, no doubt, inappropriate comment, giving him a simple nod to acknowledge my understanding. "Now, get over here, you fucking stubborn little shit."

When Bear hugged me it was like a brother showing how much he missed me. This though? It's different, it's fatherly and holy shit, are those fucking tears prickling at the back of my lids?

Nah, must the remnants of prison food.

"Don't ever fucking do that again," he repeats, and this time I grunt my understanding.

"Ya fuckin' wanker. Tryin' to grab all the fucking glory, were ya?" Sledge rubs my growing hair like I'm five before he pulls me into a chest-bump-back-slap hug and breaking the solemn moment with Prez. "Cost ya two months, you selfish prick." There's not an ounce of venom in his voice, there never is with this dude. Or maybe his British accent just makes everything he says sound better. Who the fuck knows?

I'm about to throw some sarcasm back at him when I feel the unmistakable tiny claws running up my pant leg before reaching my shirt and immediately nuzzling my neck.

Holy shit, if I missed Mackenzie more than anything in the world, Ninja is a close second. I try to pick him up but he's running around my shoulders and arms then back up again like he doesn't know where to go next. His little nose is twitching all over the place like he knows it's me, but at the same time, the scent is all weirded out and mixed with shit he doesn't recognize.

Pulling out a sucker from the bag with all my shit in it, I unwrap it and pop it in my mouth, sucking a few times before letting him lick it just once or twice. Fuck, I hope my brother didn't sugar him up while I was gone. It's not good for his health.

"Hey, beautiful boy. You missed me, huh?" I love that he purrs and whines and almost talks to me as he shows me just how much two months seemed like a lifetime to him.

"I think he's trying to say that you smell like shit, brother." Grinder grins at me like he just told me I'm the greatest of all time.

"You'd think he'd be used to it, being around you all day." It's like I never left.

"I smell like fucking roses and great sex. He never once complained." Asshole.

Lots of hugs and back slaps later, we're all on our bikes, Ninja safely burrowed in his little pouch as we ride down Highway 17 back to our compound.

Holy fuck, the feel of the wind seeping through the open visor is nothing short of orgasmic. Two months without riding is like a lifetime without laughing.

On the long stretch of highway with my brothers surrounding me, I let go of the handlebars and spread my arms out like the huge Jesus in Rio and take it all in. Not two seconds later, Grinder is causing his engine to break, popping out little explosions like he's the ringleader for the Fourth of July. Meanwhile, Sledge gives a hard twist of the wrist and I know what's coming. His front tire lifts from the ground, his bike practically perpendicular to the road when he rises on his peg and places one foot on the seat, keeping the bike steady with his weight.

Not to be outdone, Shade does the same so I decide to give Bash a little fodder for his new camera passion, if that thing on his helmet is any indication. Raising my own bike for a wheelie, I jump back so my feet are on the seat. Just as I'm passing a car full of kids with their phones out and filming us all, I release my left hand and give them the peace sign, also the universal biker sign for "Whattup, dude?"

This is the first time in months that I've felt like myself. That I've felt alive, like the weight of Mackenzie's death is no longer pushing me six feet under. That, however, doesn't mean I'm done with those fucking Rebels. In fact, knowing she's alive only gives me greater motivation to end them, one slowly dying body part at a time.

Nearby cars honk their horns, kids waving from cars and the Boomers shaking their heads at us. It all seems so normal. So uneventful. Like my life isn't a complete fucking disaster.

Grinder is next to me now, nodding for me to follow his lead. Straddling my Philia again, I watch and see what he's doing, laughing when his right leg swings over the handlebars and the windscreen so he's sitting side saddle. No one needs to see his face to know he's ginning like a fucking madman inside his helmet. This crazy mother fucker wants to play footsies.

Mirroring his position with all our brothers watching all around us, I swing my left leg over and sit sideways on my bike facing him. As we start doing the foot-shake challenge like we're back in twenty-eighteen, I can almost hear the whole fucking crew laughing their asses off. An oldie but goodie. Yeah, I needed this and Grinder is a master at putting a grin back on our faces.

When Prez goes heavy on the accelerator and gets into riding position, Grinder and I both seat ourselves correctly, and before we get into our spots, I hold out my fist and we bump. The universal sign for I love you, you crazy motherfucker.

It's not long before we're back at the compound and, just like that, two months of pain and memories come flooding back as I pop the kickstand down and see Mackenzie's car parked right where she left it.

Fuck my life.

My brain is trying to remind me that she's not dead. She's alive and... a redhead. Yeah, that's gonna have to change back.

Grabbing my little Ninja, who's all too happy to climb all over me again and plant himself in my hoodie where he feels the safest, we walk into the clubhouse. Vanessa is the first to jump in my arms and squeeze me tight. It takes me a second to realize she's crying, and that only makes me squeeze her harder. This woman... she's the backbone to our Prez but she's also the mother to us all.

"Are you okay? Are you hungry? Don't answer that. I've already asked Sabrina to cook us a feast." I'm about to argue but then remember who I'm talking to and stop. "Go shower, feed Ninja, and we'll all be here waiting." I don't have the heart to deny her so I kiss the Prez's wife on the cheek and scratch Ninja on his belly as I hold him with my other hand.

"It's you and me now, buddy." He doesn't answer, obviously, but he does purr at the feel of my nails on his belly.

My room isn't locked, I'm guessing the Khunts have been coming around cleaning the dust and vacuuming. We usually clean our own rooms but I've been a little MIA and Ninja needs a clean environment.

When I step inside, my feet stop and I take in a deep breath. It's faint, almost completely gone and replaced by some kind of candle scent that I'm going to throw out in two minutes, but it's there. The cherry of her shampoo.

Fuck.

I can't do this.

Grabbing some of my shit and Ninja's food with a few toys, I close the door behind me before making my way back down.

"Hey, V?"

Vanessa turns, worry written across her soulful eyes, her lips downturned like she already knows what I'm about to say. "I'm gonna go to my place in town. I can't…"

With one hand to my cheek, she gifts me a tiny smile that says she gets it. And she probably does.

"Go out the side door. But, Psycho?"

"Yeah?"

"Not too long, kiddo. Okay? The longer you stay away, the worse it's gonna get. We're your family, our shoulders are stronger when we're together." I nod at her words and plant another kiss on her cheek.

Before I have time to sneak out the side, Vanessa squeezes my forearm. "Wait!"

Confused, I obey. She may be an old lady, but Vanessa is not to be ignored. This woman has had our respect since day one and it has nothing to do with being the Prez's wife and everything to do with the way she cares for us all.

I watch as she opens a cupboard and takes out different sized containers, lining them up on the counter next to the outright buffet she and Sabrina prepared for my homecoming. For a hot minute, I let the guilt wash over me, knowing they've done all of this for me, until the idea of spending at least a couple of hours laughing and talking shit makes my stomach roll.

On a good day, pretending to feel something I don't is almost impossible, but tonight I can't find the will to even try.

After scooping up mashed potatoes, sirloin, beans, asparagus, and the special gravy that only Sabrina knows how to make, she packs it all up into a backpack that I add to my front.

My spirits are so fucking low that I don't care how ridiculous I look wearing two bags.

"Thanks, V. Just give me a few nights to process, okay?"

"Okay."

Turns out, I don't get a few nights to process. One night is all I need before I hunt down my sweet Cherry Pie.

But before I stalk my pretty little prey, there's a little something I need to do.

Chapter Six
Mackenzie

Keeping my brother alive for the last two months has been harder than I thought it would be. I hadn't planned on it, in all honesty, but I haven't been able to actually kill him. It's not because I feel guilty or anything, because he hasn't exactly been enjoying himself while chained by his hands and feet to a metal table in the basement.

Some would say what I've been doing is worse than murder. I like to call it Karma. And I'm not finished yet. Each slice across one of Jake's precious tattoos is actually quite cathartic for me.

Watching the thin red line of blood spill over the fresh new wound.

Listening to the pained moans as he tries desperately to stay silent.

Tasting the bitterness of retaliation and the sweetness of revenge as my brother realizes he's truly done for.

There is no getting out of this for him.

Plus side: I won't get arrested for murder because I'm "dead".

Down side: the fulfillment and satisfaction I should be getting from this whole thing is dampened because I went and broke my own heart in the process.

Taking a step back from Jake, I admire my handiwork for today and grab the pure alcohol solution from the rickety shelving unit to the right of the metal bed. I've been cleaning the wounds so they don't get infected and give him sepsis, but it's just as unpleasant for him as the actual wound-making.

"Bissssh!"

"Oh, how original. A man calling a woman a bitch. Aren't you clever?" My laugh is as fake as any devotion I ever had for the Toxic Rebels.

"You p-pay forthss." Sounding out his words over the last few days seems to have become a struggle for him. Which is normal, considering he's being allowed the bare minimum of food and water to keep his body from shutting down completely, but with the torture on top of that, he won't last much longer.

The second stage of my plan begins any day now. As soon as the next race night is announced and those location texts are sent... I just hope the cops did their job and all the Rebels are behind bars right now because I need the win.

"I think you'll find that you're the one paying for this, big brother. Every bruise, every wound inflicted on me from you and your *club* has a price. I played my part, I obeyed like the good little girl I once was, and do you know the funny thing?" Picking up the plastic cup of week-old water, I step closer to Jake, his no-longer-bright blue eyes glaring daggers at me. "I learned a few things from y'all. *You* made me this way. *You* gave me the strength to torture you like a fucking psychopath. Aren't you proud, *big brother*?"

Jake growls in response, finding the energy to jerk his body as I lift my arm to hold his mouth open for the water.

"Nottt your brotherrr, bisssh." His rough words are spoken slowly, and they make me pause with the plastic cup almost to his face.

"I wish that were true. It'd make more sense than my own blood treating me like fucking shit after practically ignoring me my whole childhood." I had stupidly thought that my brother offering to take care of me when Dad died and Mom got sick would mean a wonderful new relationship. I was wrong.

I don't even want to give Jake the water I'm holding now. Other than calling me names, he's been a useless source of information for the last two months, but telling me he's not my brother causes my simmering anger to bubble. Fuck knows why. It just does.

The cuts on his cheeks crack open as he attempts to grin, then his weak-ass laugh turns into a cough that only seems to hurt him more.

"M-om cheeeeted." More coughing. "N-nottt Dad." His dry laugh turns into a full-on choking fit and I pour the water in my hand onto his face.

What the fuck?

Hot tears prick at my eyelids, but I won't let Jake hurt me anymore. The whole point of this is for me to hurt him now. My breathing is shallow and I continue to stare at him until his cough dies down and he glares at me, a wicked grin on his cracked lips.

"H-he wsssss weeeak. Like yooo—" A quick cut from the corner of his mouth up to his ear stops his vile words. The sight is satisfying, but I cut too deep. Shit.

I need time to process what Jake said. What does he mean by not Dad? Was Dad not my dad, not his dad? Or is he just trying to get to me?

Fuck.

The landline ringing upstairs gets my attention and the volcano of anger erupting inside my trembling body begins to settle briefly. There's only one person with the number for this cabin, and that's because he owns it.

Leaving a writhing, bleeding Jake on the cold, hard table, I head up the basement stairs and into the small kitchen, picking up the landline phone from its dock after removing my plastic gloves.

"Hey, Spence."

"I have good news." His smooth tone is comforting, and I could never in a million years pay him back for what he's done for me.

"Shoot."

"Poor choice in wording there, Babe." We both chuckle, because, yeah, shooting is how we got here in the first place. "He's free, came out yesterday. I saw 'em all riding through town and, man, I can see why you fell for a biker." He sighs, probably daydreaming about bagging his own biker one day.

"Life would be so much easier if I hadn't. But thanks, Spence. I appreciate the update. You gonna stop volunteering at the jail now?" Talking on the phone with Spencer once a day is my reprieve from the basement, so I'm not quick to finish with the call.

"I might give it another week or two, but Steve's not sure I should stay."

"How is Steve?" Steve's job at the mortuary made my plan a hell of a lot easier than I'd anticipated to begin with, and I'm selfishly worried that messing with him will cause me problems.

"He's good. A bit distant, but I won't push him. More bodies have gone missing from the morgue since you and Jake, and it's all a bit of a mess at work for him at the moment."

"Do I need to have words with him to make sure he's treating you right?" I chuckle.

Spence told me, flat out, he thinks I'm a badass capable of anything. And while he's not entirely wrong—especially considering the last couple of months—I'm still just a twenty-one-year-old girl trying to figure my shit out.

"I'll let you know, Babe."

"Okay. First, though, I might need some help." *I've just remembered how badly Jake was bleeding out when I left him.*

"Is it finally time for the shovel?" I love that he's as callous as me about this whole thing. After I told him what happened that night in the Rebels' trailer, his indecision about helping me vanished. Spencer is the kind of best friend everyone needs, ready with a shovel to bury the enemy's body.

"Yeah, I think so. He was bleeding pretty badly when you called. And I've seen those videos with the inflatable unicorn costume as a disguise in this kind of situation… don't do that." I laugh, and Spence feigns insult with a sharp inhale.

"As if I would? Okay, I thought about it, but I'll just wear some old clothes." His chuckle warms my insides. It's been four days since I saw him and Aleko, and I'm craving human contact that isn't my dying, possibly already dead brother—if the lack of cries is anything to go by. That, or he's passed out. "Be there in an hour."

"See you soon."

Forty-five minutes since my phone call with Spence, and I haven't dared go back downstairs because I have this gut feeling that it's really over. And it wasn't nearly as satisfying as I'd hoped.

I've been pacing the small kitchen, trying to make a damn decision about what to put in my sandwich, like it's the most important thing in the world. What I really want to do is find Aleko, make him forgive me for not telling him what was going on, make him take me back and solve all my problems. But my dad raised me to solve my own problems... if he's even my dad at all. Either way, he *did* raise me, taught me to respect myself, to ride, to be strong in the face of my fear. Which is the only way I've gotten through the last five or so years under my brother's rule.

Peanut butter and jelly. Classic. I grab the ingredients I need, shaking myself off before allowing my emotions to get the better of me, and make my sandwich. A few minutes later, the kitchen is spotless again and I have my food in hand as I make my way back down into the basement.

Yup. Jake's dead. His eyes are wide open, glassed over and staring at nothing, his body is limp, and the giant diaper he's wearing is overflowing with shit. Fucking great. That's been the worst part about all of this. Because I know that if I'd let him stew in his own crap for this long, he'd have been long gone. The cooking utensils from the kitchen have come in handy, saving me from actually touching anything. Ugh. The thought alone makes me shudder.

The main thing on my mind now is that I'm going to have to tell Mom that her son is really dead, and not fake dead. Not that she knows if either of us is alive or dead right now. Before my "death" I told Maggie, mom's nurse at the psych ward, about my friend Spencer, said that I'd be going away for a while and he would be checking in on her—so that when I "died" he wasn't a complete stranger to them. The last time he spoke to Maggie, he found out that the staff hadn't informed Mom about the tragic shooting of her children. They're not sure how she'll cope with the information, and considering she's there in the first place because her husband died, I get it.

The strange thing is, though, Mom's noticed my absence. According to Maggie, she even asked for me by name two weeks ago. I didn't think she'd be lucid enough to realize, and I'm more convinced by the day that Jake and his cronies were giving her something.

"Honey, I'm ho—ugh!" Spence's loud greeting is quickly cut off by gagging noises, followed by his footsteps coming down the wooden staircase. "Shit, Mac, this place fucking reeks." He's holding his light-blue T-shirt up and over his nose, showing his distaste as well as vocalizing it.

Now that I really think about it, it does stink in here. I guess feces and a dead body will do that to a place. I've been totally nose-blind to it, and I shrug, pushing the last of my sandwich into my mouth and chewing. I used cherry jam because it reminds me of what else I destroyed.

"Were you really down here eating a fucking sandwich and staring at your dead brother?" He's not judging, there's amusement in his eyes that perfectly match his T-shirt.

The statement should definitely bother me more. But it doesn't. What does, is the fact that I thought doing this was worth ruining what I had with Aleko. I could have done so many things differently. If I'd have just taken the money for the street race winner for myself instead of handing it over. But no... I needed this.

It's sick, it's twisted, but I don't think I could have lived with myself just doing nothing... not after that night. Living around the Toxic Rebels as I became an adult made me think this is okay, but deep down, I know I'm messed up. I don't particularly care, but I know it's not normal. Maybe that's why I let Aleko go so easily? Because I know I'm not the good girl who needs saving like he thinks I am.

"Yeah. Peanut butter and jelly. I can make you one before we start, if you want?" I grin, pushing aside all thoughts and feelings that make me sad because I have shit to do.

"Ha. No." Spencer shakes his head in disbelief, and I imagine a smirk grazing his lips as his eyes crinkle at the corners. "We're going to need to fumigate this place when he's gone. Get rid of the stench. I brought hazmat suits for us."

"You, Spencer Holt, are the bestest best friend a girl could ever ask for, you know that?" He really does think of everything.

"I do know that. Now hurry your juicy ass up and let's get this body out of my basement." He throws me the carrier bag that was dangling from his bent elbow as he's still holding his T-shirt up to his nose.

Said juicy ass begins vibrating before I can unwrap the plastic suit to put on over my clothes, and I pull my phone from the back pocket of my jeans.

I read the text, once, twice, and excitement bubbles up inside me, mixed with a little anticipation for how I'll be received—okay, a lot—and I fist pump the air.

"That the street race text you've been waiting for?"

"It is. It's on tonight! I need to get ready!" I begin racing up the stairs, Spencer close behind me.

"Do they know who you are yet? Will you even be allowed to race?"

"I hope so." I quickly unzip my jeans and take them off before heading toward the duffel by the front door and pulling out my all-black race suit. I slide my legs into it, followed by my arms, thankful I have a thin tank-top on because it's hotter than the devil's asshole this evening, but I won't race without my safety gear.

I don't want to die… and the irony of that is always going to be amusing.

I'm also hoping to do more than race. I'll see Aleko tonight, and he's going to call me out for the top spot. When he realizes who I am, I'm praying to Aphrodite that he forgives yet another secret because, yes…

I'm Cain.

CHAPTER SEVEN
ALEKO

Returning to the race feels like someone grabbed me by the collar and dragged me back, kicking and screaming, to the exact spot where my entire world went to shit. In the span of a few minutes, my life experienced a free fall from complete and utter happiness to soul destroying despair.

The sounds are the same. Motorcycles revving, tires spinning, exhaust pipes spitting out flames from the engine brakes. It's all familiar and should be comforting since this scene was my favorite time of the month before...

Before I held the love of my life's limp body in my arms and wished I could just die right alongside her.

Except she wasn't dead, was she? She was supposed to be my partner in all things, yet the whole time we were together, she was planning on leaving me... broken and devastated on that blacktop road.

I wish I could convince myself that forgiveness is impossible. That this level of deceit is a deal breaker for me. In the five days since I laid eyes on Mackenzie, I've thought of nothing else but this. The Clash had it right all along, "Should I Stay or Should I Go?"

As luck would have it, my obsession over Mackenzie didn't even suffer a dent from this whole fucked up situation. If anything, I want to fuck the bad decision making right out of her. Teach her, with my cock, how to use her fucking words and share her plans with me. Not her best friend... *me*. I should be her confidant, the one she runs to when she needs a sounding board. The only person she thinks of when she needs someone to hold the shovel.

Me, goddammit.

Running my freshly replaced barbell through my teeth, I grin at the thought of kissing my girl again. Maybe even punishing her for breaking my fucking heart. Then I'll eat her pussy so good, she'll regret ever thinking she could go without it.

"Holy shit. Cain is back." Bear slaps me on the shoulder, nearly sending me flat on my face with the force of it, getting my immediate attention. "Nothing better to keep your mind off painful memories, brother. Beat that motherfucker for first place."

He's not wrong. My ears perk up, and for the first time since I've been here, my attention is somewhere other than on Mackenzie. I've been wanting to race and beat this Cain dude for months but he doesn't show regularly, which only pisses me off. Can't beat him if I can't race him.

Standing on the back of Vanessa's truck, I cup my hands over my mouth and bellow out my desire to kick this mystery rider's ass down that straight line.

"Cain! I'm calling you out, man. First place is mine." The crowd goes quiet as I announce my intentions, their attention turning across the street and down a few yards from us where Cain stands on a table and gives me a thumbs up.

Then the roar of the spectators rivals the booming sounds of their bikes with every engine brake on the asphalt as the race chief approaches to take the entry cash to hold for the winner. Some of it will be kept aside to go toward the grand total for the end-of-season race next month.

As long as I've been racing, Chief has been the same. Tall and lanky with a shock of white hair on his head, he looks like a living, breathing cotton swab. I watch him like a hawk as he slowly makes his way to the other side, heading straight for Cain to collect his entry cash.

Tonight's a good night. A much-needed distraction from the shitshow that is my life.

"Aww, my little brother is all grown up." Bear holds up his large palm, our hands clasping as I jump from the bed of the truck and do a one-sided shoulder check hug.

"It's gonna feel good to win this one." For more than just one reason but I don't need to elaborate, he knows exactly what I'm talking about.

Then it hits me.

Fuck.

Bear doesn't know about Mackenzie because she didn't show up at the club like I'd told her to when she visited me in jail. Not that I was expecting her to follow my instructions. I mean, I get it, she's legally dead to the world. I'm pretty sure faking your own death is illegal.

I make a mental note to come clean to Bear and possibly to the club because lying to them feels wrong. Then again, betraying Mackenzie's secret brings me physical pain.

Like I said, my life's a fucking shitshow. Well, except for this moment.

I'm going to race Cain and take that number one title, and the cash that flows with it, for myself. With the next race being the last of the season, I'll be able to infuse some cash into the club to reimburse the legal fees incurred with my stunt as an explosives expert. It's the least I can do.

Wasting no time, Bear and I jog over to the van the club wheeled my racing bike, Elektra, into at the compound in hopes I'd be here and willing to race. She's been fine-tuned by the best among us while I've been away in fucking jail. My mind was so consumed by Mackenzie that I didn't even take a detour to look at her when I got to the SOK clubhouse.

Right now, though, I'm hyper focused and that title means something to me.

I will stop at nothing to win.

Bear takes a half-sleeping Ninja out of my hoodie and rubs his soft white belly, but I don't miss his beady little eyes letting me know he's not happy about being jostled during what I'm guessing was a cheese dream where co-pious amounts of dairy were falling all over him. I have those same dreams, except instead of cheese, I'm picturing Mackenzie on top of me, naked and trembling with her need to come all over my face. Or dick. Or sliding her wet little cunt from my mouth to my chin to my chest to my abs, then impaling herself on my hard-as-fuck cock.

"Dude, are you even listening to me?" I shake the day-dream away as Bear pokes me in the shoulder, because being distracted on race night is pretty close to a death sentence.

"Cut it out, I'm listening. Just getting into the zone." My lie isn't far from the truth. I was getting into the zone... just not the racing one.

"Why's your dick hard? Man, two months in jail turned you into a preteen?" I side-eye Grinder who's full-on staring at my crotch like it's got all the answers to the world's problems.

"Eyes up here, asshole. Racing gets me hard." Why... the fuck... did I just give him that fodder? I'll never hear the end of that shit. Like, ever.

"Right on, man. I actually came in my leathers once just as I crossed the finish line." Grinder nods as he speaks, like he's reliving that particular moment in his life. I blink up at him, certain that he's fucking with me. He's not. In fact, I rarely see him this serious.

"Y'all are fuckin' weird. Now, if we could just talk racing and not niche kinks, that would be great." We both turn to Bear then jump into action, although, I do tuck that Grinder tidbit in the back of my mind for future reference.

The bike warms for about ten minutes while I suit up. The rich scent of leather reminds me of my recent freedom and my never-ending love of racing. It's not just fun, it's in my DNA. The anticipation of being one with the bike, of knowing that one stupid mistake could be my last, makes my entire body buzz with electric energy. It's the rush of that tunnel vision where nothing exists except for the finish line. It's knowing my talent will bring honor to the club, put cash in our pockets, and give me the deeply rooted satisfaction that I'm number fucking one.

"All right, listen up." My attention is solely on Bear as he gives me the downlow on Cain's racing. It's not enough to be good, you have to know your opponent's weaknesses to compensate and take advantage. "Dude is good, mostly because he's agile and his body positioning is pretty fucking perfect at the turn. He's not afraid to lean in and let the bike run to its full capacity. However..." Fucking finally. I don't want to hear how good he is, I need the dirt. "His throttle control is jerky at the turn, and although it's never happened, it has the potential to make him unstable on the way back. Push him, don't hesitate to egg him on, get him to make a mistake."

Throttle control is an art. It's delicate. Acceleration in a race has to be smooth and controlled, especially when exiting a turn. Bear is right, this is where I excel. I'll be sure to make this a teaching moment for Cain.

Minutes later, I'm straddling my beautiful Elektra. A moan escapes my throat but is lost to the cacophony of the hundreds of race fanatics hanging around this patch of road. Tonight's event is on an isolated country road where organizers are standing guard on either end. One shrill whistle from the chief and everyone disperses to avoid getting caught by the cops.

As Cain sidles up to me, I grin knowing I'm going to finally get the chance to win. When I turn to look at him, I only get his profile. He's smaller than I'd anticipated since I've never actually been up close to him. He can't be much older than a teenager. Maybe twenty? His bike fits him perfectly though, and with his low weight, I get why he's riding an inline-twin. He'll have a small advantage in a short distance race like tonight but I'll burn him at the turn when he chokes his throttle and loses precious seconds.

My vision of Cain is obstructed by the leggy redhead who walks up between us, a scarf wrapped around her bare neck and a skirt that'll give the crowd a little show when we take off. I barely give her the time of day because at this moment, Cain turns his head toward me just an inch, giving me a three-quarter view of his blacked-out helmet, and something about that move distracts me just a second too long.

We're both revving the engines, giving the crowd exactly what they're screaming for, fire spitting out of my exhaust for added entertainment, when the redhead slides her scarf from her neck. In slow motion, she raises her hand and spreads her legs hip-wide, a perfect row of white teeth blinding the spectators as she counts down from five.

Five. I need to know who this Cain dude is.

Four. Why wasn't he arrested with the rest of the Rebels?

Three. There's just something about him that seems familiar.

Two. What if he's still working with the Rebels?

One. I may need to kill him too.

When the scarf whips down, Cain takes off like a fucking bullet, but my attention was elsewhere, and instead of holding my rear brake on my acceleration to avoid the front wheel from tipping up, I have to use my clutch to ease the transition. It's finite but it's there. He's got a second on me as he handles his machine like it's part of his own body.

In no time at all, we're at the turn, and just as Bear predicted, Cain's body position is on point, leaning in and using the center of gravity to his advantage. I do the same, leaning into the turn smoothly and keeping the perfect balance. Just as I exit the turn, my right wrist rolls in a slick, practiced motion, controlling the acceleration with masterful precision, and from the corner of my eye I see Cain's jerky movement making the front wheel lift off slightly before he adjusts and we're nose to nose, a racing duel; fighting for the win.

The golden rule is to always look ahead of your immediate surroundings. The bike follows the rider's eye, so we look far and ahead to make sure we take our machines to the win. This means that, seconds before the finish line, I'm only focused on the end, ignoring everything around me. Ignoring Cain.

Just as we reach the makeshift white line, Cain inches up ahead of me.

It's close. So fucking close that I'm not sure who's won when I push both front and back brakes, creating a cloud of smoke behind me as rubber burns against the asphalt. Handing off Elektra to Bash, I run to the organizer whose job it is to catch the finish line with his camera and can't help my irritated tone.

"Whose tire?" I yell out, about to turn and talk shit to Cain about how I'm the winner. Except he's not rushing the organizer, he's sitting on his bike, all relaxed and confident.

I want to fucking punch him, knowing that behind his visor hides a smug face anticipating the announcement that he still owns the number one spot.

"Look for yourself, Psycho." Johnston angles the camera my way and I watch the video with horror contorting my face as Cain's tire bites the line mere milliseconds before mine.

Clenching my jaw so tight I get a tick right below my ears, I thank him before pushing my way through the crowd and back to my brothers. Some women congratulate me, patting me down from shoulder to ass, but I ignore them. Others ask for autographs but I barely pay any attention to them either. I'm being a spoiled little shit but I can't find it in me to care.

Just as I peel off the top half of my suit and let it hang from my waist, Cain rides up to me and stops, revving once, twice, before throwing something at me that I catch on instinct.

When he rides away, he releases his clutch and raises his arm, giving me a goodbye wave with his gloved hands.

That singular move brings me back to months earlier when someone else said goodbye before I was able to get some answers.

Frowning as my brain tries to add up numbers that make no sense, I look down at what Cain threw at me, and like a puzzle piece that makes the entire picture come to life, everything starts to click into place.

In my hand is a sucker. A cherry sucker covered with transparent plastic. My favorite candy in the world.

"Bear, bring me Philia and keep Ninja with you!" I'm running as I bark out my orders and, to my best friend's credit, he doesn't make me explain... yet.

As he rolls my street bike over, I gear right back up and I'm gone within seconds.

My Cherry Pie wants me to hunt her down. And like the animal I am when it comes to her, I make all her begging wishes come true.

Chapter Eight
Mackenzie

Racing like that again has my adrenaline pumping. The speed, the crowd... *Psycho*. It's the first time we've gone up against each other head-on—I made it up to the top ranks before he started the season, which meant until he could call me out for my spot there was no need.

The fucker almost beat me though, because of my own stupidity. For one brief second, I faltered. My concentration was on how good he looked in his leathers and the demonic face artwork on his helmet instead of my acceleration out of the turn. I can pinpoint the exact moment I fucked up. I remembered what it was like riding with him and his club, like a family instead of the shitfest I've been dealing with the last few years. Then his front tire pushed ahead of me and I thought it was all over. It was all I could do to keep his pace to the finish line. I may have got a win, but barely, and I'm going to need to work on my concentration when he no doubt calls me out next time.

His race night baby is far superior to mine, and if I'm honest, I'm surprised I won. My bike needs a lot of work, even though it's the best one the Rebels owned. As their star racer, I was given it to ride—strictly for the races only, because it was too nice for someone like me to keep. I don't have the cash for the upgrades though, but with a little tweaking, I may be able to give myself some extra speed in case I fuck up coming out of a turn next time.

All that aside... I'm hoping that my little parting gift was enough of a hint for Aleko. I don't want to reveal myself to everyone because that would defeat the point of me being "dead". Luckily, there were no Rebels there tonight—the only ones who know Cain's real identity—so they couldn't rat me out. I need to stay dead for as long as possible so Mom keeps receiving her care, and because I don't need to be investigated for faking my own death. That comes with a whole world of problems I don't want to deal with.

Being associated with the Toxic Rebels in Stonebrook Falls has its advantages, though, which is the only way I was able to get hold of fake documents for myself. I need said documents to take Mom to the doctor in New York once I win the street race money after the next meet-up.

Coming so close to losing today should piss me the fuck off, but all it does is make me stupidly proud of Aleko. If I do lose to him in the last race of the season, the second place earnings would mean I'd only have enough to send Mom to New York, which is better than nothing at all. I'm looking at the silver linings here, and one of those is an angry biker with the nickname Psycho.

In what some may call a normal world, I should be having some kind of feelings about torturing my brother for two months before accidentally killing him. I should still be the relatively meek girl I was when Isaac, Goblin, and Brick raped and beat me as my brother—*half*-brother if what he said is true—filmed the whole thing on his phone. I should probably be rocking myself to sleep in a dark corner, mad at the world and the hand I've been dealt.

But this isn't a normal world. And right now, my only focus is trying to make this crazy-ass motherfucker chasing my tail forgive me.

Slowing down on the highway, I allow Aleko to catch up so we're side-by-side, and just as he moves close enough to touch me, I drop a gear and twist the throttle. I'm ahead again, taking a sharp turn off in the direction of the beach.

We ride for what feels like mere minutes, when it's actually been almost an hour of fucking around playing catch-me-if-you-can. My entire body is thrumming with adrenaline and excitement as I slow down, pulling up by the beach area Aleko brought me to before I pretended to kill my brother and died. The vibrations from my motorcycle between my legs definitely have something to do with how I'm feeling, but mostly, it's him.

Aleko.

My own personal Psycho. One who literally went to war for me on more than one occasion, only for me to let him down.

Sighing, I watch him pull up his bike beside mine, leisurely killing the engine, knocking his kickstand in place, and lifting his left leg to climb off.

No secrets, no lies. I did both of those things.

I'm still straddling my motorcycle when Aleko pulls off his helmet, carefully placing it on his Philia before turning to glare in my direction. I almost melt into a puddle as he raises that goddamn eyebrow at me and smirks.

Holy shit, that's hot.

"Think you can run from me again, Cherry?" He shakes his head, tutting in the sexiest way anyone has ever tutted in the existence of mankind, and takes the two short steps toward me. His thighs are practically straddling my knee at this point and my clit is pulsing, demanding attention.

"There are no cameras or guards to keep you safe now..." Leaning even closer still, he whisper-growls, "There's only *me*."

In the smoothest action, Aleko lifts his hands to unclip my helmet before sliding it off my head and placing it right behind me.

Am I panting? I feel like I'm panting, and he hasn't touched me yet. Every part of him that is close to me is millimeters away from making contact and the heat radiating from him is electric, but there's been no actual touching.

Does this mean he's open to the idea of not completely hating me, or that he's really, *really* angry with me? He said he couldn't forgive secrets and lies...

I stare into his gray-blue eyes, searching for answers that are impossible to find and, like before, in jail, his gaze is dancing across every inch of me, as if checking that I'm real. There's vulnerability and pain there that makes me want to reach out and soothe him, but it's masked by the constant smirk and raised brow. It's as though he's not sure which direction this conversation is going to go so I take a deep breath, ready to apologize over and over again...

And just as I'm about to exhale, the devil on my shoulder has another thought. A more defiant one. There will be time to explain why I did what I did. For right now, my body is alight with a fire that I never thought possible for this man, and I know he feels it too. His breaths are as ragged as mine.

"You know…" My voice sounds breathier than I intended, but I'm going with it, matching his smirk with one of my own as his second brow rises to match the first. I almost think I'm managing the one brow thing myself for a brief second until his smirk turns into more of a trying not to laugh thing. "Maybe I will run again. Think you can catch me, *Psycho*?"

Without giving him a second to process my words fully, I slide my leg out from between his thighs, knock my kickstand into place, and jump off my motorcycle, the opposite side of Aleko. Then I run toward the beach. It's not easy running on sand with a full leather suit on that's too big for me, and the tide is high so there's really not a lot of beach to run to, but I spot some dunes up ahead.

I can hear his laugh from behind me and I almost turn, ready to give in and have him catch me already, but this is too fun. I don't remember the last time something was just fun.

After a few minutes of running, thankfully, Aleko finally makes contact. He wraps his arms around my shoulders and tackles me to the ground. The sand mostly breaks our fall and he maneuvers us so that he's now straddling me, my arms pinned to my sides by his leather-clad thighs.

"Think you're funny, do you, Cherry?" Unwrapping the sucker I threw at him earlier, he pops it into his mouth, and it's then I notice the silver glint on his tongue.

"Actually, I do. Made you laugh, didn't I?" I struggle—not very hard—to pull my arms out, but with all the leather and the sand beneath us, it's not easy.

"No. You thinking that you could get away from me again made me laugh."

Like some kind of stealth clothes assassin, he unzips my leather suit and slides it to my waist, then he grips my wrists, holding them together at my stomach with one hand, and moves off me, bending my knee to reach my foot. One at a time, he removes my boots, then the rest of my suit.

It's still warm out, and I was hoping meeting Aleko tonight would lead to this, so of course, all I'm wearing now that my suit and tank-top are off are my black bra and lace panties. Aleko's gaze runs all over my body, seemingly appreciating my lack of clothes, before his eyes finally rest on mine. The heat emanating from him is addictive and I'm struggling to remember why I pushed him away and let him believe I was dead.

"You won't run from me again." I feel like he wants to say more, but he stops himself, releasing his grip on my wrists and standing.

The sound of the ocean crashing against the pillars of the pier to our left is suddenly the only thing I can hear, but the rhythm of my pounding heart quickly joins in as Aleko strips off his leather suit, revealing a plain white T-shirt and tight boxer-briefs. They hit the sandy ground beside him as quickly as they appear and my breath catches at the sight of him in all his glorious nakedness.

His cock stands hard and proud, the lines of his tattoos dipping and curving around every inch of his beautifully toned body as the moonlight makes him glow like an ethereal dark angel. I swear I'm in the middle of a romance novel, because this man is almost more than I can handle—*almost*.

Without thinking too much, I rise to my knees and move toward him, gripping his thick cock in my hand and looking up at him through my lashes. There's still a hint of anger in his eyes, but it's overshadowed by amusement and pure lust as I tentatively lick the pre-cum dripping from his tip.

The deep grumble that escapes him on an exhale has a direct link to my clit, causing a shudder to roll through me.

His eyes narrow briefly, as though he's making a decision, before he grips the low pigtails in my hair, one in each hand, and pushes himself between my lips, hard and fast. The thick head of his cock hits the back of my throat and I gag, tears forming in my eyes, but I'll take whatever he's willing to give if it means he forgives me.

He holds me in place for a few seconds before releasing the pressure on my hair so I can control my actions once more. Bringing my hands up from my knees, I palm his ass cheeks, squeezing in time with the bobs of my head as I suck him in deep, running my tongue along his shaft each time I pull away. His fingertips dig into the sides of my head, urging me to move faster, to suck harder, to twirl my tongue over his tip so I can taste every last drop he has to give.

Bringing one of my hands away from his perfectly toned ass, I grip the base of his shaft and move in time with my mouth before palming his balls and rolling them with my fingers. He groans and I look up at him through my lashes again to see his eyes firmly on me. They're hooded, and I can feel how close he is.

"Fuck!" Aleko's body tenses, his grip on my head becomes firm and he holds me in place as he thrusts deeper, pausing on a loud groan. Streams of his salty cum hit the back of my throat and I suck harder, milking him for everything he has, swallowing it all down like my favorite shake.

The crunch of the cherry sucker in his mouth makes me smile as I pull away, licking the tip of his cock to make sure I have all of him.

With his hands still on my pigtails, he encourages me to stand, lifting me by the hair so close to him that I have no other option but to run my breasts up his delectable naked body. When his cock falls between my cleavage, I shudder at the sensation, wondering what it would feel like to have his cum all over me.

Now face to face—or chest to face because he's got at least a foot on me—the scent of him is overwhelming and I'm struggling to remember why I lied to him.

"You are a dangerous woman, Mackenzie Wilson." He brings his hands down to the top of my ass, his fingers delicately stroking across my skin as he looks down at me. "I should hate you for what you did. You lied to me, Cherry. Fucking lied. And I don't know how to forgive that because I've never forgiven a liar." He closes his eyes and inhales deeply and my heart sinks a little at his admission.

I did this. I made him feel this way. It's not fun.

"I'm so—" My apology is cut off by his lips on mine, his tongue taking no prisoners and demanding entrance into my eager mouth. The hard metal of his tongue bar confirms that he's had it repierced since leaving jail, and I'm not complaining. That thing is magical when it's pressed against my clit.

Aleko's firm hands slide farther down to grip the globes of my ass and he lifts me so we're the same height. I need zero encouragement to wrap my legs around his waist, loving the sensation of his hardening cock against my panty-covered pussy.

I really fucking missed this man.

The kiss is desperate, chaotic, and I need the thin cloth barrier between us to disappear so he can sink his cock inside me so deep I see stars. My nipples are rubbing against the material of my bra, needing contact as much as my pussy does as I push myself closer to Aleko.

His grip on my ass as he kneads my flesh is hard enough to leave fingertip-sized bruises, and I can't wait to wear them with pride.

Quicker than I can blink, Aleko pulls his head back, breaking our kiss, our connection, but his hold on me doesn't falter.

"Why didn't you tell me?"

Okay, not the way I thought this was going to go yet, but I'm all for an open dialogue—now that I know what a shit-show it is to keep things from him.

I make a move to get down, but his grip tightens, indicating that I'm not going anywhere.

Sighing, I quietly tell my pussy to stand down because this isn't going to be pretty.

"I've been planning it for a long time. And you were never a part of that." I lower my eyes, focusing on the lines of the octopus across his bare chest.

Aleko is quick to rectify my move, using one of his hands to place a finger beneath my chin and lift my head again.

"The moment I made you mine, you made me yours. That means I'm a part of every-fucking-thing, Cherry." His gaze is intense, but the anger and hurt are back, stronger than the lust from minutes ago.

"I know." I sigh again because I *do* know. And that's what made it so difficult when the time came. "But it needed to be believable. You helped make it believable."

"You mean you fucking used me?" Disgust fills his eyes and he loosens his grip on my ass, allowing me to slide down his body. I already hate the lack of contact as shame rolls through me.

"No. I would never—"

"But you did."

"Aleko, no. I…"

"What, Mackenzie? What could you possibly say to make it all better?" His tone is accusing, but there's hope there, as though he really does want me to make this all better.

My eyes remain locked on his, even with the small distance between our bodies now.

"You weren't supposed to go to jail, I—"

"What the fuck did you think would happen when I realized someone had shot my old lady? That I'd find the ones responsible and invite them over for coffee?"

"I thought you'd be safer by not knowing. There was no doubt in my mind you'd have killed Jake for me, and if you went to prison for my problems, well… I wouldn't have been able to live with that." My voice breaks on the last syllable, having to compete against the roar of the crashing waves. As emotion floods my tone and tears prick my eyes, it feels as though even the ocean is pissed off at me and my life choices.

"And you thought me living with your death was a better option, did you?" Hate fills his words, creating a bigger chasm out of the crack already running through my heart.

He's right. I may have thought my plan through, but not once did I imagine the fallout after he came along.

"I'm sorry, okay?" The tears finally break free and I can't contain the gentle sob. "But I'm only sorry for what I did to you. Everything else needed to happen. Jake needed to be taught a lesson, and it had to…" I inhale shakily, the tears streaming now. "It had to be me."

Aleko's expression softens a little and he steps closer, placing a palm on each side of my face and searching my eyes for more answers.

"What happened with Jake, Cherry? Was his shooting fake too?"

I slowly shake my head. "No, but he's been alive for the last two months."

His eyes widen slightly at my admission. I want to tell him everything, be completely open and honest with him, and I'm afraid that ship has sailed, but I have to try. Aleko can't forgive lies.

"Where is he?" As though he can take care of all my problems before he kicks me to the curb, Aleko's eyes are tense, narrowed, focused on the person who destroyed my life.

"He's dead now. As of tonight, actually." I huff a laugh, but it's full of pain and anger.

"So you kept him alive and in pain for the last two months while you pretended you were both dead?"

What I can only describe as pride takes over his face as I slowly nod, more tears falling down my cheeks and over his thumbs.

"Oh, baby. You really are fucked up, aren't you?" The way he says it sounds more like a proud father than an angry lover.

More tears trickle down my face as I nod again, fearful of how he's going to react now.

"Come home with me, Cherry. We'll fix everything. *Together.*"

"I can't, I—" Once again, I'm interrupted with a searing kiss. A kiss to rival all kisses as our tongues war, our bodies heat, and all sense of time disappears with my fears of losing him.

"Did you bury him?" He pulls away to look deep into my soul to ask his question, and I shake my head, knowing I left Jake's corpse in the basement so I could race tonight.

"Okay. Let's go call Grinder."

Chapter Nine

Aleko

"Woo wee! I've got some serious primal kink vibes going on right now."

I look to Grinder and shake my head.

"What the fuck is that?" I'm confused but also more than a little curious.

"Oh, brother. The chase, the hunt, the catch, and the ultimate fuck." He nods over and over again like his mental image is getting the stamp of approval from his brain. And his cock, apparently, since his palm cups his groin, making him moan.

"Dude, do not fucking come in your pants. I will throat punch you." I chuckle at Bear's threat, then reality gives me a shot of adrenaline straight to my heart knowing it's time for some serious truth.

"Did you buy this place?" Bash crouches down and takes some of the damp dirt into his hand and lets it fall between his fingers like he's assessing its worth. It's early

September so dawn comes later than the summer, but at six in the morning, there's enough light to see our surroundings.

"Nah, it's not mine. It belongs to Mackenzie's EMT partner, Spencer." I let my gaze bounce from one end of the cabin to the other. Standing here at the first light of day with the dew settling over the window panes and the trees swaying in the slight breeze, it feels like we've been parachuted into some kind of fairy tale with a Stephen King-ish twist.

"It's like *Little Red Riding Hood* meets *Pet Sematary*." They all grunt their agreement with Bear's assessment.

"It's about to get a lot weirder. But first, I need you all to not freak out." As I speak, I take a couple of steps forward and turn to face them.

"Well, that's just fucking stupid, brother. You saying that is automatically gonna get us freaked out. It's like when they're screaming 'NO!' or 'STOP!' and it just makes you wanna pound 'em harder and harder."

I look to the sky, begging for some much needed patience. Grinder's stupid comment makes Bear lose his shit.

"That's called rape, you fucking asshole!"

"Relax, brother. It's actually called role-play. You should try it. It's a cumfest every fucking time." Somebody save me.

"Christ, forget it. Why are we here, Psycho?" I nod at Bear, taking a deep breath, my hands on my hips and my head down as I search for the right words.

Except I don't get the chance to say a damn thing because my favorite sound in the world calls out behind me.

Enter Mackenzie, back from the dead.

"You're here cause I need help moving a body."

Raising my eyes and looking at my brothers through my lashes, I almost laugh at their cartoonish expressions.

Bash is wide-eyed, like a cat facing a bull with no way to run. Bear is blinking like maybe he's hallucinating or half-asleep as his mouth opens then closes, but the right words seem to escape him.

Grinder? Well, he's true to form.

"I knew that fucking ambulance was too close." We all look at him with shock in our eyes. "What? No fucking way an ambulance gets there two minutes after a call. We were out in the middle of no-fucking-where." Then he grins at my little Cherry Pie and I want to punch him in the eye for looking at her like she's his next meal. "Hey, Mac, death looks mighty fucking delicious on you." At his words, I *do* punch him. In the shoulder cause I'm not a complete fucking nutjob.

"Watch your fucking mouth, Grinder, or next time I'll rip your fucking nuts off."

Grinder rubs at his shoulder and, to his credit, manages to look a little sheepish.

"My bad, didn't mean no disrespect, Mac. I'm just sayin', it's good to see you breathing and shit." Fucking Grinder.

"Can we just go back to the fact that… she's alive?" Bear is still staring at Mackenzie as she trots down the wooden steps of the house and stands at my side.

"Yeah, it's a long story and I'll be glad to tell you as we move my brother's body." My arm automatically wraps around her shoulders, my protective stance unmistakable.

"Fuck, Mac. We really missed you." Bear doesn't even ask for permission—don't fucking judge me, she's my girl, no other man gets to touch her—as he steps forward, wraps his huge arms around her waist and hauls up like she weighs a total of nothing. I'd laugh at the sound of her giggling if I weren't put out by the fact that another man is getting this reaction out of her.

"That's enough." Everyone freezes, then four pairs of eyes are staring at me. "What? We get it. You're all happy she's alive. Now, put her down."

"Geez, grumpy is back."

I shoot Bash a death glare and, to my satisfaction, he looks away. Kid's getting a little too ballsy.

"Alright, so where are the shovels?" Bear claps his hands like we're about to play a round of Monopoly.

"Aww man, it's been so long since we've had to bury bodies. I've missed it."

Mackenzie pats Grinder on the cheek and grins. "You're welcome."

Fucking hell. This woman.

With the five of us working, Bash and I get Jake wrapped in plastic and tied off nice and tight while Bear and Grinder dig a hole away from the property and far enough from the river so it doesn't show up on a day of heavy rains.

"We should plant a tree here or something." All eyes land on Grinder.

"Why?" I ask as Bear slashes a hand in the air with a definite answer of his own.

"No."

"Why not? It'll be the only good thing he'll do… feed a tree," Bash pipes in, agreeing with Grinder.

"Because the roots will eventually dig him out at some point." We all nod, thankful Bear loves falling down rabbit holes of information.

"Makes sense," Bash whispers as we all look at the freshly moved earth for a second. It's nearing lunch time and we're all sweaty and dirty, but it doesn't stop me from pulling Mackenzie flush against my side, needing to feel her warmth.

"I think he's had enough of our time. Who's hungry?" I chuckle at Mackenzie's words but stop when Bear's words of wisdom act as a cold shower.

"We need to call church. The club needs to know." He looks to Mackenzie, and even though I know Bear would never harm a single hair on her head, my grip tightens around her waist. "Mac, you need to come with us."

We don't bother showering, so putting on our leathers after manual work with a corpse feels like Hell on Earth. The water heater in the cabin is just big enough for one shower and some change a day so it didn't make sense to waste time. That's why we have suites at the compound.

Which is where we're headed, ready to face the firing squad.

"All right, all right, calm your asses down. You sound like a bunch of toddlers jacked up on sugar." Everyone at church quiets down at Prez's fatherly order.

With Ninja running across the huge table, I tap the wood three times with a freshly cut carrot stick and chuckle when he runs to me like a well-oiled speed bike. He knows what's up. Prez's wife Vanessa prepares little baggies for me every day with different fruits and vegetables for Ninja. Apparently, while I was trying to survive in jail, they were scouring the online world and learning how to get organized when sharing their home with a pet rat. Okay, so jail ain't as bad as prison, but still.

"Sorry, Prez, we're just a little excited about getting our Enforcer back," Hoops calls out, and everyone goes back to slapping the table in unison while making obscene noises.

"How's your arse feeling, Psycho? Get a work-out in there?" I don't need to look up to know it's Sledge talking shit. The accent and the crude jab do the job perfectly.

"No more than you, brother. Heard Grinder's been practicing on you." I wink at Sledge as he throws a lighter at me hard enough that I have to duck out of the way, laughing.

"Touché, motherfucker."

The raucous being more than Ninja can handle, he rummages through the baggie, grabs an extra piece of raw cauliflower, and looks up at me with begging eyes.

"Come on, buddy." Picking him—and his goodies—up, I put him on my shoulder and let him run to the safety of my hoodie before depositing the veggies in there. I swear to fuck, I wouldn't be surprised if there's a garden growing in there one day. I unwrap a treat of my own once he's settled and pop it into my cheek.

"Yeah, yeah. We get it. Now shut the fuck up and listen." Prez's words are like a blanket over the room, the silence immediate as we all look to him for the order of the day.

The cramped room, I realize, has every one of our members here, save for Diablo and Axel. They've been up north trying to rebuild the SOK charter in New York after Marco Mancini destroyed it eight years ago. The few remaining members have tried their best to make something of it but they were barely patched in back then and knew nothing about running a club. According to Bear's regular updates, a couple of months ago, their charter president called ours and asked for help or else risk a permanent dissolution.

Prez responded by sending two of our most trusted members who are apparently running that fucking ship as tight as a virgin's pussy. Diablo's words, not mine.

Mackenzie had to see Spencer, but she said she'd be here soon and my mind is solely on her when Prez brings me up to speed with what's been going on for the last few months while I was locked up.

Sure, Bear visited every two weeks and gave me whatever updates he could get away with in mixed company, but there's something to be said about being back in the midst of the group, the unity... the family. Nothing beats this dynamic.

"Most of the Rebels are in jail, maybe all of them. Who the fuck knows? Some disappeared when they didn't get picked up since they weren't at the trailer park when the stint went down." Prez is leaning back in his chair, a snarl on his lips like it always is when talking about our rival club.

"Maybe we get lucky and they all die a slow death," Shade mumbles from beside me and everyone calls out a "hear hear".

"From what our dear Deputy Sheriff tells me, their trials won't be happening for months still since the state needs time to gather all the evidence against them. With Jake being dead, she's guessing their Prez will be getting the heat for most of their illegal activities."

I grind my teeth at the mention of that piece of shit. Nobody knows this yet, but they *will* all die. Mackenzie got her revenge on Jake but they're all guilty of her trauma. Time to collect the debts, and the only currency I'm interested in is their heartbeats.

"Hey, Psycho, how'd it feel to get a drop on that piece of shit, Goblin?"

As the Mary Jane gets passed around, I crunch down on my sucker, pull the stick out of my mouth and chuck it into the trash can. With a freshly rolled joint in my mouth I light it up with Sledge's Zippo as I consider the best way to answer Grinder's question. Taking my time, I inhale deep, lean my head back and exhale.

"Better than a fucking orgasm." The room erupts in catcalls and banging fists until Prez does some banging of his own with his gavel.

"All right, calm the fuck down. We still have a problem out there. These fuckers are in jail and yet those dangerous drugs are still out there, circulating. Now, I promised Python's mother we'd find the fuckers responsible for the lethal batch and I never walk away from a promise. The cops are working on their end but we're not getting tunnel vision. Clearly, the Rebels were just a middle man. I want the motherfucking head of the snake." More banging on the table, then a few seconds of silence as we all remember our beloved prospect. Fuck, I miss him. Being here without him breaks my heart a little.

"I never told y'all, but Python came to me as a last ditch effort to get clean. His momma was Vanessa's nurse when..." He clears his throat and rubs a hand over his beard. I recognize the look in his eyes. It's pain and loss but none of us push him for more information. "She took care of my old lady real good. So I wanted to take care of her son."

The room falls quiet as we all look inside ourselves, knowing we've all suffered in some way either before, during, or after we patched in. When it comes to our brothers, our empathy is sky high.

"Anyway, we need to keep our ears to the ground and start some dialogue with our friends out there. Someone knows something and I want that information. Now, on a more positive note, we've got new prospects that need to be voted in to join Bash." As Prez nods to Hoops, his VP gets up and opens the door. Two people I've never seen before walk in, one of them being a woman.

Well, damn. Ballsy.

"Kellan Jones, aka Jonesy is being sponsored by Sledge." The latter slaps the former on the back, nearly sending him flying across the table. Dude needs some meat on his bones. My eyes travel the length of him from top to bottom, taking in the tats and piercings, and liking what I see. From what Bear said, the kid's from a rich family up north and decided to break ranks for a life of freedom and danger. We'll see if he can keep up.

"Kincaid Ford is being sponsored by Hoops." All eyes turn on the tall chick decked out in leather and sporting chin-length blue hair. Blue. Not grandma-gray went wrong, actual Yamaha blue. Guess she's a fan.

"Dibs!" Our fascination with our first female prospect is interrupted by Grinder's outburst, and without a second thought, every single one of us throws the nearest object at him, making him duck for cover.

"Sorry." His mumbled apology earns him a chuckle around the room. Well, except from Hoops, who leans down and whispers in his ear. I can't hear him but the way Grinder's face blanches, I'm guessing it's nothing fun.

"All for?" Prez calls out as Sledge takes the minutes with the number of votes for and against.

We all raise our hands for multiple reasons. First, we need new blood. Second, having a female prospect will only be an advantage for our club. A change in perspective can only benefit us.

"Good. Welcome... for now. You fuck up, you're out. You disrespect, you're out. You betray... you're out," Prez lays down the law like he always does to fresh meat.

"Permanently." We all chuckle at whoever spoke in the back but Prez doesn't pause.

"You'll get used and abused in all the normal ways, but if anyone steps out of line, you come to me or Hoops. Got it?" They both nod and the pause that follows is my cue to speak.

"Prez? I gotta say something." Here goes nothing. "That last week in jail, I found out—" My phone buzzes in my hand and without looking, I know it's Mackenzie so I answer. "Yeah?" Prez looks at me with fire in his eyes since phones aren't allowed in church. Better to ask for forgiveness than permission and all that.

"The fuck, Psycho?" I hate that glare in Prez's eyes, but it's truth time.

"We need to go outside so I can show you." I stand, making sure Ninja isn't jostled too much, and walk to the door.

"Fucking drama queen." Bear says as he passes me out the door with the rest of the club following close behind.

"Holy fucking shit!"

"How the fuck?"

"Fucking knew it!"

"Oh my God!" I turn at the sound of Vanessa's voice and grin when I see the tears running down her cheeks. Those are happy tears and happiness is always welcome.

"Surprise?" Mackenzie mumbles, her arms out wide and her cheeks pink with either embarrassment or fear.

Prez looks at me and the glare is gone, but the questions are definitely there.

"I'm gonna need you to fill me in, son."

Chapter Ten
Mackenzie

"Fuck off! Nah, Cain's a bloke!" Sledge is propping up the bar in the SOK clubhouse, locally sourced can of ale in hand. His nose is scrunched up, his hazel eyes squinting in disbelief as he takes a swig from his drink.

"Tell her to fuck off again and I'll stab you in the hand so you can't ride without being in pain." Aleko's hold around my shoulders tightens, effortlessly pulling me closer to him, and I can't help smiling at the whole situation.

"Damn, dude, that's a bit much, ain't it? You couldn't just punch me or somethin'? No… you'll fuckin' stab me. Wanker." Sledge downs the rest of his drink, crushing the can into his palm when he's finished. "Still don't believe your old lady is Cain." He throws the aluminum over his shoulder as he walks away, shaking his head.

I chuckle, pulling Aleko back to me as he moves to go after Sledge, trying to defend my honor when it's really not necessary. Won't say I don't love it though.

"I can fight my own battles. He isn't the first and won't be the last to not believe I'm Cain. There were even a couple of the Rebels who thought an outside rider was being brought in for the races by my brother and Isa—"

Aleko's growl silences me, because it's not a sexy I-want-to-fuck-you-now growl, it's more of a scary I'm-going-to-kill-things kinda growl. He doesn't even need to speak for me to understand where his head's at. I know the mention of Isaac, the president of the Toxic Rebels, makes Aleko's skin crawl as much as mine. The way this man feels my pain with me is just one of the reasons I'm blowing my original plan to smithereens by revealing I'm actually alive to anyone other than Spence—and Steve.

Living without Aleko has been a torture I've barely endured. After just a few short weeks of knowing him, he managed to integrate himself into my very soul. Being here, with him and his friends, after they helped me bury my brother that I murdered, is all the therapy I feel like I need. They haven't made me out to be a terrible person for what I did or judged me in any way; they simply helped, patted me on the back, and told me they were happy to see me not dead.

The Cain revelation had more comments from them than killing my *Jakeass* brother. Grinder said he knew Cain was a woman this whole time, Bear's big brown eyes shone with pride as he shook his head in disbelief, and Prez asked if I wanted to prospect for the Sons. The answer was no because I know what prospects go through, and I'm not being a motorcycle club skivvy again. I did it for long enough with the Toxic Rebels. I was—and I supposed I still am—a fully-fledged Toxic Rebel member. Although, with most of them in jail, including the Prez, is the Stonebrook Falls Chapter still even a thing?

"Can I get you a drink?" The prospect, Kincaid, leans over the bar, her thin black tank-top showcasing a full-color sleeve tattoo on her right arm and a beautiful chest tattoo creeping up to her neck. She introduced herself to me when we got back from the race and I think I love her already. She's tall and unassuming, but the dark look in her brown eyes tells me she has a story. I'm not one to have girlfriends, mainly because the ones from the Rebel compound were selfish twats, but I feel like Kincaid is my people.

"No, I'm taking my old lady home." Ninja takes this moment to make his pleasure at going home known, creeping from Aleko's hood onto his shoulder to nuzzle into his neck. Then, Ninja's cute little nose vibrates as he sniffs the air and looks over to me. His tiny eyes widen—if that's at all possible—and he scurries across Aleko's arm wrapped around me and jumps onto my shoulder, where he promptly nuzzles into my neck before settling into my cleavage. It makes me giggle, and Aleko's eyes as he watches us are filled with so much love I think my insides want to burst.

My heart is pounding as I stare right back—after giving Ninja an appropriate amount of attention, of course, scratching his belly and behind his ears.

"Home?"

"Yeah, Cherry. Home."

The short ten-minute ride here was just as fun as our little game of chase last night, but in a different way. We weaved through traffic, held hands as we rode side-by-side, and my cheeks ache from all the smiling. I know we have some things to talk about, and I've personally got a hell of a lot of stuff to work through, but I no longer feel like the weight of the world is on my shoulders.

After we lock up our motorcycles in the secure garage beside the building, Ninja ignores Aleko's open palm and eyes me, his tiny nose twitching.

"Traitor." Aleko grins at his furry pet and shakes his head.

"You wanna come with me, tiny dude?" I swear Ninja nods in response to my question and I hold out my own palm, then bring him in close to my chest, where he promptly settles.

"I guess I'm not the only one who missed you." Smirking, Aleko quickly raises and lowers that one eyebrow as he pulls a cherry sucker from his pocket and pops it into his mouth.

With steady strides, I follow when he turns and heads inside the building. We go up one flight of stairs before turning left to where, I'm assuming, his apartment is. The suite he has at the SOK compound was great, easy, convenient, but this feels like he's letting me see more of him, and I like it.

The apartment is small, with two doors off the open-plan kitchen/living room—I'm guessing for the bedroom and bathroom. What really makes me smile, is the motorcycle frame with custom parts spaced all around where most people would usually have a couch and TV.

"Does this one have a name too?"

"Yeah, Dot's a work in progress." Pride fills his voice as he slides off his jacket and hangs it on a hook by the door, leaving his tattooed arms bare and the white T-shirt hugging his strong biceps.

I can't help but feel that Dot and I have a lot in common because I'm also a work in progress, still trying to figure out who I really am. One thing is for sure: I'm a lot fucked up.

Ninja shuffles around, indicating that he wants to get down, scurrying straight for the snacks Aleko is pulling from the fridge for him.

"Can I use your shower?" For some reason, I now feel incredibly awkward in this new space.

"Yeah. It's the door on the left." Aleko continues to move around the kitchen area, prepping some food and drink for Ninja.

I half-expected him to tell me to wait for him to join me, but I'm in the small bright-white bathroom now and nothing. There's no bath, but the shower is larger than average, surrounded by glass doors with rounded silver handles. A few silver-patterned tiles are interspersed with the plain-white ones on the walls, giving the whole room a beautifully elegant look.

Fifteen minutes later, I'm stepping out of the shower, my thick blonde hair dripping down my back as I wrap the thick gray towel around my body. Disappointment settles in at the fact that Aleko didn't come to shower with me, and I feel like he's still mad at me—understandably so.

Once I'm dry, I towel off my hair and decide to be bold, walking out of the bathroom completely naked. Ninja is on the kitchen counter with his head in a bowl of food, and Aleko has either run away or is in his bedroom.

The heat between us has been sizzling all day, with light touches, cheeky smiles, and longing glances, my pussy is practically begging for an orgasm. Which means any and all thoughts of actual real life shit is being pushed aside—totally on purpose because I'm not ready to truly think about what I've done.

Four pairs of red leather cuffs are laid out on the deep-gray bed sheets, and a fully-clothed Aleko is staring out of the small window at the far side of the bedroom. The sun is setting, leaving an almost angelic glow around him, and he must hear my heart beating loudly in my chest as I admire him because as he turns, his light-blue eyes slowly graze down my naked body. That hunger I've craved all damn day fills his gaze as he prowls toward me like he's a starving lion and I'm a juicy slab of meat laid out for the taking. It shouldn't be sexy, yet here I am.

His movements are fluid, and it's clear he's comfortable in his own body because he knows how to use every inch of it to make me weak at the knees. Stopping inches away from me, he seems to be holding himself back.

"Wh—"

"It's my turn to speak now, Cherry. Inside this room, we follow my rules." Aleko leans in, his T-shirt skimming my nipples that are begging for attention, and sniffs the crook of my neck. "Fucking delicious."

I smile at his approval, grateful for the cherry-scented body wash he had in the bathroom—exactly the same brand I've always used.

"What if I don't want to follow the rules?" My voice is all breathy and completely unexpected.

Aleko chuckles and shakes his head. "You think you have a choice, Cherry?"

Before I can answer, he kisses me, hard and fast. Our tongues duel for dominance and he nips at my lower lip as his hands cup my face. All too soon, it's over and he's pulling away.

"Lie down on the bed."

Again, as I go to speak, he silences me, this time by tweaking my nipple, which makes me yelp. He does it with a stern stare that suggests arguing with him is futile. The only thing holding me back is my intrigue for the cuffs.

"Fine." My sass is all bravado because there isn't anywhere else I'd rather be in this moment.

Aleko picks up the cuffs, putting all but one pair down on the bedside table as I lie on the memory foam mattress. In complete silence, he lifts my left arm and pushes it over my head, then he wraps a leather cuff around my wrist and buckles it firmly in place before attaching the other half of it to the bedpost. He repeats his actions with my other arm, then moves to my ankles.

"I need to restrain you for a while because you have some lessons to learn, my beautiful Cherry Pie." He continues as though he's talking to himself. "I'm not sure how long I'll be able to hold out for because you're a fucking vision. Those pretty pink lips winking at me." Aleko places a tender kiss on the inside of my now cuffed ankle, completely at odds with this sexy, domineering thing he's got going on, before moving to my other foot.

"Maybe you don't need to restrain me. I can be good." I try for my sweetest smile, batting my eyelashes, but his smirk and the way he rolls his eyes in disbelief make me laugh. "Rude."

"I'll show you rude, soon enough." This time he kisses the top of my other foot before crawling up the bed, still wearing his jeans and white T-shirt.

"Why are you still fully clothed?"

"Nah-ah-ah. You don't get to ask the questions tonight. My rules, remember?" He winks, and I swear my clit has a pulse, throbbing to the beat of its own personal rave party where Aleko is the DJ.

Spread-eagle on his bed, there's not really a lot I can do, so I frown to show my faux-displeasure.

Without further preamble, Aleko's tongue is lapping at my juices between my pussy lips, his large hands spread across my hips and thighs. I arch my back as pleasure rolls through my body, and one of his hands slides up my stomach to grip my breast. He pinches and twists at my nipple, then sucks on my clit so hard it almost hurts, but the immediate pleasure overtakes any pain. The ball of his tongue bar against my flesh is as good as I remember, adding an extra sensation to the already mind blowing pleasure.

An orgasm is quickly building, starting in the tips of my toes and my fingertips, and as it begins flowing through me, everything stops.

"No!" My yell is involuntary, but I was so close to coming I could almost taste it. It's like the ghost of that orgasm is now floating away, never to be seen again, which is the exact moment realization dawns on me. So, this is how it's going to go, is it?

Aleko's chuckle from between my legs makes me growl down at him, only making him laugh harder.

"Fuck, that was cute, Cherry." He dives right back in, eating out my pussy like his life depends on every drop of my cum as I buck up against his face, seeking out that delicious friction, chasing my phantom orgasm and begging it to come back.

It doesn't take him long to build me back up again, pinching my nipples and sucking on my clit as he makes my entire body tingle like I'm wrapped in live wire. Just as I'm about to worship at the altar of the big *O*, everything comes to a screeching halt.

Motherfucker.

Our gazes clash as his mischievous blues meet my narrowed glare and I swear to fuck there's an entire conversation going on between us without a single word being said.

Then he begins again...

This time when the orgasm builds, it's almost painful and I cry out for more. Aleko obliges, using his other hand and pushing it beneath him, sliding one of his fingers around my opening, but never all the way inside.

It feels like he's been teasing me for hours, when logic tells me it can't have been more than a half an hour, but this "no orgasms" rule is well past frustrating and sliding into infuriating territory.

As I'm trying to control my breaths, Aleko reaches into the bottom drawer of his bedside table and pulls out a medium-sized pink dildo.

"I hope you're gonna make me come with that thing, because you're doing a shit job of it so far." I'm being bratty and I don't care.

"Oh, baby, you're going to come so hard you'll see stars, but before that…" He turns the dildo on, so it's vibrating, and pushes it against my clit, making my hips buck again as that familiar throb closes in once more. The pleasure-pain of being held off for so long only seems to intensify it each time.

"Oh fuck, no!" Ghosted.

Aleko moves the dildo away from my pussy and licks the tip, his eyes never leaving mine.

"Tonight, *Mackenzie Wilson,* you will learn a very valuable lesson in not lying to me. Because I'm telling you now, there is nothing wrong with you for what you had to do.

You're not broken, you're not crazy, you're exactly fucking just right." His words are full of fire and they hit the mark.

My heart aches because he's not wrong, I've been feeling all of those things, but I've been pushing them aside in hopes he'd get me off with a rave party between my legs. A hot tear forms in the corner of my eye, but I blink it away.

"I'm going to edge the fuck out of you for another hour before I give you what you need. Because, baby, the first time you come tonight will be with your pussy lips squeezing the life outta my cock." The buzzing of the dildo hits my clit again and I groan, throwing my head back and trying to breathe through it. "Maybe then you'll realize how fucking perfect you are for me because you're not the only one who killed their brother."

CHAPTER ELEVEN
ALEKO

In my quest to strip Mackenzie of all her demons and open her eyes to the perfection of herself, I failed to factor in the excruciating pain of a long-term boner. It's only fair I hold myself back until I let her come, but holy mother of all the gods, my dick is about to raise the white flag.

"Scootch down as far as the cuffs will let you."

Blinking back the haze of lust, Mackenzie follows my instructions, allowing me enough space to fill my palms with the naked globes of her ass and pull her back up to my hungry lips.

The sound of my mouth devouring her pussy coupled with the scent of her need for me only makes my cock throb even more painfully. Ignoring it for now, knowing I won't be able to last very much longer, I reach back for the dildo. Instead of turning it on, I push it up her cunt and leave it there while I suck on her swollen clit.

Her screams and vocal threats only spur me on. She's right on the edge of her sanity and I can't wait to break it all down. Destroy her inner voices trying to peg her down a couple of notches.

Nobody hurts my woman, not even her own damn self.

"Fuck, Aleko, just let me come! Please." My eyes snap open and land on her scrunched up nose and pleading gaze.

I could be a good guy and let her come all over me but that's not happening. I have a plan and nothing, not even the greatest fucking thing in the world—her pleasure—is going to stop me.

"Don't move." I chuckle at my assholish ways and wink as she growls—nope, that was a snarl—at my retreating back.

"When you least expect it, I will make your balls pay for this." My chuckle turns to a choke when I reach the door to my bathroom and grab the water bottle I recently used and left on the counter. The sadist in me grins as I fill it from the tap.

"I have no doubts, Cherry Pie, that your revenge will come with a steep interest rate. But..." I kneel back down on the mattress right between her smooth, silky thighs and pull the dildo out just enough to watch her breathe through her need to come. Then I slam it right back inside.

Her juices are everywhere. On her pussy, on the bed, all over the fucking dildo, and now dripping over my fingers. Without thinking about it, I bring my thumb to my mouth and suck on it like I was sucking on her clit not two minutes ago.

The primal reaction she gives me is better than the actual taste of her, which is saying something since she's my favorite flavor in the universe.

"Here," Putting the bottle to her lips, I cradle the back of her head, "Drink." "I have to—" Her phrase dies on her lips when I tilt the bottle up and force her to swallow.

"What you have to do is hydrate." Every gulp has rivulets spilling down her chin and the corners of her mouth and I can't fucking believe I'm jealous of water.

"What the fuck are you doi—" Without looking, I set the bottle on the bedside table and crash my lips into hers. My tongue sweeps in, finding hers, and what should have been a quick kiss turns into a declaration of everything. My love, my obsession, my need.

"This mouth? It's mine. You don't get to take it away from me. You don't get to decide what's best for me. Do you understand what I'm saying?" There's no need to speak loudly, my words infiltrate like a breath through her parted lips and as her eyes flash with understanding, I give her a curt nod like we've just sealed the deal of a lifetime.

Now, it's time to keep my promise.

Pulling out the dildo, I press my palm to her lower belly and thrust two fingers inside her cunt. Just as I curl my digits in a hook, her intake of breath and screams that follow almost make me come in my fucking pants. It doesn't take long, a couple of well placed massages over that perfect spot that makes her lose her goddamn mind and her body gives up all control.

Pressing down just a little harder on her bladder, her gift is almost immediate. I don't waste time getting undressed, almost ripping off my jeans before lining my cock up to her pussy lips and slamming my fingers right back inside her pussy.

In awe, I watch as the first squirt lands on the tip of my steel-hard dick. It's fucking hot watching give up her control as it coats my skin. Over and over again, she releases all of her secrets and manipulations. Her body has never lied to me, only her mouth, and as she cries out to the gods, I keep going. I keep making her come, squirting her lies away. Howling her deceptions at the space between us until it disappears because as I lean in and swallow her curses, I remind her of who we are. I remind her that we belong to one another as my dick slams inside her pussy, thrusting in and out of her like an animal. Fuck, she feels like heaven. Like home. Like... everything.

Still, I need more.

Reaching out, I open the drawer to the bedside table and curl my fingers around the bottle of lube. It's hard to concentrate when her tongue is fighting mine for control, our kiss becoming harder, more violent and demanding.

With one palm at the side of her face supporting my weight, I sink my teeth into her bottom lip and whisper, "There's only one god for you, Cherry, and he's about to own you all over again." On my last word, I lean back on my haunches, sliding out of her cunt and palming my dick, giving it a couple of pulls and feeling the wetness of her orgasm from shaft to tip.

I wish I didn't have to add the lubricant, that I could take her with only her cum on my dick, but I meant it when I said no one would ever hurt her... not even me.

In quick successions, I release her ankles from the bondage and push her knees up until her ass is in full view.

"I own your mouth and I own your cunt. Soon, I'll own your ass, too." Squeezing the bottle, I place a generous amount of lube on my fingers and circle her opening with the tip of my index, pressing more and more with every turn. "The next time you decide to leave me, remember this moment." My finger breaches her tight little hole to the first knuckle before I pull it out and push right back inside, giving her more. "Remember the second I claimed you, that precise feeling when I took what's mine."

With total and complete control over her movements, I watch the tight features of her gorgeous face as my dick slowly, torturously glides back in and out of her cunt, ignoring her pleas to hurry up. To go faster. To fuck her harder.

I'm in fucking control of this.

For two months, she controlled my emotions by letting me believe she was dead. Tonight? I'm letting her know that her orgasms and her pleasures have always, and will forever, belong to me. In my fucking control.

"Oh my fucking god, Aleko. If you don't hurry the fu—" With a flick of my gaze, I see her panties lying on the edge of the bed right where I put them while she was taking a shower. Closing my fist around them, I bring them to her mouth and grin down on her like the fucking demented asshole I know I can be when it comes to her.

"You know, for someone who has a lot of groveling to do, you sure are being bossy." The only clue I get that she's figured out my next move, is the widening of her eyes and the snarl that makes her luscious top lip curl up right before I shove her panties deep into her mouth.

"That's more like it." With my cock buried inside her pussy I growl at the sight of it, slowly fucking the fight right out of her.

But I want more.

Pulling out, I line the tip of my cock to her asshole and press, all the while squirting the lube down her crack and over my shaft.

"Breathe, baby. Just breathe through your nose for me." My hips want to snap forward, my dick eager to breach that opening, but I have to be careful. Gritting my teeth to keep myself in check, I throw the lube on the bed somewhere and wrap my fingers around her thighs as I push myself deeper inside her ass. "Fuck, you feel too good. So tight and hot and fucking perfect for me." Letting out a pained exhale, I sink the top row of my teeth into my bottom lip and make the mistake of looking down at Mackenzie as I do.

Fighting her restraints with her head thrown back and the cords of her throat pulsing in time with her rapid heartbeat, I lose my ever loving mind.

"Fuck, baby… I can't—" I can't what? Control myself? Love you more than I do in this moment? Can't fucking lose you ever again? Yeah, all of the above.

Watching her closely, I take in all of her tells. Dilated pupils, check. Heaving chest, check. But it's when her stubborn chin lifts sharply in time with her pelvis begging for more that I know she's two breaths away from losing her fucking mind with her need for harder. For faster. For me.

With her permission, I bury my entire cock inside her ass, and just as my groin meets her flesh, I exhale in relief, although it only lasts a brief moment. My need to fuck takes complete control as I pull back and slam right back inside. Over and over again.

"Now, it's time for you to listen." My hips pump in and out as I take my time, feeling every tight ridge of her ass with her inner muscles squeezing the life out of my dick.

Even from the bottom she tops me from mind to soul.

"For two months, I grieved. The only thing that kept me from blowing my brains out was my thirst for revenge." Leisurely, I pull out then slam back inside as my thumb finds her clit and I feed on her moans. All the while, her eyes are trained solely on me, listening, absorbing my words.

"I spoke to the image of you in my mind and I made unbreakable vows to you." Ducking my head down, I take one nipple into my mouth and suck hard enough to feel her chest bow with my movements. When my teeth close in on her hard, juicy peak, I flick my tongue over the tip, letting go only when her inner walls threaten to suffocate my dick.

"So far, only one of those promises has been kept." My grin is wide when her brows scrunch up in confusion. "You don't know, do you?" Mackenzie shakes her head as my thrusts begin to accelerate, slowly at first, until her moans are back, filling the room with the sweet sounds of her pleasure. "Karma always has an agenda, and while I was in county, she brought me a present."

Fucking her harder and harder, I lean my weight on one arm and bring my hand to her heaving chest before sliding it up to her throat. Distracted by the sight of my tattooed skin, I almost miss the whimper that escapes her panty-filled mouth.

"When I saw him, it was like I had a thin veil of red over my eyes. My skin started to boil, you know like when you've got a fever?" I'm full-out slamming my dick in and out of her, the chains of her cuffs clinking with my movements, creating music as I claim what's always been mine. Only fucking mine.

"But I had that little voice in my head telling me to step back and plan. I couldn't just go in and finish him. No, I had to make sure I got out first and killed all those other motherfuckers." My grunt, mixed in with the long, seductive groan beneath me as the head of my cock hammers against the walls of her ass, feels animalistic. We're barely human at this point, and I'm not sure how I've held on this long. "But when the time came, my sweet Cherry Pie, I made him bleed until the life spilled out of him and all over that filthy county jail concrete."

Mackenzie's back arches as I squeeze her throat tighter, fuck her just a little harder, and growl at the sight of her tears falling from the sides of her eyes as drool pools at the corners of her mouth.

"I killed Goblin for you, Cherry baby. I took his life as payment for disrespecting the sanctity of your existence." Even through the panties, I can hear her cries as her thighs wrap around my neck and her orgasm vibrates through my entire body.

Ripping the panties out so I can soak up her sounds, I press my forehead to hers and let my own orgasm explode right out of me and inside her. Deep and fulfilling. Claiming her breath and owning her pleasure.

It's like I've run a marathon through the desert, my lungs impossible to fill quickly enough, but I find the strength to remind her once more.

"Don't ever lie to me again, Mackenzie, because next time, I may not be so gentle." I won't tell her that I'll walk away, we both know that's never happening. The only way I'll ever leave is if I'm carried out in a casket, and after the hell we've been through, I'm guessing she'd be in there with me.

My lips find hers again and this time I kiss her soft and tender, worshiping her mouth with every lick and nip and whispered praise.

"You're beautiful." Or, "Your scent is life." Or, "You're so strong."

"Aleko?" My lids close at the sound of her tiny, exhausted voice.

"Yeah, baby?"

"I'm sorry I hurt you." I grin because I really needed to hear that. "But this love?" Her voice hitches on the word and my softening cock begins to stir all over again. "This love is bigger than any pain. Mine or yours. I will always protect you. Even if it's from yourself."

Fuck.

Keeping my cock nestled inside her, I uncuff her wrists and pull up the comforter as I reposition our bodies on our sides, one of her legs hiked up on my hip and her head safely under my chin.

"That makes two of us, babydoll."

Later that night, while Mackenzie's soft snores reassure me that she is right where she needs to be, I force myself to leave our bed and grab a hand towel, soaking it with warm water before joining her in bed where I soothe her body and clean her up. It's only when I'm sure she'll be okay that I allow myself to curl up behind her and sigh, finally happy again. That content feeling only lasts a second before her phone dings into the silent night. Reaching back, I palm the phone and catch the message from Spencer.

Spence: Ur mom is asking for u

That protective streak in me kicks in knowing that, right now, what my Cherry Pie really needs is rest.

The outside world can wait.

CHAPTER TWELVE
MACKENZIE

Waking up this morning with Aleko wrapped around me like a monkey, and Ninja lying beside my head on the pillow, is a huge wake-up call for me. Not only did I get a full night's sleep without the nightmares that have been plaguing me, but it also just feels right. Like I'm home for the first time since my dad died.

Dad is still something I want to look into after what Jake spewed at me about Mom cheating. I've been pushing it aside with every other emotion, burying it all deep and locking it away for future me to deal with.

Past me is a dick.

"Good morning, Cherry." Aleko inhales deeply into my neck, squeezing me a little tighter with the arm he has draped across my chest and the leg he has lying over the top of mine.

"Good morning, you." I gently pry my eyes open, unable to turn my head because I don't want to jostle Ninja.

With a low groan, Aleko rests on his elbow and looks down at me lying on my back. His eyes move from me to Ninja and the most stunning smile I've ever seen graces his plump lips. The strangest sensation bubbles from my toes to my thighs, my stomach, my heart, and actual tears begin to prick my eyes.

Concern makes him scrunch those expressive brows and he tilts his head a little. "What's wrong?"

No secrets. No lies.

I sigh a little. "I'm just so fucking in love with you and I'm super happy. Okay?" I roll my eyes to make the damn tears disappear, huffing an awkward laugh at my vulnerability this early in the morning. So early, in fact, that my breath is probably rancid too.

Aleko chuckles, shaking his head. "I fucking love you too, babydoll. Let the tears fall. I wanna taste them." He wags his brows and smirks before leaning down and licking the corner of my eye, where a tiny tear managed to escape. "Delicious." Then his lips press against mine so tenderly, my nipples perk right up and I moan with satisfaction.

The way his tongue slowly gains entrance into my mouth is just as good as when he's rough with me. He's able to erase anything and everything around me with this simple connection. Bringing my hand up to his head, I cup his cheek and try to hold him in place, but he moves away all too quickly, making me pout like the twenty-one year old I am. My stomach chooses that moment to grumble loudly, and I concur; we are not amused that the kissing has stopped.

"Let's get some breakfast before you waste away." Aleko gives me a quick kiss and gets out of bed, his thick cock standing to attention. Man's got an iron will if he's rocking a boner like that and not doing anything with it. He pulls out a pair of boxers from the top drawer of his dresser and casually slides them up and over his cock, hiding some of the good stuff. At least his chest and shoulders are still on display.

"Can't move. Ninja is sleeping." I shrug, wanting to keep the real world out a little bit longer. Here, in his bedroom, the outside doesn't exist.

"Ninja, come and get some breakfast." The little traitor wriggles from his position nestled against my head and moves onto my chest, where he does the cutest stretching anyone has ever seen, then he runs over to Aleko's outstretched hand and jumps on. "Oh look, you can move now." He winks, that stupid sexy smirk etched firmly onto his face as he picks up his phone and leaves the room.

If he wants to play that game, I'll see how blue he'll let those balls of his get before he gives in.

With this thought in mind, I untangle myself from the bed sheets and look around the small room for something completely unsuitable. Aleko's T-shirts are far too predictable, his hoodie and cut are draped across the top of his dresser in the corner of the room... no, also too predictable. Fuck it. Naked it is. My cellphone is dead, not that there is anyone other than Spence or Aleko who would text me, but I put it on charge anyway. I have a couple of side quests in my game I want to complete later.

I need to use the bathroom first, so I sneak out and sleuth it next door without being seen by Aleko, who's busy in the kitchen, hopefully making coffee if the smell is anything to go by. After finishing what I need to do and washing my hands, I take stock of my reflection in the mirror.

The deep bags beneath my eyes are a little brighter than they have been, my skin a little more flush, and my grin a whole lot wider. There's still a lot of work to do, but my mental load doesn't feel quite so heavy as it once did.

Jake is dead. Goblin is dead. Isaac and Brick need to be dead, but they and the other Rebels are currently in jail awaiting trial. I do feel bad about Booker, Cameron in particular though, because they were never overall bad guys. They just got caught up in Rebel shit because they love to ride, to race, and they wanted to be a part of something bigger than themselves. Yeah, okay, they still did bad shit. But so did I until I figured out a way to swap aspirin out for the drugs I was delivering to the Stonebrook and Rockford dealers when I was the Rebels' lackey.

We all do what we've gotta do. My reasons may have been more life and death than theirs, but toh-may-to toh-mah-to.

With a deep breath, I ready myself to be my bold self and tempt my man—the thought still makes me giddy—back into bed.

Just as I wrap my palm around the handle of the door, I hear voices out in the living space. I can't make out what they're saying, but whatever it is must be funny because there's a deep rumble of a laugh mixed with the one I love so much, and there's another I don't recognize.

Fuck! I'm naked!

I quickly look around for a towel. Why are there no towels in the bathroom except the tiny one beside the sink?

As I'm trying to figure out how the small hand towel will cover my pride, there's a heavy knock on the door.

"You 'avin' a shit in there, darlin'? Only, I'm bustin' for a piss and Psycho'll kick my arse if I do it in here."

The British one. Is it Slay? I can't remember, and it's not really important because there's no way out of here for me without at least something being seen! If I ask them to turn around, they'll want to know why and... actually, that's not so bad. I'm not doing anything wrong here so there's no reason to panic.

Okay. Breathe. It's fine.

More knocking.

"Did you fall down the loo?"

"Oh for fuck sake, Sledge, go outside in a bush. Leave my old lady alone, she can take as long as she likes."

Sledge! I was close...

Also, Aleko calling me his old lady so casually is doing things to my insides that I can't explain as anything other than... right.

"Aleko?" I call through the door.

"Yeah, baby?" He's on the other side in a heartbeat, rattling the handle without waiting for an invitation inside. It's locked. "Open up for me, Cherry."

"I'm naked!"

He chuckles in response before speaking. "It's okay." He pauses, then directs what he says next in another direction.

"Thanks, Bear. Turn the fuck around, Sledge, if you don't want those pretty eyes of yours on Grinder's trophy shelf."

"That's low, mate. Proper low." Sledge laughs, and I'm assuming he turns around because as soon as I unlock the door, the handle is turning and Aleko is inside.

"You're a much better breakfast than what my brothers brought over for us." His eyes scan the length of me as his hands roam across my skin. My head. My neck. My arms. My waist. My hips. Then he grips my ass and lifts me, making me squeal a little in surprise.

He places me on the countertop beside the sink and slams his lips against mine, immediately demanding entrance with his tongue. We battle it out, hungry for each other in every way as he grips the back of my head, his hands entangled in my hair. I hook my fingers in the waistband of his boxers, ready to pull them down and guide his hard cock into my wet pussy. I don't need any warming up because this man has me constantly ready for him with just his presence.

Aleko stops me, gripping my wrist and sucking on my tongue as he pulls away to raise that damn sexy-as-all-hell single eyebrow. The smirk that joins it could burn me up to cinders right there with how hot he makes me.

"Fuck me, Aleko." My tone is breathy and heavy with lust.

"Demanding little thing, aren't we?"

I nod, giving my best innocent pout and looking up at him through my lashes.

The grin that breaks out across his face is one for the picture books, because it's the most devilishly sexy thing I've ever seen.

"What my cherry pie wants, my cherry pie shall get." In one swift move, his boxers are on the floor and his cock is thrusting deep inside my pussy.

Aleko captures my screams with his mouth, gripping my ass with one hand and the back of my head with the other as he pounds into me. The hand on my ass moves around to my front and he pushes it between us to rub against my clit. An orgasm is building pretty quickly, the deep and fast thrusts hitting all the right places, causing all the right friction as I try to contain my noises to low moans. It's difficult because Aleko is a machine and I want to scream to the heavens how amazing this man's cock feels inside me.

"Fuck, I'm so close!"

"Yes, baby, come all over my cock." We speak between kissing, exploring each other's mouths with our tongues as he pushes impossibly deeper inside me.

I raise my knees and wrap my arms around them, gripping Aleko's sides for support and scratching across his skin as he thrusts harder, faster. The tips of my toes tingle first, then it builds and takes over my entire body until I scream out in pleasure. His hips stutter as he comes inside me, then holds himself there for a few moments, his kisses becoming gentler before he pulls away and rests his head against my shoulder.

After we've both regained our normal breathing patterns, Aleko places a soft kiss against my lips and begins pulling his cock out. The movement makes me shudder, an aftershock of the orgasm giving almost as much pleasure as the thing itself.

I move to slide off, but Aleko holds up his palm. "Wait a second, Cherry. I look after what's mine." He holds up the small hand towel and runs the cold tap over a quarter of it before encouraging me to open my legs up for him.

The coldness is a shock at first, but it's soothing as he wipes me clean.

"Go and pee."

I don't need to be told twice. Even though the whole reason I ended up in here to begin with was to pee.

Thankfully, Aleko turns away instead of outright watching me, but it's still a little odd to me that he would want to stay while I use the toilet.

"I'll go and grab you something to put on, Cherry."

"Thanks."

Aleko winks on his way out of the bathroom, quickly returning with a large black T-shirt with the SOK logo in white on the short sleeve. He also hands me a pair of his boxers, probably more for his own sanity than my modesty because the T-shirt is pretty big and covers everything.

"You all good to go, babydoll?"

Now semi-dressed, I nod and take his offered hand in mine, linking our fingers together as though it's something we do every day.

I could definitely get used to this.

Bear and Sledge are sitting on the leather couch on their phones, and Kincaid, the new prospect, is standing by the front door like a sentry, but her tough façade is cracking a little with Ninja in her palm as she feeds him sticks of vegetables from the pocket of her prospect cut—no doubt prepared by Vanessa before they all came over.

"Good to see ya, kid. We're here to help ya plan shit."

Sledge's accent is confusing at the best of times but, "What shit are we planning?"

A knock on the front door attracts all our attention and Kincaid leisurely opens it up. I'm half-expecting a dozen more SOK brothers to walk through the door—may as well have a party at this point—but it's none of them.

"Spence!" I run over to my best friend and jump into his arms for a squeeze. "What're you doing here?" It's just dawning on me that there's no reason for Spencer to even know where Aleko lives, let alone actually be here.

I move back and rest my hands on my hips, looking not very menacing at all in my oversized tee and boxers, but Spence knows I need answers.

"Your man called me this morning. Time to Shawshank your mom, Bitch!"

Chapter Thirteen

Aleko

"You sure this is the right address?" With his arms crossed against his chest and one hand scratching at his thick beard, to say Bear's not buying it would be an understatement. Can't blame the guy. Usually, when we're sent out for some enforcer business, it's the lowest of lowlives hurting the good people of Rockford Beach that get the special Psycho visits.

Prez called while we were arranging the details for Cherry's mom, and when the Prez calls as riled up as he was, we answer. A friend of the club, Jimmy Collins, came in asking for help. It's what we do, chip in for this community that has accepted us throughout the years. Hell, every year we do charity runs and even did one for Jimmy when his wife's cancer treatment almost ruined them. So, when one of our townspeople shows up with pictures of his daughter lying in a hospital bed because she was kicked and punched to within an inch of her life, we just can't ignore that shit. I mean, regardless of whether or not we know the person, an innocent getting the fuck beat out of them deserves our special brand of intervention.

And here we are, ready to dish it out. Although, I'd rather be breaking my mother-in-law out of the psych ward than retaliating against these pricks.

Yet, here we are, having to deal with entitled rich bastards who like to beat the shit out of women. Fuck, I'm irritated.

I mean, sure, we're used to going in, shaking up and torturing deviant fucks in their homes, but... this? Not your typical humble abode. That being said, not all lowlives are poor. Exhibit A: a fucking mansion in the old money neighborhoods of Stonebridge.

"According to the GPS, we're standing right in front of the address Jimmy gave Prez." As I speak, I double check on my phone screen, just in case. "Preston Beaufort, 1242 Oleander Drive."

"You know these big plantation-style homes have never been good to my kin, right?" Slicing a look to my right, I smirk at my best friend, reading between the lines. Being Black in the south comes with its own moments of generational PTSD.

"Well, I guess Karma's about to ring that fancy fucking bell and wreak some havoc in the name of justice, brother." We fist bump, both sporting demented grins with the anticipation of fucking some shit up. Looking over my shoulder, I call out to the others.

"This guy decided to beat Jimmy's daughter to a bloody pulp and leave her for dead. I don't fucking care how much money this asshole has, we're here to collect. Blood and money. Those hospital bills won't pay themselves."

Behind me, Grinder's hyena laugh has me chuckling as I pull up my face scarf and wink at Sledge. "Let's go fuck with society's crusty hole."

With Bear by my side and Grinder, Sledge, and Boner behind us, we take our time making a beeline for the front door. To anyone else, the double-panel white doors would feel oppressive for how high they are, but what we lack in height, we make up for in strength, and between the five of us, the mass is impossible to ignore.

Comically, I press my index finger to the doorbell and keep it there until the door flies open and a red-faced twenty-something comes at us like a bat out of Hell.

"What the actual fuck is your pro—" It's not every day that five bikers with their neck scarves pulled up over their noses and eyes squinting with unfinished business make an appearance at some fancy-pants house. This guy's sudden change from confident to about-to-piss-his-pants is not surprising. Also, brownie points for shutting his whore mouth.

At least this guy's not a dumb motherfucker.

Yet.

"You Preston Beaufort?" I look him up and down like he's dog shit stuck on my boots.

"Who the fuck are you?" Yeah, not so smart after all.

"You Preston Beaufort?" Fucking hate repeating myself.

"Yeah, what's it to you?"

We don't talk, we don't explain, and we sure as fuck don't ask for permission before Bear pushes both his palms against the door and opens it wide enough for us to barrel in one-by-one. As I take my first step, I raise my arm and curl my fingers around blonde preppy boy's neatly coiffed curls before dragging him deeper into the huge fucking house. His whimpers are already annoying me because I can guarantee that Jimmy's daughter didn't get any leniency from him.

The ceilings are so high, my first thought is... damn, the electric bill must be a bitch. Then I remember I don't actually give a fuck.

"Who else is in the house?" I ask, Preston Beaufort, the poor excuse for human excrement. Even his name makes the hairs on my arms stand on end. "And don't fucking lie to me or I'll just kill you all without losing an ounce of sleep." I wouldn't kill innocents but this fucker doesn't need to know that.

"D-does th-the maid c-count?" We all come to a screeching halt at this nutsack's words, his eyes flitting briefly to the upstairs like he can see her from here.

"The fuck is that supposed to mean?" My fingers tighten in his hair as Grinder spits his question into the dude's profile. Literal spit flying across his cheek. Not gonna lie, I get a bit of a boner when he recoils and makes a face like we just fed him rotten eggs.

"I-I mean, I'm the only one in my family h-here." Tsking at his answer, I pull him a little harder as I drag him to the nearest room where I can sit the kid down and play with him. "If it's money you're looking for, I know the code to the safe." I pause, look at Bear, and grin.

"He knows the code to the safe." We all nod at each other because, yeah, we're gonna need that to help pay Jimmy's medical bills.

Scraping a chair from under the thick, wood, table, I'm none too careful as I push him to a sitting position and let Boner tie his wrists flush against the back of the chair.

"Maybe we'll let him live after all." Bear shrugs as he circles Preston's chair, all tall and intimidating.

"Maybe." My eyes are fixed on this rich kid and although his hands are shaking and his leg is bouncing up and down like he's tripping on something, he's not looking away from me. In fact, this asshole is staring me down. Ain't that scared, is he?

"One of y'all need to find the employee." Without taking my eyes off Preston, I speak over my shoulder.

"On it." Of course Bear would be the one accepting the job.

Knowing my brother, he'll find her, tell her to play along, and promise we're just here to get answers from her employer. It works every time.

Narrowing my eyes at the kid, I try to figure him out. He's playing the part of a scared innocent but something is off. It's in the way his chin is still held high and his gaze doesn't bounce from each of us. Most times, in this scenario, our marks are constantly verifying our positions, like they're keeping tabs of where we are so they can be ready for attack. It's a survival skill that kicks in when terror fills your veins. Preston here... well, he's only looking at me and, for some reason, this makes me really fucking happy.

"Tell me something, Bougie Boy." Placing two fingers under his chin, I make sure he can only see me and the venom in my glare. "You get off on beating the shit out of girls? Does it get your dick hard when your fist crunches against bone?" Pushing the point home, I jab him in the nose, hard enough to hear the pop.

The top half of his body swings to the left with the force of my fist, and he yells out in pain that's music to my ears as he sits back up again. His eyes are wide, scared, red and beginning to swell. I'm digging this look on him.

"What–What are you talking about?" His words are gargled as the blood that's now leaking from his nose seeps into his mouth between cries and unintelligible words.

"Oh no." I look at Grinder, who's standing behind the perp, and scrunch my eyebrows like maybe... just maybe... we got the wrong guy.

We don't.

"Did we fuck up again? I told you to check first." Grinder plays along, what I'm guessing is a cocky grin hidden behind his scarf making his eyes shine bright with amusement. Or maybe that's a touch of madness, because this guy loves to take home souvenirs.

"I mean, all of these houses look alike, you know?" Cocking my head to the side in confusion, I bring a hand to my hair and scratch my scalp.

"I dunno, man. It sure smells like the right house." Grinder's nose sniffs at the air like he's a bloodhound. "Hold up, Imma check." My gaze follows him as he leisurely walks over to a life-sized marble representation of a Greyhound. In the years I've known Grinder, I've learned not to question his oddities. The shit he comes up with seems to make sense to him and who the fuck am I to question it?

Turning back to Preston, I whisper, "Don't worry, he's real good at his job. We wouldn't want to dismember the wrong filth, would we?" The kid doesn't answer, his furrowed brows slanted in confusion, that bouncing leg keeping a strong rhythm.

"What the fuck are you doing, man, do you know how much that thing costs?" With his nose still running a steady stream of red, his words aren't perfectly comprehensible but I get the gist. Dude is livid.

The distinct sound of liquid splashing against a hard surface makes me grin but I keep my eyes on our target.

The more Grinder pisses on that statue, the more I wonder if Preston's behavior is all an act. Sure, he's doing all the right things by stuttering and shaking, but the truth is always in the eyes, and his reveal only darkness.

"Nope, no mistake here, boys." Grinder makes a show of shaking off the last drop before he tucks his dick back inside his leathers and buttons the whole thing up. "The trick is to piss on white, if it turns yellow then we're right. See? Even the carpet changed colors." I have to fight the urge to either roll my eyes at the absurdity of Grinder's show or bust a nut laughing. Possibly both.

"That's fucking ridiculous, you fucking psychopath!" Preston's words are directed at Grinder, which is a little insulting, to be honest.

Grabbing the kid by the hair again, I bring his attention right back to me. "I'm the Psycho here, asshole. Don't fucking forget it." My humor from seconds ago is completely gone. In its place, putrid hatred for men like this one settles deep in my bones as I bitch-slap him hard across the cheek. It's demeaning and condescending and exactly the message I want to send. "Now, explain to me why you would beat the shit out of a young woman and leave her to die on the dirty street."

Right in front of me, his boyish features morph from frightened, confused, and timid to cold and calculating with zero life inside. He's not even trying to hide it anymore. It's easy enough to recognize cold-blooded monsters since I spent my entire childhood surrounded by them. Evil chameleons who know exactly which persona to play in any given situation are a rare breed, thank fuck. On the outside, they adapt, but inside? There's nothing good left there.

"Bitch wouldn't do what I told her to." I grin at his words because, since the minute we stepped into the house, this is the first time he's been his true self.

"Huh. Boys, did you hear that? Bitch wouldn't listen so she got the beat down." Nodding as if we're on the same page, I look over to Bear as he leads a bound and blindfolded woman from the other room. She's not dressed like a maid, but maybe I've watched too much porn. Leading her to the couch and gently pushing her to sit, he whispers in her ear as she nods, sitting with her knees pressed together and her spine like a steel rod. She definitely got the speech and is playing along with little to no fear showing through the façade.

"You want the honors, brother?" At my question, my best friend snarls like he's some kind of fantastical creature about to transform into its animalistic being and wreak havoc on Earth. "Nah, just washed my hands. Don't wanna get this motherfucker's slime on them."

On any other day, I'd play with our food, but we need some fucking answers here. Nobody beats women like he did for shits and giggles. It was personal. From what her father told Prez, her wounds were intimate and he wants retribution since she's been curled up in her bed refusing to talk.

My attention returns to Preston, all pretense gone.

"So what's the deal? She wouldn't spread her legs? She told you to go jack yourself off? She wasn't interested?" Small dick energy is usually the culprit.

"Fuck off. She wanted me, alright? Wasn't complaining when I had her mouth around my cock." I roll my eyes then look to Boner with a nod of my chin.

Boner grabs the chair and tilts it so it's balancing on the two back legs.

In this position, Grinder is able to get real close and personal with his blade.

"Do you know what happens when a sharp blade enters your eye?"

Aww fuck, here we go.

"Hey, we ain't got time for a story, G," Bear calls out from his vigil at the couch.

"When done right…" Grinder ignores Bear's protest and our low-grade moans, but then again, this is his happy place and we don't really want to take it away from him. "The blade can slide in and avoid all major life-threatening areas. It's all about the angle, ya know? Kinda like when you fuck. Size don't matter, bitch, it's all about the angle." Grinder turns to us and winks. "Right, boys?"

Fucking Christ, can we just get on with this? I've got my girl to go home to.

"You won't even feel any pain, man. You'll be conscious, your eyeball will be intact and you'll be sitting here, no worse for wear." Preston furrows his brow and is about to say something—snarky, no doubt—but Grinder cuts him right off. "I know what you're thinking. How fucking boring is that?" Tapping the blade to his palm, Grinder stands to his full height and nods like a professor considering a student's theory on molecular science. "And you'd be right. If I wanted boring, I'd've joined the fucking circus."

I look to Bear, who just shrugs. We don't question Grinder's monologues.

As quick as a viper, Grinder rears back his hand and makes like he's about to stab Preston exactly there, in the eye. He stops himself about half an inch before the tip of the blade touches the cornea, and I can see the rapid blinking of Preston's lashes swinging against the metal that's so fucking close to him.

"Aww fuck. Did you piss yourself?" I look down at Grinder's whining, and sure enough. Dude might act like a sociopath but really, it's all fucking show if that wet stain growing by the second down Preston's leg is anything to go on.

"That's your only joker, Preston. I suggest you start fucking talking and don't leave out the details."

With his stare fixed on the blade that Grinder hasn't removed, he sings like a fucking bird.

"We were at a party. She was looking to score something to have a little fun but didn't have enough money. I told her to suck me off and we'd be even." The blood from his broken nose is now dried up but still restricting his airway, giving him a nasally voice that's starting to irritate me. Fuck, I just want to go home. "When she started blowing me, she gagged then pulled away and threw up." Without moving, he slices his gaze to me like I'm going to understand his state of mind.

"She fucking puked on my dick, man. So, yeah, I taught her a lesson." I blink then shake my head because it's not adding up.

Grinder must be thinking the same thing because he just leans in as I push the back of the guy's head closer to the tip. "I think you're holding out on us, asshole. And let me tell you. Whether you live or die, it's no fucking skin off our backs."

"My dad will fucking destroy you." His confidence is almost touching.

"We'll kill him too." I say this so matter of factly that the truth of it seeps into his pores, making his skin turn an unhealthy shade of white.

"What else aren't you telling us, Pressss-ton?" Grinder drags out the letter *S* like he's a snake about to strike.

"Fuck, okay, okay. I slapped her around a little then took her to the nearest room and made her clean me up." He pauses, and we all know he's not done but when his lips curl up at the corners and his dead eyes meet mine, I know this guy needs to be put in the ground. "I hope she took a long hot shower and washed her dirty cunt out. Pretty sure vomit shouldn't be up in there."

Did he just admit to rape, too?

I don't think. I don't hesitate.

Pushing Grinder's arm away, I start punching down over and over and over again until Preston's just a gurgling mess of red liquid. Boner is having a hard time holding the chair from the force of my punches but I don't give a shit.

The cracking of bone and cartilage are like music to my ears and I don't even feel what I'm sure are deep cuts on my knuckles, but I do see a tooth or three pop out of his mouth.

Bear pulls me off of him but I'm fighting it with everything I've got.

This motherfucker thought it was okay to beat and rape a young girl with zero remorse or empathy. Well, guess what, asshole! Fucking same when it comes to you.

We leave him there, bloodied and limp, barely holding onto life as we guide his housekeeper outside. No fucking way she should see the mess we left.

"You okay?" Bear loosens her roped wrists and removes the blindfold. "Wait until we're gone then call the cops, okay?" The last thing we want is to implicate her in our crimes. Not that she would be. No way that tiny girl could do that much damage.

"Look, if you're worried about your boss, he's not dead." Unwrapping a sucker, I stick it in my mouth and give her my most charming grin. "He's a piece of shit and he hurt a young girl." I shrug, hoping my boyish good looks will make her wide eyes go back to normal.

"He's not my boss." With everything going on, that's what she chooses to tell us? I mean, sure, technically the kid's father would be her boss but I'm not getting hung up on semantics here.

"All right, sure. You wouldn't know where the safe is, would you? That young girl has some major medical bills to pay and he owes her at least that much." My chin tilts up like my entire body wants to argue in favor of Jimmy's girl.

"Um, yeah. I... yeah. Follow me." At her words, Bear glances at me and I nod. The five of us don't have to be up there, he can get what we need and ride the fuck out of here.

As I climb on my bike, I wipe my bloody hands on my leathers and shake the rage out of my system. Motherfucker made me lose control, but that's a good thing; this whole episode just reminded me that I've got a list full of names to be crossed out. With Goblin and Jake dead, now I just need their Prez, Isaac, and his little bitch, Brick. The others, that I added for lesser offenses, can wait.

Those two motherfuckers touched my woman when they were supposed to be protecting her.

Two motherfuckers that I can't wait to punish.

With a duffle bag secured to his back, Bear comes strolling on out with the maid standing at the door, watching us.

"Let's go tell Jimmy the good news, brothers. Justice has been served."

Chapter Fourteen

Mackenzie

"She'll answer, Mac. Maggie said she'd make sure of it when she called me last night. Your mom was insistent on seeing you, something about having a bad feeling." Spencer hands me a foam cup of steaming coffee he and Kincaid picked up from the shop on their way back from visiting Mom. They dropped off a burner phone so I can speak to her after Aleko and the others had to leave when the prez called, rather than me blowing my *I'm dead* cover and walking right into a building full of doctors and nurses.

Ninja is snuggled into a cute little ball on my lap after his vegetable feast, and I'm thankful for his silent support. They say animals are great companions in times of need, they can boost your serotonin and dopamine levels, and fussing beneath Ninja's soft chin just confirms that for me. I'm calmer and more relaxed than I feel like I should be.

The nurse, who was always kind to me, Maggie, had been on my wavelength with thinking something strange was going on with Mom and her care. She had kept me up to date with any visits from my brother and his cronies, especially those rare times she was becoming lucid. Which, funnily enough, did have a pattern. I just couldn't find anyone, other than Maggie, willing to listen to me and help me prove it.

Maggie had obviously done everything I'd asked of her in my letter before I "died", because Spencer was being kept up to date and allowed to visit at any time—something that would never have been allowed while my brother was in control.

It seems the doctors on the Toxic Rebels' payroll no longer held an interest in mom's case once the cash stopped coming because she's been more lucid than ever for the last few days.

Aleko took it upon himself to delete the message Spencer sent me last night and arranged for things to get moving this morning. I'm a little pissed that he kept it from me to begin with, but I also understand his reasoning.

And I'm never going to complain about multiple orgasms.

That being said, there's no way I'm letting him get away with making decisions for me. While there are days his over-the-top obsessive behavior makes my pussy wet, when it comes to my free will the line gets real thin, real quick. But that's a tomorrow problem—another one.

"But what if she's not lucid anymore? It's just a fluke and I was wrong this whole time? There's a chance I won't win the last race, so I can't afford that doctor in New York, and all of this will have been for nothing, then what if—"

"Mac, babe. Stop. You're rambling. I saw your mom a little over an hour ago, handed her the phone myself. And you know what happened...?" He pauses for dramatic effect. "She said, thank you. My daughter is lucky to have a friend like you." Spence preens a little at the last part, never one to turn down compliments. And I can't blame him, he deserves all the praise he gets.

Everything he's done for me is nothing short of amazing and well above the usual best friend duties. The words from my mom though...? Wow. A lump forms in my throat and the backs of my eyes heat up. Ninja snuggles further into my lap, and gets himself comfortable, closing his tiny black eyes as he rubs his head against my stomach.

"Caidy, could you pass some tissues from the bathroom please?" Spencer brings his attention straight back to me, cupping my cheeks with his palms. "Cry, get it all out, but when you call your mom, you stay strong, okay? She's confused and she needs you. If you need to cry again afterward, I've got a bottle of wine in that brown bag in the kitchen."

I can't help chuckling as a few tears roll down my cheeks. It's been so long since Mom formed full sentences, I barely remember what she sounds like.

"Thanks." Spence takes the offered box of tissues from a silent Kincaid, pulling a couple out and passing them to me before leaning in to whisper, "That girl is bad ass. Did you know she murdered her husband?" Kincaid is standing beside Bash again by the front door. Whereas her arms are folded across her chest, Bash is casually leaning against the wall.

"Really?" Sarcasm drips from my tone, because Spence's picture would be next to *gullible* in the dictionary, but the fact he's already on nickname status with the newest Khaos prospect is just like my best friend.

"Whatever. I believe her." He pulls out some more tissues and throws them at my face. "C'mon, clean up. Let's make the call. I have to work tomorrow night, ya know."

"What does working tomorrow night have to do with anything?" I dab at my cheeks, drying the wetness from the few tears that spilled.

"First, I just thought I'd remind you what us living and working folk need to do, and that my new partner is awful. Thanks for that, by the way. Secondly, if you ponder whether to make the call for much longer, it'll be next week before you do it. Wine?" Laughing, Spencer stands and walks into the kitchen, pulling out two tall glasses from one of the high cupboards. "These will have to do. Seems your man isn't equipped for wine yet. I'll bring some of my glasses over next time. Because there *will* be a next time." Spencer continues to talk as he pours out two red wines before coming back to the couch and passing one to me. "I like this you. You're happier, lighter, but we've still got work to do." Holding up his glass, he encourages me to clink mine against his, then we drink.

I have more than a couple of mouthfuls, but the glass is huge, so it won't run out anytime soon.

"Okay. I've got this. It's fine. We're all fine." I shimmy to prepare myself, picking up the cell I bought in the name of Scarlett Green and pressing to call the saved number while Spence shakes his head and laughs at me. He's even more amused when I flip him off with a mouthed, *"fuck you,"* as the dull tones of the phone ringing sound against my ear.

Ninja moves to the arm of the sofa, onto what Aleko told me was one of his favorite sleeping cushions, walks in a few circles, then settles again, his head resting on his front paws as he keeps his eyes on me.

"Hello? Is that really you, darlin'?" Mom's voice is scratchy and weak, sending a mixture of joy and fear through my body. I fear for what I have to tell her, for what she's been through, for what she could still probably have to go through, but I'm happy because she's actually talking and she sounds fully lucid, like the Mom I can barely remember.

"Hi, Mom. Yeah, it's me." I have to inhale deeply to steady my breathing before emotion gets the better of me.

Killing my own brother didn't even have this effect on me. I guess that's the difference between someone important and someone lower than shit on my shoe.

"Oh, thank God. I knew it wasn't true or that nice lady, Maggie, would have told me. Those doctors give me the creeps."

Holy shit, the way Mom's talking... I couldn't bring myself to imagine it was possible. And I totally know what she means about those doctors.

"You knew what wasn't true?"

"Doctor Alley told me that you and your brother had died." She stops and sniffs, a little stuttered as though she's crying. "But as with everything else, they lied."

"Everything else?" I'm curious as to how much Mom's actually been able to take in over the years. She's been practically comatose, but then she was always a very smart woman. She was a special education teacher at Stonebridge High School. Until the love of her life died.

"We can talk about all of that when you come and get me out of this damn place. They want to discharge me, under supervision—because I don't always have complete control over my body yet—by the end of the month."

Being so close to me on the couch, Spence can hear every word, and what my mom just said makes him balk on the gulp of wine he just guzzled.

"Wow! That's amazing, Mom." And it really is, I just need to get a few things organized first. *Fuck, I need somewhere to live.* I'd still like to get Mom seen by a reputable doctor too, one not on the payroll of dickheads. A thousand things run through my brain at once; the news definitely not what I was expecting with this phone call. "We'll get it all arranged. You'll be out of there in no time." I'm actually giddy at the thought.

"I wouldn't like to stay at that biker compound you've told me about with your brother and his friends, though."

"Err..." *How do I tell her?*

"Is everything alright, darlin'?" She seems so happy, and I'm about to burst her bubble. The whole reason she's in that place to begin with is because she lost her husband. Maybe it's best to tell her now while she's still there... just in case.

Sighing heavily, I ready myself to tell Mom some semi-truths.

"Jake's dead, Mom. That part was true. I'm so sor—"

"Oh thank the Lord that evil has gone." The relief in her voice and interruption were absolutely not what I was expecting. If I'm honest with myself, I'm a little—no, a lot—shocked, and I kinda wanna laugh, but that would show my crazy.

"Mom, did you hear what I said?" I feel like I need to make sure she's understanding me.

"Yes, darlin'. Your brother is dead. I also heard everything you told me about what he and his friends did to you on your visits." Her voice cracks a little toward the end, but I won't point it out.

Mom may have been in a psych hospital for years, but before she completely broke down, she was always one of the strongest women I knew. Still is.

"So you're okay with that?" My question is tentative, and I feel like all I've done so far is question my mom when

I should just be happy to have a whole conversation with her.

"No. I'm not okay with any of it, but I can't live like this anymore, darlin'. Your brother and his friends were my jailors. I longed for your visits. I wanted to take away all your hurt and pain, and now it's gone. Mine too." She sighs sadly. "I still miss your father though. Always will."

"Me too, Mom. Me too." I don't feel like now is a good time to bring up what Jake said about Dad not being my dad. As much as I really want to, now's not the time.

"So earlier, when you said we'll arrange it, did you mean you and that nice boy who's been coming around to see me? Spencer, is it? He's very good looking, darlin'. Well done." Masterfully changing the subject, Mom's tone brightens a little.

Overhearing this, Spence begins wagging his brows suggestively, holding a hand to his chest and pretending to be bashful, like, *"Who? Me?"*

"I didn't mean Spencer, no. He's my best friend, not my boyfriend." I stick my tongue out at him and flip him off again when he fakes shock and offense at my denial.

"That's a shame. *We* who, then?"

"My actual boyfriend, Aleko." *Is he my boyfriend though?* We haven't exactly had a discussion about it, but

I'm also not a dumbass. He's claimed me as his old lady, which I'm well aware is a big deal in the motorcycle community. Fuck it, I've said it. It's out there.

"I can't wait to meet him, then." I can hear the smile in her voice, clear as day, and it soothes my soul to know I haven't destroyed hers by killing Jake—not that she knows exactly that, but it's fine.

My mom and I talk for another fifteen minutes about the weather and the puzzle Spence took to her last week. Seems puzzling was a bit of a thing for the two of them. It was mostly Spence to begin with, but as Mom became more lucid, she started helping and they've built a budding little friendship.

I finish the call with promises to keep in touch on the phone, not yet having the chance to explain why I can't visit in person. Although, I was adamant about her not telling anyone that I'm alive, with promises of answers once she's out of there.

Everything is moving forward a lot more quickly than I'd planned. I mean, I had my suspicions about Jake and Co. being responsible for my mom's situation, but to have it basically confirmed for sure? Well, I'll have to give that doctor in New York a call or email to see if he has any advice. As for now, there's nothing I can do tonight, so tomorrow's me can deal with it.

Spencer and I finish off the bottle of wine he bought after Bash and Kincaid refuse our offerings. Instead, they stand like sentries by Aleko's front door, on their very best behavior. They're taking their prospecting duties seriously, rather than fucking around, and I can respect that.

A few hours later, Aleko, Bear, Grinder, and Boner arrive home, the rumble of motorcycles before they walked in was drowned out by the loud thumping of *Rayne Over Knights* playing through the bluetooth speaker. Which means Spencer and I were found mid-dance, having the time of our lives.

Apparently, Sledge had some work to finish in the garage so he went straight back to the compound.

Grinder and Boner need no invitation, and they both join us dancing behind the couch as Bear chuckles with a shake of his head. At the sound of his timber voice, Ninja perks up from his cushion and scuttles over to Bear, who immediately picks him up for a belly rub.

"Fucking love this song, man." Grinder raises an arm in the air as the chorus drops, as does Spencer while Boner's dancing is a little more like what I'd dub Dad-dancing, but he's trying. I can't help laughing at them, mimicking their moves just as a strong arm wraps around my waist from behind me.

"You look fucking delectable, Cherry." Aleko's deep voice is at my ear just before he pushes the sucker in his hand between my lips. I groan and lean my head back against his hard chest, enjoying the warmth being close to him brings.

We dance, I suck, and when the song is over, Aleko encourages me to continue swaying. Grinder walks to the fridge and grabs a few bottles of water, passing them out to Spencer, Boner, and Bash before taking a huge swig of his own. Aleko and I both declined the offer, too entwined in each other to bother.

"We're gonna split, Psycho." Boner nods toward the door as he pushes his arms into the sleeve holes of his cut.

I look over and see that Bear and Kincaid have already gone. I'd been so caught up in my own little world I didn't even notice. Ninja is already asleep too, curled up on the gray cushion on the sofa, his tiny body moving slowly up and down as he breathes.

"Do you need a ride?" Grinder's addressing Spencer, and I notice a little disappointment in his eyes when Spencer shakes his head.

"Nah, I'm good, thanks. I've got an Uber waiting and I need to get back to my *boyfriend.* Besides, as an EMT I try to avoid death traps on wheels." I take note of the way Spencer says boyfriend, because he definitely emphasized it, meaning he can sense Grinder's interest in him too and this is his way of letting him down gently.

"Cool. Later!" With a tilt of his head toward Bash, they both leave.

"I'm not going anywhere without a hug." Spencer opens his arms out, waiting for me to come to him to say goodbye. With a little resistance from Aleko, I peel myself away, pecking him on the cheek before wrapping my arms around Spencer. "You did good today, babe."

"Thank you. For everything."

Our words are mumbled into each other's necks, but we know what we're saying.

"You still owe me one... or ten, so don't thank me yet." Spencer laughs as he pulls away, ruffling my hair and blowing a laughing kiss to the growling man over my shoulder. "Learn to share your toys, Aleko." Spence winks before grabbing his jacket and cell, then walks out the door.

"I missed you today." Aleko's arms snake around my waist again, his whole front pressed against my back as he whispers into my neck.

"I missed you too." Spinning in his hold, I face him, looking up at the tall, tattooed man I'm lucky enough to call mine.

This time, I kiss him, not waiting for his move first. I devour him, taste him, but it doesn't take long before he takes control again. Breathing heavily, we separate, and I rest my forehead against his chest. Aleko takes hold of my hands and brings them up to his mouth, kissing my knuckles with a seductive grin.

I notice his knuckles are bloodied, but I know what he does, what his job with the MC is, and I also know he'd never harm an innocent man, so I don't ask questions because I really don't care.

"Now, about sharing my toys... I have some new ones I think we should try, but I'm not sharing any of those either."

CHAPTER FIFTEEN
ALEKO

"Please tell me your mother's not a vegetarian."

Bear's question has Grinder's head whipping around looking to Bear then to Mackenzie and back again, eyes narrowed and mouth opened in shock before she even has time to answer.

"I have no idea, really. I mean, she's been medicated for years with constant IV drips. She's Pharmatarian." Now it's my turn to look at my girl who doesn't even laugh at her own joke because it's not funny. Not to her, not to me, and definitely not to her mother. But to Grinder? That fucker throws his head back and barks out a sincere howl of laughter quickly followed by a choking sound as Bear punches him in the gut.

The sound is so sudden it wakes Ninja from his nap in my hoodie. Running to my shoulder and sniffing out the level of danger in the vicinity, he then presses his little nose to my neck and goes back to sleep in the hood.

"Get back to work, asshole," I growl, pulling Mackenzie's back to my front, my arms crossed over her chest as I run my nose over the top of her head. Fucking cherries will be the death of me and I'm okay with that.

"Why aren't the prospects doing this? What's the point of having them if I'm doing all the grunt work?" All the while complaining, Grinder turns back to our most valuable possession besides our racing bikes, and starts banking the coals to one side of the grill big enough to feed every hungry member of our club, Boner mimicking his every move.

"They're helping Sabrina in the kitchen, piling up the pork shoulders for me." Bear is our official barbecue master. He's got generations of experience smoking North Carolina style barbecue for the club. As an implant from New York and Greece before that, this whole war happening between the two Carolinas has always been fascinating to me.

"So, are we doing North or South Carolina style?" I like fucking with them.

"Shut your whore mouth." Grinder doesn't even turn around, too busy lighting the coals.

"Low and slow, baby. Low and slow." At Mackenzie's words, I chuckle in the crook of her neck when she shows her North Carolina born-and-bred colors.

"I knew I liked her for a reason." Bear winks at my girl and I barely suppress a growl.

"Have you ever been to BBQ Camp?" I frown at her question.

"What's that?" It's my turn to get mocked by the whole crew.

"Fucking Yankee," Sledge calls out, carrying a huge cooler filled, I'm guessing, with ice and beer. A true barbecue is an all-day affair. "And a lazy one at that, mate. Make ya self useful, will ya? Being in love ain't no excuse for standing there doin' nuffin'." I flip him off, knowing damn well he's right but having zero desire to walk away from my girl.

"It's a two day camp held in Raleigh every year in late spring. Apparently, the Department of Food at NC State teaches them the art of perfecting a North Carolina style barbecue." Mackenzie answers my question with fire in her eyes and excitement in her voice. "Have you been, Bear?"

"Nah, I learned from the best: my mama and her mama before her and before her. It's a family affair and one day,

I'll pass it on to my own kids." I don't know if Mackenzie hears the sudden melancholy in my best friend's voice but I certainly do. Anytime he talks about his mother, his mind goes to a dark place for a minute, then he's back to his normal self. Whatever that means.

"That's so cool. I once told my dad to go and bring me so I could learn with him but we quickly realized it's very much a boy's club so..." I feel her shrug below me and have the sudden urge to throat punch every one of those men for making my girl feel like she wouldn't belong.

"Speaking of family, you must be excited about your mom coming home." Bear's statement makes Mackenzie squeal a little and I can't help grinning along at her happiness. Her happiness makes her look younger than her age, and that's saying something.

"I can't wait. She deserves a little normalcy." For the last two weeks, we debated and discussed all the avenues possible for her mother's care. Getting her an apartment seemed too risky. We weren't quite sure of the trauma she'd suffered and even less about what kind of PTSD she might manifest. Living with us wasn't an option since my apartment is too small; one bedroom would cramp everyone's style. Mackenzie suggested she get a place for just the two of them and I shut that shit down with a kiss and a hard fuck against the wall.

After asking Prez and putting it up for a vote at church, we settled with having her in a suite on the compound. It's the best of both worlds. She'll have round-the-clock care with people always around, but also some much needed privacy. This means we'll be spending a lot more time here than in my downtown loft, which is fine. A small price to pay for seeing my girl so happy.

"I need all the hands available to set up the exterior," Vanessa calls out to everyone within hearing distance, and it's like she's kicked an ant hill. Suddenly, everyone is running around helping with chairs, tables, plates and cutlery... me and my girl included.

It's only ten in the morning but it takes eight good hours to smoke the pork shoulders to perfection, and while Bear regales us with his cooking prowess, we make sure everything else is perfect for Darlene's "welcome to your new home" party.

And yes, there's an actual banner being made by the Khunts and my old lady.

"Not to *rat* him out or anything, but it looks like Ninja wanted to help with the sign."

I pause in my tracks, carrying yet another fucking table from inside the clubhouse to the outside eating area and glance at the banner. Right there from one side straight through to the other, are little paw prints in orange, red, and yellow.

"How long have you been waiting to make that joke, dude?" I quirk a brow at my brother in arms, Hoops, and scowl. Although, it quickly morphs into a full grin.

"From day one, man. From day fucking one." Getting a chuckle out of me, I slap him on the shoulder and lean in.

"Don't ever do it again, it's like a dad joke on crack."

"Duly noted."

Six hours later, Mackenzie and I are driving down Highway 17 on our way to grab my mother-in-law and break her out of the loony bin because, clearly, there's nothing medically wrong with her. The only problem she had was a clinically psychotic son.

Beside me, Mackenzie's leg is bouncing up and down like she's about to meet her maker, and instead of stressing me out, all I see is bare flesh begging for my hands.

"Why are you so nervous, Cherry Pie? This is a good thing, right?" With one hand on the steering wheel and the other now clamping down on Mackenzie's smooth skin, I let my gaze sweep from one side of the road to the other.

It's a two-lane road with multiple side roads going who the fuck knows where, and while Vanessa's truck is older than my parents, it's got great potential for a little late afternoon snack.

"This is huge, Aleko. Like, fucking gigantic."

I know she's not talking about my cock, but touching her, no matter how platonic it may be, gives me hard-cock brain. You know, when everything said or implied is immediately translated to my hard cock inside her sweet cherry pussy.

"What time are we meeting Spence at the clinic?" I know what time we're meeting but I'm buying myself some extra minutes before I pull over onto a side road and make a second turn onto a secluded dirt road that probably leads to someone's house. Right now though, I don't fucking care if we're parked on the goddamn president's pristine White House lawn.

"At five thir—what—where are we going?" Her leg stops bouncing up and down and her entire body tenses like she's expecting danger to jump out at her.

"We've got an extra fifteen minutes before we need to be there." I turn off the engine and face the love of my life. "Straddle me, Cherry baby. It's been way too long since my cock kissed your cunt." I grin when her cheeks pink up and her nipples instantly harden beneath her T-shirt. Fuck, she's a sight to see. And touch. And taste and fuck.

"You want to meet my mother smelling of sex and bad decisions?" Her voice drops an octave and I don't believe, for one fucking second, that she's going to resist me. In fact, as she tsks her delicious little tongue at me, she's lifting her ass and pulling down her jean shorts before kicking them completely off.

"May as well greet her with my true self. She'll soon learn her little girl is getting thoroughly fucked morning, noon, and night." Releasing my cock from the constraints of my own jeans, I wrap my fingers at the base and get comfortable just as she lifts one leg over my groin and pulls her panties to the side.

The head of my cock slides up and down her wet lips and we both groan at the perfection of it all.

"God, you feel so damn good." Her words are moaned out, filling the cabin with the sounds of her need for me.

"Show me how good, Cherry. Fuck my cock like you can't get enough of it." With my hands clamped on both of her thighs, I dig my fingers into her flesh and lean my head back on the seat. There's nothing more beautiful than this woman bouncing up and down on my dick. Every guttural sound she makes, every bounce of her tits so close to my mouth.

"That's it, baby. Take everything you want from me." From below, I meet her thrust for thrust as she uses my shoulders for leverage. "Give me your mouth."

In half a second, we're kissing. Our lips sliding and tongues dancing to the sound of slapping skin and chirping birds. The scent of her is all around us, making it so fucking hard not to come it's almost embarrassing, but that's all a testament to her, isn't it? She's so fucking sexy that I can barely control my dick and it sure as fuck can't control itself.

"I'm so close, baby. I love feeling you so deep inside me. Christ..." Her words are whispered over my mouth as we fight for control of our kiss. When she tries to pull away, I bite her lip and pull her right back to me.

"I said give me your mouth, Cherry. Give me your orgasm now, too."

"Yes, yes... fuck yes." Sliding my hands from her hips to beneath her panties and onto her ass cheeks, I press her as close to me as humanly possible as I grind my groin into her and almost lose my fucking mind at the feel of her hot little pussy squeezing my cock like it can't get enough of me.

Hot liquid drips down my shaft as I lose my fucking mind and shoot my cum deep inside her cunt.

Our shared groans feel like the last sentence in a perfect chapter. The end of a past life leaving room for the future.

Suddenly, the thought of our future filled with babies and hours and hours of making them flits through my mind. Only last year, the idea of me being a father would have scared the fuck out of me, but now? With Cherry riding my cock like a fucking queen? Well, in this very moment, the mere idea of her belly swollen with my kid inside is a picture I'm not willing to forget.

"Okay, big boy. Time to go." With one last kiss with her swollen lips, Mackenzie pulls me out of my reverie, but not before she notices the big, fat grin on my face. "Oh, you've got a great post-coital face." Another kiss and I don't correct her because telling her I want her pregnant soon and often might very well get me a kick to my balls and we can't have that, can we? I'm gonna need them in mint condition if I want my plan to work.

By the time we make it to her mother's current habitat, for lack of a better word, Spence is there waiting and tapping on his watch when we pull up. As soon as we're close enough, his face lights up like the northern skies during a solar storm and he winks over at Mackenzie. Again, it takes me a beat to remind myself he's her best friend and in no way making a move on her so I force myself to loosen gritted teeth.

"Down boy. I'm not into the girly parts. Also, you have great sex hair." Okay, so maybe he was winking at me.

"Quit flirting with my man."

"You're no fun." Spence rolls his eyes then taps on his watch again. "Let's go before they change their minds and we have to blow up the place to get her out." I frown at Spencer's words.

"You watch too many movies, man. It's all good." With one last kiss to Mackenzie's lips, Spence and I head inside and bust Darlene out of this fucking joint.

This place smells like fucking death. In fact, it's the exact same thing as that horrendous day I had walked into the morgue and saw Mackenzie lying there... dead. A shiver runs down my spine at the memory and I have to consciously remind myself that she's fine. We're fine. Every one is fucking fine.

"Good morning, Maggie. Looking stunning as always." I raise a brow at Spence as he puts on a whole fucking show for the nurse who's just come to get us.

"Oh, hush, you." She pats her heated cheeks with a bright grin plastered on her face and does a double take when her eyes land on me.

I do what I do best. Flashing her Mackenzie's favorite grin, I nod just as Spencer goes in for a hug.

"No ma'am, I will do no such thing. Compliments are like vitamin C, you need them every day to feel good." Fucking hell, this dude knows how to work a room. Although, I would argue the same thing for orgasms, but this is neither the place nor the right public to announce all the ways I want to give my girl her daily dose of vitamins.

"Come on, now. Let's go get Darlene, she's been very excited about leaving." Her words are whispered behind the back of her hand like she's an accomplice in a bank heist.

Now, I get that the look I've got going on isn't always to everyone's taste, but until now, I've never given a fuck what others could possibly think about me or my tattoos. We're in the twenty-first century, for fuck's sake. Yet, here I am, a little nervous as we're going down the hall and veering into the left wing. I'm suddenly aware that whatever

Mackenzie's mom thinks about me is going to matter to my girl.

What if Darlene doesn't approve? What if she convinces my little Cherry to find someone more suitable?

I almost laugh at that. *Right.* Like I would ever let her go.

"Hey there, Darlene. I've got these two handsome boys here to take you home." Maggie's southern drawl is everything I love about North Carolina.

"Oh, my. I think I have everyth—" Oh fuck, here we go. Darlene's word ends on a cliffhanger and I'm suddenly feeling shy, my feet shuffling and my gaze everywhere except on her.

"Hey Momma Darlene! This is Aleko. Remember, I said I'd be here with him?" Spencer is trying to make things less awkward but is failing miserably because she's barely paying any attention to him at all. Her sole focus is on me and more specifically, the cross under my eye.

"Goodness, that's a lot of tattoos! And yet you are one handsome young man, aren't you?" The laugh that escapes me tastes like freedom. Like my lungs aren't frozen and my heart is no longer afraid of being rejected by my future mother-in-law.

"I guess beauty's in the eye of the beholder." What the fuck am I talking about? I'm Aleko fucking Kastellanos aka Psycho. I don't get fucking flustered like this. *Christ.*

"Hmm, I guess it is. Tell me…" she looks over at Spencer, a deep frown marring her otherwise flawless skin. The resemblance to Mackenzie is staggering, like seeing thirty years into the future through a crystal ball.

"*Aleko*. I know, Momma Darlene, it's kinda weird but, meh, it fits." Fucking Spencer.

"Tell me, Aleko. Do you make my daughter happy?" At her question, my spine stiffens, because no one is supposed to know she's still alive, but it's then I realize that Maggie has disappeared somewhere and it's only the three of us.

"Yes, ma'am, I'd like to think so." Ma'am? Holy shit, who am I right now?

"Well, then." Darlene steps right up to me and pats my face with the palm of her hand. It feels like approval and acceptance and everything I didn't know I needed. "That's all that matters. So, let's get out of this joint, shall we?"

Indeed, let's.

CHAPTER SIXTEEN
MACKENZIE

Tears prick my eyes at my first sight of Mom in over two months. The huge smile on her face is magnetic as she walks toward the truck with Aleko and Spencer on either side of her like bodyguards. Her arms are linked through each of theirs until I make a move to get out of the truck, opening the door and sliding out. Then, I practically run into her now-open arms, and sob into her neck.

"Hey, now. Why are we crying, sweet girl?" Mom pulls back, wiping the tears from my cheeks as she takes me in.

I shake my head, fighting more tears, sucking it up so she doesn't worry. Now's not the time to go into everything.

"I'm just happy you're finally out. You're... well, you're you." And she really is. Her eyes are brighter than I've seen them in years, her dark hair bouncier, and the pallor of her skin makes her look ten years younger.

"Of course, I am, darlin'. Now, I hear there's a party going on in my honor? It's been too long since I tasted good food, so are we making a move?" I don't blame her eagerness to get out of here, this place holds nothing but crappy memories for her and I'm sure she'll be glad to see the back of it.

The sun is shining, so my baseball cap and sunglasses aren't out of place, but I'm still conscious that someone could recognize me out here. I was, after all, a regular visitor to this place. Meaning, I'm good to leave too, and I open the passenger door so we can all file inside.

"There sure is. Let's go, Mom."

Spence hugs Mom and they say their goodbyes before he drives off—he has to work tonight—and we're finally leaving this place behind us and on our way to the compound.

Most of the club members are around back, the barbeque already on the go, and Aleko heads off to find Ninja so I can show Mom around her new home without overwhelming her with people. After laughing at the irony that she's gone from one psychiatric hospital to another, she takes in her new suite, lovingly decorated by Vanessa and Sabrina. There are bright colors everywhere, oranges, yellows, pinks, completely opposite to the bland white and beige that she's been used to.

"This is beautiful, darlin'. I love it." She runs her palm over the soft sheets of the large double bed, then pushes down on the pillows and cushions, bringing a hand to her chest before looking up at me standing in the doorway. "Thank you."

This whole day is more emotional than I had imagined it would be, but seeing the happiness in my mom is worth everything.

"Actually, Vanessa and Sabrina did most of this." I can't take the credit for how beautiful this room currently looks.

"Are they—"

"The food is almost ready, Mac," Vanessa calls down the hall as she approaches, before coming to stand beside me and grinning when she sees Mom. "Hey, Mrs. Wilson. I'm Vanessa. It's lovely to meet you, Mackenzie's told us so much about you. How's the new room?" If I'm not mistaken, Vanessa is a little nervous about Mom's reaction.

"Oh, sweet girl, it's beautiful. Thank y'all for making me feel so welcome." Mom seems to hesitate for a moment, something briefly flashing across her face, but it's gone in an instant and she walks toward us and opens her arms to hug Vanessa.

"Phew. I wasn't sure if it was too much, but Sabrina insisted it was all good. She doesn't speak... ever, but you'll love her." Vanessa winks at Mom as they pull away. "Shall we?" She holds out her elbow for Mom, and I swear, the way this woman accepts new people into her life is staggering. One of the most beautiful souls I've ever known for sure.

"Oh yeah, let's! Mackenzie tells me your boys make the best barbecue in the state." Eagerly, Mom takes Vanessa's elbow and we all head outside.

The 'Congrats on your break out' sign makes Mom laugh as soon as she sees it, and one-by-one, the club members introduce themselves with a handshake. To begin with, she lets go of Vanessa and grips onto my arm like her life depends on it, the situation completely overwhelming, but it gradually loosens. Then Grinder approaches right after Boner, and he plants a lingering kiss on her knuckles before walking away with a wink that makes her cheeks heat.

There's a little hesitation in Mom's steps, but for now, she seems to be dealing with all the people and this new situation just fine. And as we settle into the afternoon, my cheeks ache from all the smiling.

"We've heard that the Rebels have got themselves some protection in jail. Some big wig from outta town. Means we can't get to any of 'em, but Veronica says they're moving soon to prepare for their trials." Hoops swigs at his beer, throwing the glass bottle in the recycling bin Vanessa insisted on keeping out here before picking at the leftover pork on his paper plate.

"Okay. So we find out when they're moving and hit them hard." I don't know how this conversation even started, but Aleko's fists are clenched as he speaks and I can see how ready he is to do exactly what I had been trying to avoid by keeping my original plans from him. Being out of jail and knowing I'm alive has only slightly soothed his anger toward the Rebels, but he still very much plans to kill them, Isaac and Brick in particular.

It makes sense, I want to kill them too, which should in no way be something I'm okay with. Murder... being responsible for taking a soul from this Earth...

What am I thinking? Those fuckers have no souls, and neither did my brother.

Looking over at my mom sitting at the table beside us, laughing and smiling with Violet, Sabrina, and Crow, I decide to continue ignoring the fact that I'm more than okay with everything that's been happening. Future me really is gonna have some shit to deal with soon, but for now, I have zero fucks to give.

My mom is here, no longer cooped up inside a psychiatric facility. She's talking, and though her movements are a little stiff from years of, well, mistreatment, she isn't showing any other outward signs of her previous condition. It does all seem kind of overwhelming for her though, which is understandable. I can see it in the way she keeps checking her surroundings, jumping whenever someone approaches from behind her. That was until I suggested she sit with her back to the building so that she can see everything going on around her. It seems to have helped her relax a little, and while she may have people directly next to her right now, I'll still be keeping an eye on her. The damage that place did could be invisible.

"Hey, Cherry baby." Aleko nudges me to gain my attention—I must've zoned out watching Mom—and I turn to face the man who holds my heart. He grins, that dangerous half grin that I can't resist, before planting a too-short kiss on my lips. "Did you want more food before the prospects start wrapping up the leftovers for tomorrow?"

"Ooh, yes please. Is there any more potato salad?" I don't know what they put in it, but it's like crack. I swear, I'm addicted.

Ninja chooses that moment to scurry back to us, climbing up Aleko's pant leg and into his lap, where he settles in for a belly rub. He's been spoiled this evening, each of the brothers feeding him carrot sticks or apple wedges and fussing over him when he does his cute paw thing.

"Sure is." While scratching at Ninja's tummy, Aleko leans forward again and kisses my cheek. "Jonesy! Get your ass over here."

The new prospect drops his can of local brew in shock at Aleko's yell, and immediately jogs over to the low brick wall we're sitting on.

"Yes, Sir Psycho?"

I can't help it, I end up spitting out the water I was drinking and laugh.

"Drop the sir. My old lady would like some more potato salad."

"You lazy shit." I lightly hit Aleko's shoulder and Ninja stands and abandons his lap for mine.

"What?"

He knows exactly what, and the smile he's trying to hide tells me so.

"I can get my own food, you know? You didn't need to send a prospect."

It's a moot point anyway, because Jonesy didn't need telling twice, he's already disappeared.

"I didn't need to, no. But I wanted to. He looked bored and I'm comfortable with you nestled in beside me." He shrugs, completely unapologetic. I fucking love this man.

Maybe it's the way he carries himself, the way he does what he wants when he wants, the way he accepts every single inch of me, mind, body, and soul, that makes all the fucked up shit seem trivial.

Wordlessly, Jonesy returns with a bowl full of potato salad and a fork, handing it over to me with a small, worried smile. It seems out of place, because he has an intimidating look about him. His head is completely shaved, like Bear, but it's also covered in tattoos, and he has more piercings in his face than I've ever seen on one person. The man is a walking contradiction because he's sporting a pair of baggy, colorful beach shorts along with a Hawaiian-style shirt and his leather cut.

"Thank you." I take the bowl and return his smile, ignoring Aleko's low growl beside me until Jonesy goes back to what he was doing before he was summoned—covering the leftover food and stacking it on the cart to take it inside.

"Hey, Prez!"

I don't know who it is, but it's loud, shouted across the courtyard jovially, and everything kind of hits the fan so quickly that I barely have time to blink.

My mom's chair is thrown backward as she stands, screaming incoherently, then she moves faster than I thought she could, waving a knife in the air. Hoops approaches and tries to calm her, holding his palms up to show that he's not trying to harm her, and she fucking stabs him.

While all this is happening, I'm frozen in shock with no clue how to handle this. Ninja jumps and runs up Aleko's arm into his hoodie. My potato salad goes flying to the ground and smashes on impact, and Sabrina, of all people here, is the one who grabs Mom around the waist to pull her away. Sabrina holds on tight, pressing her whole body up against Mom's front in a tight squeeze, then Mom breaks down and begins sobbing.

Shaking myself out of my inaction, I quickly stand and approach the pair. Hoops is sitting on one of the tables with Vanessa putting pressure against his new wound, the knife is on the ground, and my whole world may as well have imploded. Again.

I don't, and won't, blame her, but Mom just fucked this up for both of us. By trying to kill one of the members of this MC, she is forcing their hand. I know how this all works.

Silently, Sabrina passes Mom over to me, unwrapping her arms to slide them around me instead.

"I-I'm sorry, I thought it was... *him*. I... I..." Mom is trying to apologize through her sobs, her body giving out on her as she collapses to the ground.

"Hey, Mom. It's okay. It's okay." Falling to my knees, I cradle Mom's head against my chest. Tears prick at my own eyes because I know this short but happiest time of my life is going to crumble around me after this.

Behind me, Aleko approaches, kneeling on the ground and wrapping his arms around both of us as he gently kisses my head.

Everything around me feels like it's on pause. I know there's bustling and talking, but nothing's important to me right now other than Mom's wailing sobs and shaking body.

I don't know how long we're sitting here for, in our strange cuddle-huddle, but sounds begin filtering in and I realize I need to try and help. Hoops could be bleeding out and I've been ignoring the fact that my mom stabbed him. Hugging the attacker isn't the way these things usually go down.

The sounds are filtering in because Mom is now silent. Her body is still trembling, jerking on the occasional intakes of breath, and as I pull away I see what she's doing. She's shutting herself off, unable to deal with what's going on, and I get it.

"Mom, I'm gonna take you to your room. Okay? It's been a long day and you need some rest." *One thing at a time.* I remind myself to breathe, my EMT training kicking in.

Aleko unwraps himself from us and stands, holding out his hand to help me and Mom up. Looking around, I see Hoops flanked by Prez and Vanessa. Prez looks pissed, which I understand, it also cements my thoughts on how the club is going to want to handle this whole thing.

There's a gentle tap on my shoulder, making me turn to Sabrina, who is waving a small piece of paper at me. Her brows are furrowed in concern as she silently urges me to take it.

I'll take her to her room and stay with her for the night.

I know Sabrina is mute, or chooses not to speak, but this is my first kind of communication with her like this. The club trusts her, Vanessa thinks the sun shines out of her fucking ass—her exact words—but I don't want to put someone else in the same position as Hoops.

"No, it's fine. I can do it."

As if she pre-prepared for my response, she produces another piece of paper from her back pocket and holds it out to me.

It's fine. I've got this. I think Hoops needs stitches.

I shake my head in disbelief, because I have no doubt that she has more pieces of paper stuffed into her pocket, ready to argue her point.

"Okay. Thank you." I turn to Mom, who is now standing stoically beside me, her gaze unfocussed and her cheeks patchy from the tears. "Is it okay if Sabrina takes you to your room and stays with you? I just have some things to do first, then I'll come too."

Mom waves me off as though I'm speaking nonsense and holds her hand out to Sabrina. They must have done some serious bonding in the few hours we've been here.

With a quick hug, I let Mom go, watching as they disappear through the doors into the main building where all the suites are located.

"You good, baby?" Standing directly in front of me now, Aleko cups my cheeks and searches my face for I don't know what. I can't believe I'm going to have to give him up. *Again.*

I nod as he wipes a thumb across my cheek where a tear has escaped. "Is Hoops okay?"

The blinding grin Aleko gives me is one for the history books because it's fucking beautiful. "Of course he is. Could probably do with a few stitches, if you're up for it?" He winks before leaning down to kiss me, so softly, like a goodbye...

I nod once more, trying for a light smile but probably failing miserably, and pull away from him to head for Hoops, Prez, and Vanessa. The other brothers and the Khunts are all still enjoying themselves, drinking, laughing, the smell of weed beginning to overpower the barbecue scents.

"How are you doing? I'm so, so—"

"No need to apologize. Just wrong place, wrong time. But I'm good. It's not too deep."

"Can I see?"

Vanessa moves her hand away from where she has some cloth pressed against the wound. He's right, it's not too deep and a couple of stitches is probably all he needs. As an EMT, I'm not trained for this but I had fun practicing on Jake when I held him prisoner. So, yeah, I have limited knowledge. Guess we'll see how good I am.

I notice some other scars across his ribs, but he quickly lowers his shirt a little to cover himself when he sees me looking. Neither of us says anything, mainly because I don't want to piss him off any more than my mom stabbing him already has.

Luckily, I have the supplies I need to fix him up inside.

After a long-ass day and night, Aleko leads me to his suite, gently placing Ninja in his tiny bed on the dresser once we're inside.

"It's not your fault, you know?" Aleko breaks the silence first as I undress. He's already naked, lying back against the pillows on the bed.

"Hmm." As I'm pulling my dress over my head, Aleko grabs my hips and pulls me onto the bed with him, making me squeal.

"Don't *hmm* me, Cherry. I know you. I know you're blaming yourself and feeling all kinds of things that you don't need to be feeling." Wrapping his arms around me, he holds me close, the big spoon to my little spoon. "Now I'm going to help you feel some things that will make you smile before you pass out from being cum-drunk, then we can deal with this tomorrow."

More shit for future me to deal with, and I know I'll be cussing my past self out again for burying my head in the sand, but the way Aleko's fingers trickle across my skin is too intoxicating to ignore.

So I give in to him. Over and over... and over again, until I do, indeed, pass out.

CHAPTER SEVENTEEN

ALEKO

"Stop staring at me, it's creepy." My grin is instant at Mackenzie's mumbled, sleepy, words.

All night, every night, I sleep on my back with her draped over me in various positions. Leg hiked up on my waist and an arm either around my chest or tucked under her chin with her elbow digging into my ribs is the norm. She's a constant weight of comfort and even unconscious I can feel her presence, which is the only reason I sleep so well. This morning, however, she ended up facing away from me.

So, here I am. Propped up by my elbow with my front flush against her back as I watch every breath she takes in and every exhale she releases. The regularity of those sounds tend to calm my usually overactive heartbeat.

"It's not creepy when it's done out of love." Tracing the back of my index finger down the column of her neck and over her shoulder, I pause at the underside of her breast. Heavy and warm, the smooth skin makes my dick hard in a second.

"Yeah, that's what stalkers say."

I pinch her nipple hard enough to wake her completely. Her answering scowl only makes me harder. "Don't fucking talk about other men in our bed, Cherry. Do I need to fuck some respect into you? Need another orgasm to remember that you're mine?"

She rolls her eyes and turns back around, giving me her back again like the little brat she likes to be in the morning. "I have a message for you."

My mood shifts without preamble, the words ominous and too dangerous for my liking.

"From who?"

"My vagina wants you to keep your dick away so she can rest."

It takes my brain a couple of seconds to understand her words. When I do, I have to work really fucking hard at not laughing loudly enough to wake the whole fucking compound.

"Is that so?"

"Yeah, she'd appreciate a little down time, maybe a hot bath to relax her. Maybe then she'll be ready for round..." I can practically hear her counting in her head, so I do what I always do when it comes to her. I help.

"Round six."

"Damn, Aleko. Are you actively trying to drown me in my own orgasms?" The back of my finger returns to her silky skin, leaving goosebumps in its wake as I trace the story of my love for every inch of her.

"When you..." I have to take a breath and remind my heart and mind that it was all a ruse before I can even say the word. "When you *died*." I swallow down the lump of fear that never completely disappeared, even with her return. "It was like riding in a tunnel that never ends. The sound of the exhaust is so loud, it's enough to drown out every other noise around you. And your vision is singular, fixed ahead to the exit as you ride through, full speed ahead. Except, no matter how fast I was riding, the exit—the light—never came closer."

Changing the mood wasn't my intention but, for some reason, the words just come spilling out like I have zero control over them.

"Aleko..." My name on her parted lips is the sweetest sound, the most soul-soothing balm in the world.

"So, yeah. I watch you. I always know where you are, like I'm the planet that revolves around your sunlight. I growl and I snarl and I swear to fuck, Mackenzie, I will kill without a thought if it means keeping you safe. Mark my words."

Turning in my arms, Mackenzie wraps all four limbs around me and without either one of us deciding anything, my cock slides into her warm, wet pussy, pumping in and out, slow and steady. With her on top of me, blonde hair spilling all around like a cocoon just for us, we make love. Our mouths are fused together, our breaths feeding each other's lungs, and our moans healing each other's bruised souls.

"I take it back." Her words are soft against my lips.

"What do you take back, sweet Cherry Pie?"

"My vagina can rest when she's dead." I chuckle at her seriously fucked up words and decide being all sweet and cuddly is enough for now.

Flipping us over, I look down at her and grin like the psycho they've branded me.

"Good. I think she needs to be punished for thinking I could ever stay away." I don't waste time pressing my body to hers and attacking her mouth with my need for her. Gone are our soft kisses and sweet words. We are only frenzied craving and bottomless need for each other.

Rubbing my naked skin over her, it takes a Herculean effort not to rear back and slam my cock inside her. I will, but not this second. In fact, right now, the only thing I want is to feast on her cunt and feel her juices run down my chin. I want her so wet she's slipping and sliding all over my dick. I want her at my mercy the exact way I'm at hers.

Kneeling between her legs, I flip her over once more and grin at the immediate squeal that escapes her.

"Ass up." In a fraction of a second, she does exactly what I tell her and presents me her perfectly round ass, her pussy and asshole on display just begging for my mouth and fingers and cock. "You are a fucking sight, Cherry, and the best part is that you're all mine."

Running a gentle hand over her ass, I pause before pulling back and connecting again, this time with a reverberating slap that takes her completely by surprise.

"What the fuc—" The second slap cuts off any of her protests, her surprise turning to pleasure as my fingers dig into her skin and knead her recently pink flesh. "Oh, God. Do that again."

Fucking Christ, my dick cannot get any harder. This woman will be the death of me in the best of ways.

With the reactions she's giving me, it's difficult to stop, impossible to take my eyes off her reddening ass. So, I don't. Instead, I bring my mouth to her pink cheek and soothe the sting of my hand with a kiss from my lips. Then, I bite hard enough to make her squirm but not enough to break the skin.

It's only when she's absolute putty in my hands that my mouth travels to the crack of her ass and licks a path right down the middle, taking my time circling her puckered hole before lifting her high enough to bury my tongue inside her succulent little cunt.

I don't eat her out, I fucking devour her. My entire mouth consumes her with licks and bites and sucking sounds that are pure music to my ears, and combined with her moans, I lose myself at this woman's mercy.

Reaching around her, I tap out a soft beat on her clit to prepare her, warn her, that she's about to come all over my face. At the same time, I press one thumb to her puckered hole with my other hand and don't let up on her pussy until she's screaming for me to stop or continue or something, something, something.

If I weren't so fucking desperate to come inside her, I'd chuckle at her confused orders. Just when I think she can't take anymore, I give her the trifecta of pleasure.

In one move, I press two fingers to her clit and rub just as my thumb breaches her hole and my tongue disappears into her hot little pussy, my entire face buried between her lips. Is it possible to suffocate from eating pussy? I may very well find out and be okay with the consequences.

Her orgasm is swift and powerful, her cum instantly coating my mouth and nose and chin. It's fucking Heaven and I never want to let her go. This, right here, is everything I want, all the fucking time.

"Ohmygodohmygodohmygod!" she chants over and over, her ass and pussy grinding against me, seeking out more... always more.

Without a second's hesitation, I force myself to separate my mouth from her cunt and immediately replace it with my cock. It's deep and it's hard as stone, making her cry out again and again, alternating between God's name and mine. Not gonna lie, the familiar pang of jealousy throbs in my chest because God has nothing to do with the way she's writhing beneath me or the way her body is melting at my touch.

Her orgasms are mine.

Her pleasure is mine.

Her compliance is all fucking mine. I *am* her god, in and out of the fucking bedroom.

The thought has me rearing back and slamming inside her without any finesse. I don't fuck her pussy, I pound it with unleashed need and want and refuse to apologize for the way she makes me feel.

Unhinged. That's what she brings out in me, and it feels too right to question.

The next time she comes, I join her. My body draped over hers, my front to her back, and my dick emptying out inside her cum-thirsty cunt.

Our suite smells like sex and our breaths are the only sound I can hear as my heartbeat pumps inside my ears.

Goddamn, she's everything. Every fucking thing that matters in my life is right under me. With a soft kiss to her shoulder blade, I roll us over on our sides, keeping my dick inside her, and pepper her skin with my lips.

"I love you, Cherry. Don't ever doubt that."

"I don't doubt it for a second." Her response comes between two heavy breaths and I wait a beat before pinching her nipple.

"Ow! What was that for?" She tries to turn her head, I'm guessing so she can read my face.

"Say it back, Cherry." With a roll of her eyes, she faces away from me again and presses herself even closer against me before giving me what I want.

"I love you, too, you big buffoon." Honestly, I don't even care that her sweet words are dripping in sass. In fact, I kind of love it just like that.

"Your shot is soon, isn't it?" My question may seem out of the blue, but it's not. It's been bouncing around my head for days.

"Huh?"

"Contraception, Cherry. Next week, you're due for a shot. Correct?" I may have snooped around before all the shit went down. I figured she'd had the shot while hiding out and next week would be the logical time for her next shot.

"How the fuck would you even know that?" As soon as her words are out of her mouth, she stiffens in my arms.

"What's wrong?" I can feel her trying to pull away but instead of letting her go, I clamp her arm around her waist and hold her to me. "What's wrong, Mackenzie?"

"I need to look at the calendar." A warm feeling grows in my chest at the panic in her voice. An obsessive man like me can only hope...

"I am your calendar, Cherry. Next week is when you're due for your shot."

"Well, Mr. Knowitall, with everything going on, I haven't had my shot." With every one of her words, her pitch grows with panic.

"Is that a bad thing?" My first concern, in this situation, isn't what I want. As much as I want her pregnant with my baby, I definitely don't want her unhappy about it.

"It's not like we've been using condoms, Aleko. Once we knew we were both clean, we just kinda went at it like feral little bunnies. So, yeah, this is potentially a problem." Wiggling away from me, she tries to get away but, again, I keep her flush against me, my mouth at her ear and my words barely a whisper.

"Nothing bad can come from me loving you, Cherry. If you're pregnant, I'll follow your lead on this, but you need to know that you carrying my baby is nothing less than perfect for me." This time, when she springs off the mattress, I let her go.

"I'm only twenty-one, you fucking caveman!" Her outrage is dimmed by her wide eyes and nervous grin on her face.

"Hate to break it to ya, babe, but my sperm is probably in there swimming like a champ and poking at your eggs like a lunatic." I shrug with zero shame in my tone. "To be honest, I wouldn't be surprised if you're already pregnant with a little Psycho making room in there for the next however many months."

"I'm not pregnant. I would know. Jesus, I'm an EMT, I would fucking know if I'm—" Her gaze is fixed over my shoulder and she looks like she's calculating some equation on quantum mechanics. "Fuck."

I grin.

"When was your last period?"

"Fuck, fuck, fuck." Mackenzie bolts from the bed and picks up her phone.

"When was your last period, Cherry?" I'm right behind her in a nanosecond, looking over her shoulder as she opens up her cycle app.

"Fuck, fuck, fuck." I'm starting to love that chant.

"Well, damn. Guess we're taking a trip to the drug store." I don't even bother to hide the smile in my voice.

"No, no, no!" When she turns around, the fear in her eyes is real but I don't miss the way one of her hands flies to her stomach like she's already protecting it. "I thought it was all the food Sabrina was making me eat."

"She *is* a supreme cook." I wink, half expecting her to snap at me. She doesn't though, and I can see the shadow of worry in her eyes as she looks up to me for guidance.

"But what if the club kicks my mom out? What if we have to move out? I'm not leaving her alone, she needs me. But I don't have a job anymore and I can't live under a bridge, I mean... I know the Red Hot Chili Peppers think they're great but we don't have good bridges here in Rockford." I'm trying really fucking hard not to laugh because what the actual fuck is she talking about? As If I'd let her go, let alone live under a fucking bridge.

"It'll be fine, baby. It's you and me, we'll be great." My hand rests right over hers as my lips whisper-touch her lips. We don't kiss, not in the conventional way and we definitely don't talk but for a calming moment, we just take in the possibility of what's to come. Of what we will be... together.

Hell, maybe I'm wrong. Except, I know I'm not. It's in the way her belly rounds ever so slightly at the bottom, all hard and tense. The way her breasts feel so fucking full when I cup them and bite on them. The way her cunt milks my cock like it can't get enough of me.

And I'm not even going to start on her mood swings because I like my balls right where they are.

All that aside, before we can begin living a life together, we're definitely going to need to address, in church, the fact her mother just stabbed our VP. And that's a whole lot of worms we can't put back into the can.

"There's so many of them."

Bear and I are at the drug store, standing in the aisle for all the feminine products, as we both stare down at the three fucking shelves filled with pregnancy tests.

It takes me a second or ten to respond to him because he's right... who the fuck needs so many tests?

"Which one should I take?" There's a red box, a dark pink box, a green box, a blue box. So many fucking blue boxes. I pick a random one up and read the instructions.

"One line, you're not pregnant, two lines, you are. Results in one minute. Sounds simple enough." Bear's only response is a grunt and I'm pretty sure that means, yes.

Snatching up a second box, I read those instructions. Wait three minutes and the word "pregnant" tells you everything you need to know.

The third box is a combination of both of the others, boasting its success rate of ninety-nine percent accuracy.

"Get one of each, I guess."

Head cocked to the side, I look at Bear because what he just said makes perfect sense. When I stepped out of our suite earlier, I made a beeline for Bear's room and banged on the door before swinging it open and barking out orders to my best friend. He was face down on the bed, naked, with some Khunt using his back as her pillow. Without even questioning my sanity, he got up—careful not to jostle his partner too much—and took a four minute shower before he was dressing and walking out the door with me.

That's the thing about Bear and me... we've got each other's backs no matter what.

"Yeah. I'll let her choose, right?"

"Right." We both nod like the decision was easy to make. It wasn't, not by a long fucking shot as evidenced by the fact that we've been here for over twenty minutes just staring at boxes.

"Come on, I wanna know if I'm gonna be an uncle." I grin because I love the sound of that.

Grabbing no less than six boxes, we make our way to the register when something catches my eye and forces my feet to stop dead in their tracks.

On tiny hangers, are those onesie things for babies, each with a different slogan. Two make me grin so I swipe them up before grabbing a handful of cherry suckers and putting everything down on the counter for the cashier.

"Will this be all?" The tiny woman with a ponytail so tight it looks like her eyes are pulled into slits and she's trying to self-face-lift doesn't even look at me. She's so busy ogling Bear that if this were a cartoon, she'd have hearts in the place of her pupils.

"Yup."

"That'll be seventy-four ninety-five." I blink at the cashier who, again, isn't even looking at me, before swinging my gaze to the numbers and back at her.

Beside me, Bear chuckles. "And so it begins, brother. Better start a little nest egg 'cause it's gonna get real expensive real quick."

My answering grunt is all I can give as I fish four twenty dollar bills out of my wallet before my phone starts screaming, "Answer the fucking phone!" over and over again in Prez's distinct, smooth, and no nonsense voice. Fishing my phone out of my pocket, I grin at Ponytail Lady, who is finally giving me some attention—narrowed eyes and open mouth counts—and shrug.

"Guess I better answer the fucking phone." I make no apologies for who I am. "'Sup, Prez?" Swiping the five dollar bill, I drop the dime in the plastic box collecting change for St. Jude's Hospital and head for the door.

"Get yer asses back here, we've got a situation. Church is in fifteen." Without even giving me time to respond or ask questions, the line goes dead and anticipation grows deep in my belly, getting bigger and bigger as the seconds go by. When Prez calls like this, it means shit just hit the fan. Honestly, the possibilities are endless.

"What did Prez want?" We hop on our bikes before I stash the loot in my backpack.

"Something's up, we need to head straight to church."

"Let's go, Daddy."

My head snaps to the right so fast I almost dislodge my spine as I narrow my gaze into heated slits. "No, dude. Never again."

In sync, we both pull our helmets down, Bear laughing the whole time.

But when we get to the compound and take our seats at the central oak table, the laughter has long since died as I replay Prez's words over and over again in my head.

"First order of business before we get to today's disappointing news, is the shitshow of Hoops getting stabbed by..." Prez narrows his eyes on me, distaste curling his lip, "Your old lady's mother." Rubbing my hands over the top of my head, I groan at the mention of Darlene's unfortunate decision-making.

"She's really sorry about that, Prez." As if he can feel my tight fit between the rock and the hard place, Boner passes me the last of the joint going around the table. "It won't happen again." Lifting my chin to our VP, I ask. "You okay, Hoops?"

"All stitched up and ready to go, Psycho. I'm fine, man. But Prez is right. Our priority is the safety of our members. I get that she probably has PTSD but the issue is that she's a liability." I stare at Hoops, processing his words and hoping I'm not about to get some really fucking bad news.

"What's the PTSD about? You know anything?" This is church. What is said here, stays here but still, it's Darlene's story to tell.

"It's really fucking personal, Prez, but I can tell you this... we'll make sure it never happens again." I nod to Hoops, hopeful he'll get that I intend to keep my promise. "And right now, she's shaken up about it, too, and refuses to leave her room." Fuck, I hope this'll buy us some much needed time.

"Prez, if there's one place she can heal, it's here with us." I nod at Bear's words, he's right about this. We're all misfits who fucked up at one point or the other and Darlene is another victim of injustice, just like the rest of us.

"What about the Khunts? If we let this go, some of them might get ideas." Boner lights up a cigarette and shrugs, knowing he makes a good point.

"We do need to think about the girls, although none of them have an ax to grind. Right?" It sounds like a question but it's more of a warning.

"I wouldn't put violence past Rea, especially since your boy found himself a sweet old lady." Crow jumps into the conversation and I can't disagree with him. Rea has always been a bit of a wild card. I don't regret much in my life but fucking that girl on the regular is my biggest to date.

"All right. It's a club vote so let's do it." As Prez slams the gavel down, I look around the table and make eye contact with each of my brothers. I need them to know they can trust me to take care of this. To always have their best interests at heart.

"All for keeping Darlene at the compound, say aye."

One by one, my brothers lift their hands. All of them look me straight in the eye as they do and I know I've got my answer. They trust me.

"Unanimous. She stays. But, Psycho?" I already know what he's about to say but I listen carefully anyway. "No more."

"No more, Prez."

"Now, this is going to be more problematic and I need you to keep your shit together." Again with the index finger but this time he points it only at me. "Some high roller bailed out the Toxic Rebels last night. They're all back at their trailer park." Prez's finger hasn't moved an inch. "You... you don't fucking leave the compound. We'll handle this without you."

"The fuck you will!" I stand so fast the heavy chair flies out behind me. "They're mine, Prez. Their last breaths are mine."

"No." I whip around to look at Bear and snarl, actually fucking snarl. *Et tu, Brute.* "Their last breaths belong to Mac."

Motherfucker. Fucking true words, right there.

Chapter Eighteen

Mackenzie

"It won't take long to put weight on if I keep eating like this." Mom tips up her bowl for the last drops of the Vanessa-made creamy mushroom soup before using the rest of her soft bread to scoop up the dregs.

I've got to say, I agree with the sentiment. Although, after this morning, I'm now thinking my own weight gain is due to something else. It's worrying because I'm unsure of how the club is going to deal with Mom stabbing their Vice President. If Mom has to go, or worse, they decide she is too unsafe for this world, then I won't lie down and allow that. I can't.

Everything I've done has been for her, to fall at this hurdle would completely break me. More so than I already am. My brain is already working in overdrive to keep everything that's happened, everything I've had to do, safely locked away in the dark recesses of my mind.

Sabrina takes Mom's now-empty bowl and stacks it with the ones we already finished, then, in ASL, she signs something which Mom immediately translates for me.

"Where do you think these wide hips came from? Vanessa missed her calling as a rabbit." Mom's laugh is a thing of wonder, something I never thought I'd hear in all its glory like this again. "I'm going to go ahead and assume you meant chef? Here, this is how to sign *chef*." She slaps her right palm down against her left hand, like a clap, then flips her palm up, before placing both palms so they are facing each other, as if there's an invisible box being held between them.

Sabrina repeats the action, silently giggling and rolling her eyes at herself for the mistake.

Neither of us brings more attention to the mistake, because it really doesn't matter.

Before today, I had no idea that Sabrina could sign, but Mom explained that's because none of the club members know how, so it's just easier to write notes. Sabrina isn't deaf, she can hear perfectly well, but she chooses not to speak for reasons that are her own. To be fair, I haven't really had time to spend with many people here like this to find out; Aleko is a needy man—not that I'm complaining because I'm just as needy.

Mom and Sabrina have built a lovely relationship in the short time she's been at the compound, and the fact that Mom is able to pull up on her training and knowledge from before she was admitted to that place is nothing short of amazing. I think Sabrina likes being able to speak to someone without writing it down, and I know for a fact that Mom is enjoying the opportunity to use her learned skills.

While I've been here for the last hour, I've witnessed them both correcting each other on certain words, but for the most part, it's been surreal to have Mom here.

The irony of where we are isn't lost on me, though. Mom's gone from being admitted to a psychiatric hospital to being confined to her suite in an *old and restored* Psychiatric hospital. But stabbing someone doesn't come without consequences... well, not when there are witnesses anyway.

"Now, darlin'. I know you've been trying your hardest not to ask about what happened. I can see it all over your beautiful face." Mom pushes her chair away from the small desk beside her, then stands and comes to sit beside me on the king-size bed. The mint-green sheets were Vanessa's idea. She had insisted on making sure my mom was comfortable and had bugged me to tell her Mom's favorite color before she moved in.

Bet she's regretting that now. It all seems like such a waste.

I swear, my emotions are so up and down, I'm surprised I'm not nauseous.

"Yeah." I can do nothing but shrug and pick at my fingernails, concentrating on my hands as though they're going to change the world, and feeling every bit the sixteen-year-old child my mom left behind five years ago.

The warm embrace as she wraps an arm around my shoulders and pulls me close is something else I thought could never happen again. A lump catches in my throat and I'm struggling not to be sad in any way about what has been missed. Instead, I lean my head against her chest and listen to her heartbeat as she rubs the top of my arm.

"Something triggered my brain to go into defense mode. When your brother would visit with his friends, they..." She pauses, taking a moment before continuing. "They took advantage of me being unable to fight back or move. It became a game. I won't go into detail because it's all in the past, and to be honest, I can't go back to that dark place in my mind. But now that I'm no longer in that position, I *can* fight back. I'm sorry, darlin'. It was like an instinct to protect myself. I realized what I'd done by the time Sabrina brought me back here." She sighs and we sit in silence for a few moments.

Me? I'm absorbing the information she's just given because knowing this... well, my brother didn't suffer enough.

"Do you think speaking to someone about everything could help?" Maybe explaining and apologizing to the club is enough. Maybe they won't vote to kick her out or... I shudder. No. They wouldn't do worse, would they?

"I've been talking with Sabrina, if that counts." Mom laughs, and it's a little scary to see how easily she's moving on from what happened to her, last night *and* at the Psych hospital.

Like mother, like daughter.

Let's all push aside our feelings in hopes of moving for-ward... but that's not going to help Mom. Not after last night's outburst.

"It does a little." I smile against her chest, still in her hold, until I shoot up as a memory hits me. Broaching the subject is something I've been putting off, waiting for the right time, but let's be real, when exactly is the right time to bring up your dead brother and his last-second spewings? "Jake told me something. Before he died."

"Okay? Would you like to share, darlin'?"

Hesitant, I nod as her hazel gaze searches my face, her love and encouragement filling my chest with the warmth I've been missing for so long. Unconditional love. I open my mouth to speak, but she holds up a hand.

"For you to be looking this worried, I think I know what he told you. Was it about D-Dad?" She's trying to be so strong as she brings him up, his death being the reason she was admitted in the first place, but the subtle tremble of her chin gives her away.

I nod again, feeling like one of those wobbly head things, unable to do anything else.

"Before your dad, there was another man. An older, married man. He was a mistake, but after the first time, he refused to take no for an answer. Your dad was my best friend, and he persuaded me to move away with him to a new town. It was the only way to get away. Restraining orders were ignored, and for a short while, things weren't safe. A few weeks after we had moved, I realized I was pregnant. With your brother. Your dad immediately whisked me away to the town hall where we were married, and he agreed to raise the baby as his own. Over the years, there have been glimpses of the man, and I know he was in contact with Jake because I never told him, yet he knew. So yes, Jake is—was–your *half*-brother."

Relief floods me because I hated the thought that I could have a different dad out there somewhere, that the dad I knew as my own had lied to me for my whole life.

"Wow... Mom, I love you." There really isn't much else to say because my mom is stronger than I ever gave her credit for. It's no wonder she broke down when Dad died; he was her glue, holding her pieces together... just like Aleko for me.

And now it's completely clear as to why I'm not crumbling every second of every day. Aleko would never let me.

"Do you remember his name?" I'm curious. I'd love to find out more, to see what kind of man Jake's father was. This is definitely one of my downfalls, my unhealthy need for knowledge.

"No." Mom closes her eyes, her head shaking over and over, as she pulls me in for another hug.

I hadn't noticed, but Sabrina must have left the room at some point. The empty soup bowls have disappeared so I'm guessing she's taken them to the kitchen, where the Khunts will wash them. I think Rea is down there today. My least favorite of the ones I've seen around here so far. Rude as fuck.

Mom's shut down at this point, slowly rocking backward and forward as she holds me, intermittently kissing the top of my head, and I decide no more questions for today.

It's like the fates have decided the same thing because there's a persistent knock at the door, followed by a shout, "Where's my Cherry Pie?"

The door flies open as Mom finds herself again and invites him in with a quick, "Come in."

"I need to steal you away for like, an hour or two, Cherry." Aleko raises that sexy as fuck brow, telling me everything I need to know without a single word escaping his mouth.

He and Bear went to the pharmacy for "supplies" before church was called for something important. That must all be over now, so Aleko is clearly back with the goods from his shopping trip.

Lucky for me, Sabrina chooses that moment to come back into the room with a fresh pot of coffee. As much as I want to stay with Mom for a little longer, right now, I need to see what my future actually holds.

After some goodbyes, and assurances from Sabrina that Mom will be okay, Aleko and I head toward his suite.

There's something on his mind other than the whole possible-baby thing, and I'm pretty sure I know what it is. Because it's on my mind too. This is probably what their whole church thing was about.

"How long does Mom have left before she's got to go?" I won't even entertain the alternative option.

"What the fuck are you talking about, Cherry?" Aleko unlocks the door to his suite and holds it open for me, gesturing for me to go first.

I sigh, he's going to make this harder than it needs to be,

"She stabbed your VP, I know the rules, she's got to be dead to you guys now. She ha—"

"Let me stop you right there, babydoll." Closing the door behind him, Aleko prowls closer to me, placing his hands either side of my face and forcing me to make eye contact. "The Toxic Rebels don't run under any kind of rules like the rest of us. Not in any universe would you or your mom be told to leave here. You're family. You get that, don't you? Which means *she's* family. We've all had our fair share of trauma, so we get it. The Prez said so himself. Hoops is fine, no one died, we know she didn't mean to and that she's sorry. We'll get her some help." He shrugs as if it's no big deal.

"And that's it? No repercussions?" I'm skeptical, because this isn't what I know.

"That's it." Holding his hands palms-up and out to his sides, he turns to grab a paper bag sitting on his dresser.

As he passes it over to me, the sheer number of boxes inside almost floors me. The task ahead is suddenly super daunting.

"Wait, if church wasn't about kicking Mom out, is everything okay? Because you seem a little on edge." And he does, even though the playful glint I love so much is still there in his beautiful blue eyes, there's a tenseness to his neck and the way he's carrying himself differently than usual.

"I'd say not. No. But it will be. We can and will come up with a plan for all that though. Right now, I need you to take these and piss on every single stick." He winks, but I'm not buying it.

"I'll piss on sticks when you tell me what's wrong."

"Incorrigible. That's what you are, Cherry. Incorrigible." Snatching the paper bag from my hand, he places it on the bed behind me. Then he puts one hand against my waist as if to steady me, and the other against my cheek. "The Rebels have been bailed out, awaiting trial." I have to remind myself to breathe, but it hurts. "Jonesy is trying to find out who it was, but our lawyer didn't have much info to go on..."

My heart is beating out of my chest, my head pounding, my hands trembling against Aleko's strong, bare arms.

"Baby, we'll deal with them together, okay?" Eyes dancing between mine, Aleko kisses me, hard and fast, before wrapping his arms all the way around me so we're pressed so close together that my heartbeat becomes his.

Adrenaline is flooding my veins, and it's not because I'm scared like I thought I would be. The thought of now being able to get to Isaac and Brick without the constraints of bars and police in the way is exciting. The possibilities running through my mind seem endless, and with Aleko by my side, they really are.

The fact that what Mom did is basically nothing to him, my fears completely alleviated, is a huge weight off my shoulders. I swear, this man would forgive me anything.

"Promise?"

"I promise. Now, will you go and piss on those sticks already?" He grins, pulling my face to his to kiss me, all tongues and teeth, before resting his forehead against mine. "I fucking love you." He turns and grabs the paper bag again, shoving it at me and spinning me toward the bathroom, slapping my ass to get me moving.

I don't.

Instead, I turn to look at him over my shoulder, a disapproving look on my face, trying desperately to do his one eyebrow thing.

I'm failing. I know this because he's now laughing at me.

"Too cute. Fuck off. Piss on sticks." Shaking his head, he gently pushes me into the bathroom, then stands in the open doorway with his arms folded across his chest. The loose black tank top he's wearing is showing off all his neck, chest, and arm tattoos, and I wonder if this can wait until later... not that I'm trying to put off knowing at all.

Okay, I am.

As I approach him, he smirks, unmoving, and does the eyebrow thing. He knows what he's doing.

"Bastard."

He chuckles at my insult, and I huff.

"Are you really going to watch me do this?" Pulling my short-shorts and panties down, I sit on the toilet before pulling out a box from the bag at random.

"Did you really think I'd do anything else, Cherry?"

I roll my eyes because no, I did not.

"Okay. Fair."

It takes longer than I imagined, but after peeing in a cup and dipping six different sticks into it for their allotted time, the first one is ready. If the timer going off on Aleko's phone is any indication.

"I don't wanna look."

"Why, baby?" We're both sitting on the bathroom floor, me in Aleko's lap, and it's just dawning on me what's going on.

I might be pregnant. I might have a real human growing inside me. One that I'll be responsible for. Having children isn't something I envisioned for myself, but now that the possibility is here, I really want to have Aleko's baby. I want a family with him, and every single thing that comes with being his and him being mine.

What I'm scared of, in this moment, is that I'm *not* pregnant.

We stare at each other for a few minutes, his question going unanswered, but I think he sees it in my expression, in my eyes, because he just smiles and kisses me before pushing me up to stand along with himself.

I take a deep breath and look at the first stick, Aleko right behind me, keeping my back warm with the feel of him, and my stomach jumps into my chest at the sight. Then I take a look at the second, third, fourth, fifth, sixth...

Holy shit.

"We're pregnant!"

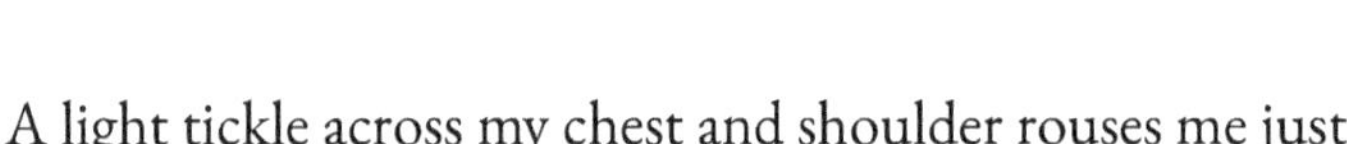

A light tickle across my chest and shoulder rouses me just before I hear, "Cherry Pie, you awake?"

I quickly realize the tickle is Ninja, just as eager as Aleko to wake me up this morning.

"I wasn't awake. No. Go away. Ninja can stay though," I grumble out my words, keeping my eyes closed because I just don't wanna.

Aleko chuckles, then the feel of his soft lips press against my forehead, my cheeks, my mouth, and my nose. "C'mon. We have to go and see the doc."

I groan, knowing we already talked about this last night. He's insisting we go to see the doctor right away, so we can better plan and prepare for our new arrival. After Aleko spent most of the night practically worshiping my body, I agreed we'd do it today before we announce it to anyone. I'm looking forward to telling Mom she's going to be a grandma. When I was younger, I distinctly remember her and Dad discussing it once, and how excited they were with the thought of spoiling their grandkids someday since Jake was well on his way to adulthood.

The fact that my baby's only got one grandparent is upsetting, but I know Mom and I will be able to tell the little bump all kinds of stories about Dad. On the other hand, I doubt Aleko will want to divulge anything from his family, considering the whole Greek mafia thing he told me about one night when I couldn't sleep.

Although I'm not exactly innocent these days; I broke the law and have a fake identity. To the law, I'm no longer Mackenzie Wilson, I'm Scarlet Green. My fake IDs are great, I mean, they were good enough for me to see Aleko as a visitor in jail, but it feels wrong to use them for this. For this baby's mom to be listed as Scarlet Green is like a kick in the teeth, but of course, Aleko has a solution.

The doctor we're seeing is the Sons of Khaos club doc. He's on their payroll for any medical needs that the law doesn't need to know about. I have no idea how it's all going to work, but I'm rolling with it.

I'd rather it wasn't at whatever stupid time it feels like right now, but as I open my eyes to Aleko's smiling face with the feel of Ninja snuggled into my neck, I'm not going to complain.

"Here, drink this and put those on. I've already got the keys to Vanessa's truck." Aleko holds a glass of orange juice over me, waiting for me to sit up and take it, then he plants a firm kiss on my lips and practically jumps off the bed. He throws a pair of pale blue sweats and one of his black SOK T-shirts at my now-bare legs, because of course, he's pulled the sheets off, making me squeal.

I can't be mad, it's endearing. Fucking beautiful, in fact, how excited he is about this.

An hour later, we're sitting in the doctor's office waiting to be seen, while Ninja is living his best life having a play-date with Crow in the SOK garage. There was no appointment booked, but Aleko insisted we do this today and the doc agreed when he realized he was dealing with the Sons of Khaos Enforcer.

"Mr. and Mrs. Kastellanos?" A nurse calls from the reception area, smiling as Aleko and I stand to follow her through to the doctor's office.

"Mr. and Mrs.?" I whisper as we walk hand in hand behind the nurse down the hallway.

"Soon, baby." Aleko winks, pushing me into the room before him, ever the gentleman.

The appointment goes as expected, and I answer any questions about my last period and how I've been feeling recently—which isn't any different so I guess I'm one of the lucky ones because I hear morning sickness sucks. But maybe that's still to come? Ugh. The joys.

After rolling the ultrasound machine over to the bed I'm lying on, the doctor instructs me to lift my T-shirt and lower my pants a little before squeezing on some really cold gel. He takes a few minutes rubbing the stick across my stomach, typing something on his screen, then looking at his date chart.

"Looks like we're already in your second trimester, Mrs. Kastellanos. You're fourteen weeks along. Congratulations. Would you like to know the sex?"

"Yes!"

"No!"

Aleko and I answer at the same time, and I understand his excitement, but fourteen weeks is over three months ago... before I fake died... around the same time as... oh God. There's a chance that Aleko isn't... I think I space out for a moment because my ears start ringing as I try to do the math. Tears begin to burn behind my eyes and I look at the amazing man beside me, gripping my hand so tightly I think he knows too. Seconds pass, where I think we both stop breathing, before Aleko's expression softens and determination sets in.

"Cherry, baby? I see you. And it's a null point. This baby's ours. Okay? Me and you."

I focus on Aleko, my rock, my shining star, and wonder how I got so lucky. I nod gently, but I'm going to need some more convincing because my good luck seems to come with consequences of the fucked up kind. Which reminds me…

"Can you write it on a piece of paper and put it in an envelope, please, Doc?" I look up at Aleko, eyes brimming with unshed tears and a goofy smile that makes him seem ten years younger. "Babe, we should maybe…?"

Our gazes lock and his brow cocks up. Gone is his smile, a smirk firmly in its place.

"Ain't worried, Cherry. My sperm can outrun any of those fuckers. But if it makes you feel better, then take whatever you need."

In sync, we meet our doctor's gaze as one and ask him to put our minds at ease.

"Of course, I'll get two envelopes ready for you, one with the reveal and the other with a few pictures from the ultrasound. When we're done here, I'll have the nurse take your blood and a swab from Dad. Now, let me just turn the sound on here."

"Oh, God." My hand automatically flies to my mouth in shock at the steady beat coming through the speakers, and the doctor turns the monitor around to show us the tiny blob.

"My sweet Cherry Pie. I fucking love you, and I love *our* baby." Aleko grips my hand, bringing it to his lips and holding it against them. I can feel him trembling along with me. His hold is tight, and I get it; this is scary as shit, but we're in it together.

Tears prick my eyes and I decide that no matter who this baby's bio-dad turns out to be, they will have the best life full of love with Aleko as their dad.

There are just a few things we need to do first, to make this world a safer place for the baby growing inside me.

Chapter Nineteen

Aleko

"Seriously? Are you even hearing me right now?"

Oh, I'm hearing her, all right. I'm just choosing not to fucking listen. Big difference.

That being said, she's tired and not really thinking straight. Maybe there *is* such a thing as too many orgasms. Fuck, did I break her on that last one? Now that I think about it, I'm pretty sure she blacked out for a moment, there.

"Look…" Taking in a deep, steadying breath, I place my hands on my jean-clad hips and hang my head long enough to gather my thoughts. Now is not the time to lose my cool.

"Don't you dare 'look' me. *You* fucking look. I'm not looking at shit right now." Wow. Okay, so she really feels strongly about this or…

"Is this..." My index finger does a recap of the whole room like I'm showing her pieces of evidence in a courtroom. "The hormones?"

I'm going to blame this on my age. Or maybe the fact that I've never been around a pregnant woman, or any woman on an intimate level for very long. But I've never regretted my words so quickly before in my entire fucking life.

"You did not just say that." Her stance as she aggressively whispers those heavy-as-lead words to me is like an MMA fighter goading her opponent. The fuck am I supposed to do or say now?

"Nope. I did not. That was Ninja." Sorry, buddy, but she'll spare you, and with the way she's peeling my skin off with her glare, I don't think she'd have the same kind of pity on me.

Raising both her brows at me when she means to raise only one, I fight the urge to chuckle because... well, I like my balls right where they are.

"Google says no long trips but, at three months, I can totally get on my bike for a short, ten minute ride. You're just being all..." Her hands are flying around like she's the one pointing out the evidence and obvious errors of my ways. "Over-the-top protective and shit. I'm pregnant, not fucking incapacitated."

Now she's the one standing with her hands on her hips, one hip cocked in a battle stance and two fingers tapping on her waist like she's begging the universe to give her the strength to refrain from killing me.

"If something happens to you, Cherry, I won't survive it." There. It's been said. It's out there. Do with it as you see fit.

Right before my eyes, she melts into a puddle of water that cools down our argument and gives us both some much-needed perspective. It also, however, scares the fuck out of me because who can change moods like that, so quickly and without effort?

Aw, fuck. Now, she's crying and I don't... what the fuck am I supposed to with that?

Needless to say, I will never say it out loud again, but I'm pretty sure the hormones have kidnapped her, which means this is going to be my future for many months to come.

Another thing I won't mention—for obvious reasons—is that I fucking love that my little swimmers made her this way. That I put a baby inside her and now the entire chemistry of her brain has been somewhat altered.

Because, yeah. I don't give a fuck what those dates at the doctor's said, that baby is mine. Just like Cherry is mine. There's no fucking way my sperm didn't make it to her egg before those motherfuckers got there. Even if it was a tie, my little dudes would have beat their asses right back to the tiny dick hole that dared touch my woman.

End of.

Mackenzie practically tackles me, wrapping her arms around my neck and sobbing into my chest. The way she climbs my body until our mouths are sealed in a hot, desperate kiss that electrifies my entire nervous system has my dick rock hard in an instant.

"I'm sorry, baby. I just... I'm gonna miss riding and I just want to feel her between my legs one last time before I have to... ya know..." I know exactly what she's doing and I'm choosing to let her win this little battle, if for no other reason than her mouth is fucking magical. "And race night is in the next couple of weeks, right? So I won't even be able to win my money." Yeah, I'm gonna let that slide, too. First off, no, she's not fucking racing and two, who says she would've beat me?

"Ten minutes to town, we take a pause, then ten minutes back. And—" Like a little monkey, she squeezes her four limbs around my neck and waist, peppering tiny kisses all over my face. "And…" I pause until I have her full attention. "The brothers come with us. Those Toxic fuckers are out there and there's no fucking way I'm tempting fate and risking any of them recognizing you."

"Deal. I'll agree to your conditions and add the wig for when my helmet is off as a peace offering." I don't mention the fact that the wig was already a given because I just want this to be her win right now.

"Okay, baby." She slides down my body, and as she lands on her feet, I fall to my knees and place my hands on her waist, my mouth on her belly and my words for my future.

"Make sure Mommy doesn't do anything stupid on that bike or else you're gonna be born grounded until you're eighteen." I look up at Mackenzie and grin before unwrapping a sucker and popping it in my mouth. And just like that, we're back to me and her. Her and me. Cherry and Psycho gearing up for a ride into town.

"Oh! How about ice cream at the river? That way it's private and I don't have to be all stealthy and shit."

Rising to my full height, I pop the sucker out of my mouth, kiss her grinning lips and murmur, "That sounds perfect, Cherry Pie." Then I push the cherry flavored delight between her lips and watch as she sucks on it, her tongue twirling, her eyes mischievous.

She wouldn't.

The unmistakable sound of crunching has me narrowing my eyes at her.

"Rude."

The earlier, cuter grin turns devilish as she springs onto her tippy toes, kisses my lips and a second later she's straddling one of our spare bikes.

I've never seen her suit up so quickly and didn't realize she liked to sing while doing so. There are a million things that Mackenzie does like a fucking boss, but singing just ain't one of them.

I'm not telling her that, either.

"Don't forget Ninja. He loves going to the river, right?" She looks up at me with expectant eyes like she's doubting her memory.

"Yeah, he's a regular water nut. Maybe he'll swim on his back for you." I cluck my tongue and Ninja comes barreling from his little castle cage, running around my leg and up my belly until he's nuzzling my neck and finding his favorite spot in my hoodie.

"I hope he doesn't bite off our baby's toes." I freeze. What the actual fucking fuck is that supposed to mean?

"Uhm, Cherry baby, why the fuck would you say that?" Now I've got horror images swimming in my brain of mutilated body parts and Ninja going all Count Dracula on my kid.

She shrugs and slaps me on the ass. "I'm just fucking with you. You ready to go?"

Fucking Christ.

Some of the brothers were working at the garage on a couple of late orders so I rounded up the ones that were lazing around the rec room. The prospects were chomping at the bit for some riding time and I'm pretty sure going to the river for some ice cream beat reality television for Grinder. Although, his attention was rapt on whoever had been eating the grossest fucking insects on the planet.

In the end, Bear, Sledge, and Crow decided they wanted some down time before we geared up to slash some Toxic throats. The plans are in the making, but Prez is meeting with the deputy to put all of his ducks in a row. So to speak.

The sounds of our engines roaring as we file out of the compound's circular drive bring an automatic grin to my face. It may not be climate change friendly, but the revving engines and burning rubber always pulls my blood pressure down to reasonable.

In order of rank, we follow each other to the river downtown and as soon as we hit the main road, our antics begin. Since Python's passing, Bash has taken up the role of tech dude. Nowhere near as good as our lost brother, but he's holding his own and researching and learning as best he can. Another thing he's been keeping up with are the videos of us riding and doing tricks. He'll be earning his full patch very soon, no doubt.

Like right now. Grinder is making some lewd Magic Mike moves on his bike like he's fucking his way through traffic without caring that he may or may not have caused a fender bender three cars back.

Not to be outshined, I rev my engine once, twice, then give the throttle a sudden twist of the wrist and speed by him on my back wheel, fast enough to make him lose the tiniest bit of control. No doubt the consequences to my actions will be quick and amplified because when we're on our bikes, we regress in mental age. It's not about boys will be boys, it's all about bikers and their need to feel the power beneath them, push the boundaries of their machines, Hell, push the boundaries of all the things.

Except for Mackenzie. She needs to be a good girl and ride the speed limit.

Which she obviously doesn't because, of all the riders out here today, she's the one I can least control. But dammit, I try. As I bring the front wheel back down and look to my left where I know Cherry is flanking me, I pump my palm down in the universal sign for slow the fuck down. As expected, all I get in return is another universal sign. Only, hers is telling me to fuck right off.

Growling in my helmet at the risks she's taking, it doesn't escape me that Bash takes this very second to catch up and film her giving me the middle finger.

Fucker.

Thankfully, most of the way to the river is small downtown roads, which means we try our best not to be assholes and ride like normal humans. I say "try" because we're still us, and "us" is too far from normal to be boxed into anything specific.

By the time we make it to our favorite spot, the prospects head to the ice-cream shop as the rest of us settle on the shallow banks and get comfortable.

"Come here, baby." I pat my thighs as she places her helmet on a small rock, careful that it won't fall over.

"What about Ninja?" At the sound of her voice calling his name, my little buddy pokes his head out of my hoodie and sits on my shoulder, his tiny nose sniffing the air like he's investigating our surroundings. Grinder pats his leg and my travel partner abandons me quicker than I thought his little legs could go. Guess he's going swimming.

Around us, Bear, Crow, and Sledge all sit in various positions and it's not long before Sledge starts rolling a joint and Crow lights up a cigarette.

We asked Darlene and Sabrina if they wanted to come out with us, but apparently Mackenzie's mom isn't comfortable leaving the room yet. Sabrina wrote down the word "agoraphobia" and nodded like it was the explanation to everything. A quick web search told me it's about fearing crowds and open spaces, which I guess makes sense. That being said, in her position, I'd have a fear of white coats and hospital beds, but whatever.

"Dude, smoke that over there. We don't want the smell here." All eyes turn to me before I even finish my order, my eyes locking with Bear and having an entire conversation without a single word being spoken.

"Well, I'll be damned." Fucker grins at me, and without even looking, he reaches to Crow, takes his cigarette, and crushes it into a soda can.

"What the fuck, man? Do you know how much that shit costs?" Crow's too laid back to be really pissed off, and Sledge's booming laughter at the scene only makes it all seem funny. What they don't know is that nothing is more important than my Cherry's and our baby's health.

Not a fucking thing.

"Before or after health care costs? Those things won't just kill you, they'll take all your fucking money, then kill you." Bear, ever the level-headed one.

"Save lives, smoke weed, mate." Fucking Sledge missing the whole fucking point.

"Ain't about that, brother." Bear grins but doesn't elaborate and I know why. It's our secret to tell. Not gonna lie, I'm bursting at the seams with my need to make it official to the club, choosing to ignore the little growl coming from my not-so-sweet-Cherry. Sure, we agreed to wait until Darlene was in the know before announcing it to everyone else but... Did I mention patience isn't my forte?.

"Aleko." Mackenzie squeezes my hand hard enough to cut off my circulation, my name sounding like acid in her mouth, but my lips start moving before my brain has time to add up the consequences.

"Ain't good for the baby." It's all I say, waiting to see how long it'll take them to catch on. "Ow! Fuck, Cherry, I need my leg to ride back." Chuckling as I rub my shin from where she's kicked me, hard, with her fucking Docs, I flash her the grin I know melts her panties because she's made it abundantly clear in the past.

"We're the only ones here, man. C'mon!" Crow reaches for his pack when Bear punches him in the upper arm and growls.

"Read the room, man." He can barely keep a straight face as his eyes look pointedly at my large hand lying protectively on Cherry's belly.

It takes them a second, but both Sledge and Crow start hootin' and hollerin' at the news. It doesn't escape my notice that Sledge doesn't put out the joint. Instead, he moves farther down the banks. Without apology, he shrugs like... *congrats, man, but I'mma take a toke anyway.*

The prospects come back with full hands, and barely arrived, we're on them like we've got fire ants crawling up our asses. The most feral of all being Mackenzie, who's been jonesing for some Rocky Road since we first mentioned our little outing.

"What're ya gonna name it?" Sledge asks on an inhale.

"Not Sledge." Raising a brow at my answer, he nods his head and blows out the smoke.

"I wasn't even gonna suggest it, mate. What about Rainer, though, ey?" Sledge watches the smoke leave his mouth with rapt fascination.

"Still no."

"Fair, fair. Although, he'd get some high-quality tail with that name. I would know." Grinder comes back with Ninja in his hand, cuddling into his chest.

"Who's getting laid?" Dude has some on-point comedic entrances. "Well, besides me on the regular?"

"Psycho's kid." At Crow's words, Grinder stops and does a double take.

"Are you fucking serious?" His voice is barely louder than a whisper, like saying it out loud might anger the gods.

"Yep, already in the second trimester according to the doc." No doubt my pride can be heard, felt, and tasted a mile away.

"Fuck yeah! I'm gonna be the best fucking uncle who ever uncled in the history of all uncles. You mark my words, assholes." As if to agree with him, Ninja crawls up his arm and sniffs at his neck. Then I remember Cherry's ridiculous joke, and bloody toes and fingers flash around in my head.

"I'm so fucking mad at you right now." My words are only for Cherry.

"What did I do?"

"You planted a horror movie in my head with your Ninja comment." She laughs and it takes me a moment but, eventually, I laugh with her. But still, the worry doesn't completely escape me.

All good things must come to an end and, as promised, Mackenzie didn't grumble when we decided it was time to head back.

Apart from slaloming in and out of traffic, we remained responsible riders on our way home; waving and honking at kids as we passed them by. Grinder even got close enough to fist bump a teenager in a beat up truck before opening the gas and bolting away.

As we turn a few blocks from our neighborhood, I almost have a coronary as Mackenzie comes to halt, the back tire sliding across the asphalt and her leg planting on the road before she steadies, puts the kickstand down, and jumps off the bike. It's like watching a disaster happening in slow motion and not being able to stop it. Except, of course, my woman is in total control. Still, she's pregnant with my baby and anything apart from moving slowly and deliberately scares the fuck out of me.

I'm so focused on her that I don't see the kid lying on the sidewalk, convulsing and puking his guts out. There's no one around so he's lucky we were coming this way at this very moment. And of fucking course, Mackenzie would stop

"Call 9-1-1, hurry up." Mackenzie's EMT training kicks in immediately. To my untrained eyes, it doesn't seem that all those months away has slowed her down or made her rusty.

Crow is the first to have his phone in hand, giving the dispatcher all the information Mackenzie is calling out to him.

Young man. Early twenties. Unconscious. Seizing. Vomiting. Possibly drug related.

When the dispatcher tells Crow an ambulance is on its way, I look at Cherry and growl. "We need to go. They can't see you."

Conflicted but still reasonable, she gives Crow instructions and he takes her place as they wait and she jumps on her bike, worry etched over every one of her beautiful features.

I think it's what I love most about her... her empathy.

And that thing she does with her tongue.

That's when she silently hands me the baggie with the smiley face on it and my teeth grind in anger.

Fucking hell, this shit again.

Chapter Twenty
Mackenzie

The sun is hidden by the clouds, but it's warm enough for a short walk around the gardens with Mom. Most of the club brothers are working in the garages or on deliveries and so this area behind the main building is beautifully secluded enough for Mom to be comfortable. It's full of shrubs and flowers, mostly overgrown now, but I imagine this is where they used to bring patients when this was a working Psychiatric hospital.

"Are we going to talk about what's on your mind or continue to walk in silence, darlin'?" Mom squeezes my hand where it's linked through her arm. "I'm well aware that I haven't been myself for the last six years, but I'm still your mom. I know when my girl's got something to say."

I chuckle, because she's right, she's always had a sixth sense when it comes to her kids. It's just that I'm not sure how to tell her. Do I build up to it with a long speech, or do blurt it out without explanation?

"It must be good news to give you a smile like that." She's grinning too, and I love her enthusiasm already.

"I'm pregnant." Blurting it out, it is!

My feet freeze when I notice I'm just walking alone now because my mother is no longer by my side. Then I breathe out a sigh of relief when I hear her squeal.

"Oh my goodness! My baby's having a baby!" Mom's excitement is a little overwhelming as she immediately wraps her arms around me, but I hug her back and allow the happy tears to flow.

It's a mixed feeling of relief and joy flowing through me because as much as I was looking forward to telling Mom, I also had the fear of judgment that she'd think I'm too young.

"How far along are you?" She steps back, tears brimming in her eyes too.

"About fourteen weeks. I have a favor to ask though." As the only living grandparent, I think this responsibility is the perfect way to keep Mom involved.

"Of course, darlin', anything." Confusion combined with eagerness crosses her face, the curve of her smile unbreakable.

"The doc wrote the sex of the baby in this envelope." I pull it from the small pocket of my summer dress. "Would you take it and keep it safe until we're ready to find out?"

Her hands fly to her face in surprise, the tears that she was fighting before now falling down her cheeks. "Oh, darlin', what an honor." She takes the offered envelope, clasping it to her chest as though it's precious when she realizes I've handed her a sonogram picture as well. "What a beautiful thing."

In this moment, with both of us crying happy tears, hugging each other so tightly, it's as though the last six years never happened. This is how we should have always been, but that time was stolen from us.

"I love you."

"I love you, too, Mom."

"How many have gone missing from Steve's morgue since last count?" I sip at the fizzy lemon drink Vi made for me as Spencer and I catch up in a booth in the SOK clubhouse bar area. Vi is a whizz behind that bar, like a freaking magician with her knowledge of drinks.

"Another two in the last month. Steve said he's seen some armed men talking with the CEO of the hospital on the regular, so he's assuming they're paying her off for her silence. He's reported the missing bodies to the hospital authorities, but all the paperwork just goes missing. It's how he got away with 'losing' you and Jake so easily." Spence rests his head back against the soft cushion and rolls it to look at me with a shrug. "There's definitely something going on, but no one knows what, exactly, that is. Weird as hell though. I'd go so far as to say that helping you fake die to then torture and kill your half-brother was less of a mind-fuck."

When I called Spence to tell him I'm pregnant, he insisted on coming over so he could meet his new niece or nephew and get them used to his voice early on. I told him about the whole different dads thing too, but he was way less interested in that.

Aleko and I have been staying at the compound since Mom arrived so that she has me nearby if she needs me, and I don't hate it. There's always someone around to talk to, so I'm never alone when Aleko goes off with his brothers to work or deal with club business, unless I want to be. Sometimes Ninja goes with him, sometimes he stays with me, and I love playing with the tiny ball of joy. He's great company.

As of right now, Aleko and Ninja are somewhere outside of town with Bear, Boner, and Bash. I have no idea what they're doing and I'm acutely aware that it's none of my business either.

"I mean, I still stand by the fact that you're the best friend in the world." The mention of what I did doesn't bring any of the emotions I'd consider normal. Instead, I'm impartial. Okay, no, that's a lie. I'm happy about it. I'm glad it happened and feel like the world is a better place.

"I know. I am pretty amazing." We both laugh, then Spence's phone pings, vibrating against the table. He picks it up to unlock it and glance at the message that's come through. "I've gotta go. Steve and I have to get ready for the new pharma convention that'll be in town over the next few days for this new medication. Supposed to combat the seizures or some shit. Like I said. Weird." He downs the rest of his coffee—yeah, Vi is a whizz at those too, but Aleko is refusing to let me have more than one cup of the black life-force a day. Even then, it's decaf. Ugh.

"Which company thinks they have a cure to street drugs then?" Because, essentially, that's what is causing the seizures, the deaths...

As far as the missing bodies from the morgue goes, I have no fucking clue what that's about.

"I think it's called Risus Pharmaceuticals. They're based in New York but they've had office space just outside of town for the last year." Spence picks up his car keys and phone before standing.

"Well, sounds like fun. Hope you and Steve find some time to enjoy yourselves while you're there. I'm assuming y'all are staying at the venue?"

"Yeah. Got my next shift covered too, so I'm ready to just get away for a few days." His smile doesn't quite reach his eyes, but he's clearly eager to leave. I know when he gets in his own head about something he likes to squirrel about it for a while first. I'll save my questions for the next time we speak, because something's up with him. I just don't know what yet.

"Hey, sexy. Where have they been keeping you hidden away?" Rea appears from nowhere, her hand sliding up Spencer's chest.

Now, though, the smile does reach his eyes as we look at each other and burst out laughing.

"Oh, sweet thing. No, thank you." He's gentle as he peels her off him, trying to let her down gently.

"Are you sure? You shouldn't waste your time on this one, handsome. She's got a crazy mom and a—"

All my patience for this particular Khunt disappears in an instant as I step forward and punch her in the face. The satisfying crack makes me smile, and she wails like a banshee, throwing back her arm to return the favor. Obviously, I step out of the way, because I'm not about to stand there and get punched in the face, but it was a redundant move anyway because Kincaid is immediately restraining her with expert finesse.

"Don't touch club members or old ladies without their permission, Khunt. Got it?" Kincaid's words are seething, but they're spoken with such a deadly calm that my respect for her has skyrocketed.

"She fucking punched me!" Rea squirms, but Kincaid's hold is firm so she isn't going anywhere.

"Don't talk shit about my mom, and we won't have a problem." My fists are clenched against my hips, as though I'm ready to go another ten rounds... I'm not. My knuckles ache and I won't risk our baby for this dumb fuck.

Rea isn't moving her hands away from her face, blood is beginning to drip between her fingers, and rather than feeling sorry for what I've done, I smile.

"I'm gonna let you go and you're gonna get the fuck out of here. Okay?" Kincaid's tone remains steady and Rea replies with a light nod before she's set free.

She storms toward the double doors that lead into the room, turning with her palm resting against the glass panel.

"Fucking psycho bitch!" Rea spits, then quickly exits like the fucking coward she is.

Okay, so she was made to leave, but still. She's the only one of the Khunts that I don't vibe with. I never really had any feelings toward her of any kind, I was neutral, so to speak, but now? Well, she can sleep on a bed of rusty knives for all I care.

"That was exciting! I was about to insist she let me take a look at the damage, but she can deal with it herself. Just, wow. Anyway, I've really gotta go, Steve's blowing up my phone. I love you, girl. So much." Spence wraps his arms around me, kissing my forehead before gently patting my stomach.

"Talk to you tomorrow when you arrive? You can give me a tour of your hotel room."

"Absolutely, babe." He winks and starts walking away, but he pauses beside Kincaid, who is now sitting down again at her table with a beer in hand, as though that whole thing with Rea didn't just happen. "Thanks for having my girl's back, Caidy. And that tiger tattoo on your neck is beautiful by the way." She responds by tipping her bottle with a small incline of her head, and Spence nods in response before walking out of the room.

I head back to my seat and nurse my leftover drink. I'm bored.

Working with Spencer was one of the only things I used to look forward to, and now that's all gone. I love that we still get to spend time together but I feel like I'm lacking purpose.

Mom is out of the psych hospital, which means I no longer need to take her to New York for second opinions on her condition. The street racing season is nearly over, after the next race night, there'll be no more official meets until March next year. Which means, I no longer have a goal because this win should set Mom up in a great new house—that's if Aleko even lets me race. And I have no job, no way of working anywhere in this town without being recognized, which means I'm fucking useless.

Ugh. I hate being on a self-destructive spiral. I need to do something. Maybe I can look into the whole smiley-face-drug thing. Ooh. Spencer's convention...

I pick up my cell from the table and type Risus Pharmaceuticals into the search bar. There are thousands of results, so I start at the top, the one that appears to be their official website. It all looks very dull, an average website with basic information, links to articles... I tap on the *scientists* tab because now that I'm down this rabbit hole, I'm curious.

Why do I recognize that dude? Harrison Beaufort. Who are you and why do I recognize you?

I type his name into my search bar and the results popping up seem to point toward him being the CEO of the whole company. There's a local article I click on and it loads to show this Harrison dude outside a huge white house, with tall pillars framing him and the front door. He's standing beside a petite woman wearing a deep-blue knee-length pencil dress, and a fake smile covered in a pretty rouge. The small print says this is his home in Stonebrook Falls. Holy shit, I know where that is!

Where better to get information on this antidote than straight from the horse's mouth.

Shit, there's no way I'm getting off of this compound to speak to a random man about some pills. Kincaid may appear to be enjoying her beer, but she's basically my bodyguard and that woman has the eyes of an eagle.

"Hey, Kincaid, wanna come get some ice cream? I have a huge craving for some mint chocolate chip." I don't, because as with the lack of morning sickness, I seem to be getting through this with no cravings so far, too.

"I can get it for you. It'll be quicker." She stands, picking up her cell and sliding it into the back pocket of her skin-tight black jeans full of rips and tears.

"Okay, I just need to get out of here for a bit. I'm feeling a little claustrophobic, if you get me." Not a total lie.

"I'll grab the keys to one of the club trucks from behind the bar. We go, you stay in the cab with your wig on while I grab the ice cream, then we head straight back." There's no conversation to be had, and I stand, a big smile on my face.

If I can somehow figure out all this pill shit, I'll feel like less of a waste of space. The club is taking such good care of Mom and me, and I know the sheriff's department is on their case about dealing with the problem. Keeping dangerous pills off the streets of Rockford beach is one of the deals SOK and the law have to keep the peace.

"Did someone say ice cream?" Grinder, who is sitting in the far corner of the bar room, lifts his head from his phone with wide eyes as he stands.

"Yeah, taking Psycho's old lady to get some. You wanna come?" Kincaid takes charge, now with the keys in her hand, waving them above her head as we walk through the door without waiting for Grinder to reply.

"Fuck yeah, I do." His shout can be heard, clear as day, and he's behind us as we reach the courtyard and head toward one of the trucks used on race nights.

"Can I drive? I'm kind of a bad passenger." Another lie. I'm racking them up with Kincaid, and I do feel bad about it, but it's for the greater good. "Plus, you had that beer in the bar and I haven't had a drop of alcohol. Obvs." I pat my stomach and laugh.

"Sure. Here." She throws me the keys and slides into the back seat. Grinder hops into the passenger side, and I climb into the driver's side, starting up the engine once we're all settled.

"Boner not coming?" Having fewer club members on this little field trip of mine is ideal, but Grinder and Boner usually go everywhere together.

"He will be as soon as Eden's ready to spill his ballsack before he heads back to the garage."

I don't know why I ever expect anything other than this kind of comment from Grinder, but it makes me laugh and shake my head.

Fifteen minutes into the journey, they're both suspicious, and I'm not going to be able to hide my true intention for much longer.

"We've passed at least three places we could've stopped for ice cream, Mac. Where are we going?" Grinder is first to question my motives.

"Oh, have we?" Let's see how long I can play it dumb for...

"Yeah, we have. Where are we really going?" Kincaid is in there with the next question. She's not pulling any punches or dancing around the subject, she's straight in there. Direct. I like it. But I also don't. Not in this moment, anyway.

"Just to do a bit of research is all. Then we can still get ice cream on the way back." I shrug as if it's no big deal really.

"Research for what, Mac, and where? Because the library is in the other direction and I *know* you've got access to the Internet on your cell." I've never heard Grinder be so serious.

I sigh, heavily. Resigned to the fact that I'm going to have to spill something.

"The smiley pills. There's this scientist guy—"

"I don't think so. Pull over. Psycho would have my fucking nuts for breakfast if he finds out I'm letting you go all rogue investigator. Not on my watch, darlin'."

"Sorry, can't pull over. There are no safe places to stop." I smile smugly and shrug again.

"I swear, Mac. I'll take control of the wheel myself. Don't test me." Angry Grinder is kinda hot. Not as hot as my very own Psycho, of course.

"If you do that, you could cause an accident. Aleko would be much angrier with you if you caused an accident, now, wouldn't he?" I look suggestively down to my stomach, resting a hand against it softly. It's a low move, I know, but I'm determined to figure out what this guy knows, if anything.

"You don't play fair, Mac." Grinder huffs and folds his arms across his chest, his eyes narrowed and looking straight ahead.

"I know. If it helps, I'm sorry?"

"If you were sorry, you'd turn around."

"No can do."

"Didn't think so."

Another thirty minutes later, the small and pointless gates of the house from the picture come into view. It's a large plantation-style home and the surrounding property is beautiful. A lot of greenery and shrubs. I think the back leads out to the river, where they probably have a beautifully picturesque view of the sunrise and sunset every day.

I park the truck a few yards down the road and jump out, heading straight for the gates being manned by some kind of security. Not that they're really keeping anyone out of the property because the waist-height gates are literally only in front of the drive.

Grinder is hot on my heels saying something about recognizing this place, but I'm on a mission.

"Hi, is Harrison Beaufort in? I need to talk to him." My question is directed toward the tallest one. They're both wearing all black, bomber jackets and combats, combined with shit-kicker boots and an earpiece to match.

"No, he's out of town, so you won't be getting in today, little girl. Not even with your little buddies." His face scrunches up in disgust and disdain, and it's only now that I realize this probably wasn't the best idea. I thought I had caught a bone and I wanted to chew on it, but I should regroup and spend more than like, fifteen minutes on the Internet.

"Less of the little, man." Grinder speaks from directly beside me, grabbing his crotch and causing both men to put a hand to their hips. *Shit.*

"I really think we should go, Mac," Grinder whispers in my ear as he tries to turn me around. I definitely concur, if the looks on these guys' faces are anything to go by.

"Okay, thanks." I'll find another way. Easy. No need to bring the big guns out, probably literally in this case. I almost headbutt Grinder's chest, pushing him to move in the direction of the car too, where Kincaid is standing with her arms crossed over her chest and a grim look on her pretty face.

"I'll drive back. Keys." She holds out the palm of her hand as we get closer and I roll my eyes, throwing them over to her. She catches them with impeccable reflexes, and I just know she's the kind of woman that can turn other women gay.

With my palm on the handle of the door, I pause at the clicking sound beside my ear. The freshly cocked gun keeps me frozen in place, my fight leaving me quickly because I don't want to die.

From the corner of my eye, I see the other security guy pushing a gun into Grinder's mouth, and one that appeared from nowhere holding a gun against the back of Kincaid's head.

"Where do you three think you're going?"

Fuck.

Chapter Twenty-One

Aleko

"We've had the cops up our asses because of added traffic to this area, but aside from that, shit's running smoothly." I'm looking around Jed's warehouse, Boner's cousin who took over the shipping and transportation of our merch a few months back. It looks clean and the numbers are impeccable according to Bear who does our books.

"What're you tellin' 'em?" Boner asks as he puts his long-ass hair into a man bun.

"That business is boomin'. What else? I mean, everything looks legit from the outside. I make sure of it." I can't deny this ship is sailing much smoother than the fuckfest down in Myrtle Beach last year.

"Thanks for the tour, man. Appreciate it." Because of the massive influx of stolen parts that we're laundering through here, he's had to build a new storage area, with our help, of course.

Prez will be happy that shit is going right; one less thing to worry about.

"All right, boys, time to head home." We shake hands with Jed before Boner goes in for a shoulder side-hug and I can't hold myself back.

"Is your helmet gonna fit with that bun on your head, Boner?" For my trouble, all I get is a middle finger in response.

"Touchy," I whisper-yell to Bear, who's chuckling, the sound muffled by his ever-growing beard.

"Come on, boys, I've got an old lady waiting for me." Shouts and hollers ring out and instead of making them shut the fuck up, I bask in the feeling of having someone who loves me waiting up for me.

As usual, a somewhat long-distance ride always means one or all of us engage in some kind of one-on-one racing or showing off our wheelie skills. That being said, when we're outside of our county, we try not to fuck up too badly since we don't have our deputy looking out for us as best she can.

Plus, now I have someone to go home to, something to look forward to, so getting pinched by the law for any-fucking-thing isn't on my to-do list.

About halfway down 17, we stop in Jacksonville, where New Bern Highway becomes Rockford Highway, to get gas. Bash fills us up while Boner, Bear, and I go into the station to get drinks.

My phone is out as I wait in line, tapping out a message to my Cherry Pie, making sure she's wet and ready for me.

Me: I'll be home in 45. I want you on our bed. Naked. Legs spread, cunt open and wet.

Depending on her mood, she'll either respond with her usual sass, telling me she takes orders from no man, or she'll make me hard in an instant, telling me she's already wet and waiting. No matter which it is, her responses are always swift.

"That'll be all?"

I look up at the cashier and nod, handing him a fifty to pay for our fill-up and bottle of water.

Looking down, still no response. Little brat is making me wait.

When I look back up, hand out for my change, I notice the cashier's bored expression from seconds ago is gone and in its place is something close to worry or fear.

That's when I realize I'm grinning and I don't need to look in the mirror to know it's not a normal, happy-go-lucky grin. I'm planning a million ways to punish my girl in the very best ways.

But he doesn't know that.

"Thanks," I throw over my shoulder just as Bear and Boner walk up behind me, ready to pay. "See you two outside."

By the time we get home, I'm a one-track mind heading straight to my suite without even rubbing down my beautiful Philia. I can do that later, after I've shown my girl all the ways we can put her hormones to good use. Like orgasms. Lots and lots of brain-altering orgasms.

With Ninja in my hoodie and a spring in my step, I swing open the door to our living space and call out a classic, "Honey, I'm home!" and chuckle at Ninja's beeline for his food. While we were up in New Bern, he'd finished his carrot sticks so I'm guessing he's starving.

My musings are interrupted by the utter silence in our suite. No music or humming, no rustlings of sheets or running water. I can feel that Mackenzie's not here but I check anyway. Room empty. Bathroom empty.

Before worry sets in, I remember that my mother-in-law is only a couple of doors down, and because my little Cherry Pie gets bored real fast, I smile at the thought of her finally spending quality time with the only family member she has left.

Two minutes later, I'm standing in front of Darlene's room knocking three times in quick successions.

"Come in." At her voice, I peek in my head and grin.

"Hey, Darlene. Just wanted to steal my girl away for a little while. Do you min—" As I step into the room, I notice it's empty and it takes my brain a minute to comprehend.

"Oh. She's not here, honey. You know her friend Spencer came by earlier so she went to get a drink downstairs with him." Her smile is warm without a worry etched on her skin. Since she's been here, I've noticed the tension dissipating more and more as the days pass. I can't imagine the kind of fucked up hell she had to live through while in the hospital, but one thing I do know: we'll make it right. There are a few Toxic Rebels that need to feel the wrath of the Psycho, and in due time, they will.

Prez has ordered me and the others to stand down for a few more days so that any kind of attack is planned out and can't be tied to us. He understands my thirst for revenge but he also has no plans on losing yet another member. We're all like sons to him and every loss takes a mental and physical toll on him.

It's the only reason why I'm not going rogue... my respect for him is strong enough to keep my psycho at bay.

For now.

"'Sup, Vi?" Trotting into the clubhouse bar, a quick scan of the place tells me she's not there. No Spencer and definitely no Mackenzie.

"Hey, Psycho, need a drink?" Shaking my head in guise of an answer, I sweep the room with my gaze once more. Brothers are playing pool or darts. Some are getting their dicks wet, others are smoking weed. None of them are hanging out with my girl.

"You seen Mackenzie around?" My question is directed at Violet but my eyes are everywhere as my gut begins to churn. Something's not right, I can feel it in the tightening of my muscles and the immediate acceleration of my heartbeat. My body is already reacting to what my mind is refusing to accept.

"Yeah." My head whips around to look at Vi, hope springing to the forefront as I hang on every word she's about to say. "She was here earlier with her friend, the paramedic, I think?" I nod, trying really fucking hard not to shake the rest of her answer right out of her. "But she left with Grinder and Kincaid about..." Trailing off to look at the clock hanging on the far wall, she nods to herself, and in those mere seconds I've got a million different ways Mackenzie could be in trouble running through my head. "Yeah, about an hour and a half ago. Man, you should've seen her punch Rea in the fucking nose. Brutal and totally badass."

Immediately, my phone is in my hand and Mackenzie's number on my screen. Pressing the green button, I clench my jaw when it goes straight to voicemail. I want to react to the fact my girl is now, apparently, getting into fist fights, but I'm pretty sure that's the least of my worries.

Motherfuckers. I'm going to tear Grinder's balls off one at a time then feed them to him. And fuck, Kincaid may be a prospect, but she's the level headed one of the three. What the fuck was she thinking?

"They say where they were going?" With my eyes still on my phone, I question her at the same time as I pull up Grinder's number. My voice is eerily calm, but only because I'm using all of my fucking energy to keep myself in check. At this rate, it won't be long before I'm losing my ever loving mind.

"Ice cream, I think?" Sucking in a breath, I remind myself that Vi isn't to blame and force a clipped thanks her way. Although none of this is her fault, I want nothing more than to shake her over and over again in hopes of getting more answers out of her. Which is fucking ridiculous, but here we are.

My gut twists again at the sound of Grinder's short and far-from-sweet message on his voicemail.

"Ain't got time for your shit, leave a message." Goddammit, why the fuck did they think it was okay to go into town knowing damn well the Rebels are out? If anyone sees her…

No. I cannot go down that spiral path or I'm going to burn this whole fucking place to the ground.

Practically running down the outside stairs and heading for the garages, I search out Kincaid's number on my phone and realize I don't fucking have it.

Hoops is the first brother I see, half of his body inside a Mercedes where the engine should be. I only know it's him because of his height.

"Who the fuck's got Kincaid's number?" My body is buzzing with rage and worry and probably love but also… when I find her, she's getting a fucking spanking like no other. Pregnant or not, she's gonna have the imprint of my hand on her ass for days.

"Fuck!" I barely register the sound of skull against metal as Hoops eases his way out of the Merc's hood and glares at me. Dude is never angry, he's the most level-headed one among us, but when he's pissed, his face transforms into something close to animalistic.

I should apologize but I'm not in my right mind. I never am when it comes to Mackenzie.

"Kincaid?" This comes from Jonesy, who's jogging up to me with his phone in hand. I'll vote for him to patch in just for this.

"Yeah, call her. Now." It doesn't take a mind reader to know I'm losing my shit, but Jonesy doesn't blink an eye at my fucked up attitude.

"The fuck's wrong with you, Psycho?" I raise a brow at Hoops like my name should answer his fucking question. It's not lost on me that he's my VP and could easily sway a vote to strip me of my patch and kick me out for being an asshole, but I know he wouldn't. Also, I don't really give a fuck right now.

"Mackenzie's missing." Those words out of my mouth and becoming real almost have me puking all over the garage.

"She ain't missing, you fucking idiot. She's with Grinder and Kincaid. They took one of the club trucks and went for ice cream. Jesus fucking Christ. Keep this up and she's gonna bolt." Stunned, I stand there staring at Hoops who never—fucking *never*—talks like this. What the fuck is *his* problem? And yeah, I'm not ignorant to the hypocrisy of this situation and the thoughts running through my mind, but this is Mackenzie we're talking about.

My entire fucking world is out there and I can't reach her. There is no exaggerating. If there's one reason for me to lose my fucking mind, she's it. She's my reason. For everything.

"Oh yeah? Then why the fuck is nobody answering their phones? Grinder practically has it welded to his hand and never fucking turns it off. Explain to me why the fuck it's going to voicemail." Every word out of my mouth rises in pitch as the realization that something is not right seeps into my bones. Into the very fabric of my existence.

"Shit." Hoops knows it, too. Because I'm right. Grinder never lets his phone run out of battery. He never turns it off. Not once, in all the years I've known him, has that fucker ignored my calls. Hell, until today, I had no idea what his voicemail message sounded like.

"Yeah. Shit." All this is happening while Jonesy is calling Kincaid over and over again. Hers is ringing but she's not picking up. This could be normal, if she were on her bike. But she's not. Vi and Hoops both said they'd left in the spare truck.

A quick sweep of my gaze confirms this when I see both bikes sitting exactly where they should be.

"Fuuuuuuuuuck!" The roar that barrels through my lungs, up my throat, and out of my mouth doesn't even sound human to my own ears. It's part animal, part creature, a lot monster.

That's when I realize Bear is there, his huge arms around my shoulders, and I can't understand why the fuck he's holding me down. When did he get here? Oh yeah, we're in the garage... New Bern... He's the treasurer.

I can't exactly form coherent thoughts, everything is coming at me in chopped up intervals.

"Fucking calm down, Psycho." Thrashing around, fighting his hold, I blink, over and over again, desperately trying to clear away the dark edges and red filter of my vision. The fuck is happening to me?

"She's gone, Bear. She's fucking gone. A-fuckin'-gain!" Through the red haze, I see the crowd of brothers and Khunts surrounding us. The sound of Prez's voice is piercing through the ringing in my ears as he speaks, calmly, with Bear.

They're all isolated words. "Calm. Plan. Trailers." But the one word that brings me hyper-focus is the last word I hear. "Rebels."

Without allowing any of the consequences to keep me from getting my girl back I take a step toward the entrance of the garage, only to find myself completely trapped.

"What the actual fuck?!" My words are a feral mixture of a scream and a growl, which is the exact moment Bear gets in my face.

"Had to tie you to the titanium pole so quit ya movin' before you hurt yourself." This time, I do fucking growl. No, it's a snarl and it promises long, drawn-out pain for this treachery.

"If anything happens to her, Bear, I swear to fuck I will—"

"You'll what, Psycho?" Now Prez is in my face and the rage he's letting me see shocks me into brief calm. "Remember the last time you went in half cocked? Remember what happened to you? You wanna do that again and leave your old lady alone? What about ya kid, Psycho? Gonna leave him alone, too?" My lip curls up but I hold it in because it's one thing to go ballistic on Bear, it's a totally different story when it's Prez in my face.

"No."

"No. You're not. Now calm the fuck down and let's do this right." His words have their intended effect because "do this right" doesn't mean, we wait. It means we plan. And we do it now.

Relaxing against the pole, I keep my mind busy by watching the brothers run around gathering their bikes and running to the storage unit where we keep our small arsenal.

"Prez, we don't have the spare truck, Vanessa's home with hers and the vans are loaded with parts for transfer. Want us to take it all out?" Boner's looking at our President for wisdom when Jonesy speaks up.

"My old roommate's got a van. She lives about ten minutes away, I can go grab it and we can use that. It'll be faster, no doubt."

Prez takes a second to think about it before he reacts. "Go."

Jonesy runs, not jogs, to his bike and within less than two minutes, he's gone. Dude is definitely getting my vote for a patch.

"I can help. Unchain me so I can help load." Now that the haze of rage has dissipated enough for me to look at my surroundings, I understand why Prez was so pissed off.

Around me are tools, car and motorcycle parts all over the fucking place. It looks like a tornado came through and we were the epicenter. I don't even remember doing it. How fucked up is that?

"We go in at sundown, so we need to wait another couple of hours. If we go now, the only place we'll end up is six feet under or locked up for life. You get me?" I'm nodding at Prez because my logical brain understands everything he's saying, but my gut? My gut is filled with dread and deep, soul-crushing fear.

They're right though, going in like a maniac will get us absolutely nowhere.

Against every bone in my body and cell in my brain, I clamp my jaw and do as I'm told, knowing damn well that if they let me loose, I'd be on my bike and out of here faster than you can say "Kill those bastards."

The wait was fucking unbearable.

Jonesy came and went with his van. The brothers loaded up on all kinds of weapons, some making my trigger finger itch with the need to spill blood.

No brother was spared, all lined up behind Prez in our normal hierarchy, we rode out in a roar of engines with a blur of dust left in our wake.

The whole way I blocked out images of Mackenzie lying dead in a pool of blood. It's not difficult to imagine it, I've already lived it and it was fucking brutal. Knowing it was fake doesn't erase the pure agony of finding her and being told she was gone.

If anything happens to her tonight, it won't be from a plan she had. It'll be real and there's no fucking way I can live with that. So I push the thoughts back and only concentrate on getting those punks, maybe killing them all.

Rockford and Stonebrook are like sister towns, the line that separates them a natural boundary: The Cape Fear River. The name has never felt more apt.

As we arrive at the Rebel trailer park, we don't aim for stealth, we want them to know we're here and we're not coming in peace or quiet. We're coming in force.

Before I'm even off the bike, Jonesy has the van stopped at the entrance, blocking anyone who'd try to ride off and is running to the back to open up for us.

A crowd of women has already formed as the Rebels run around trying to organize themselves against the raid of pure rage that are the Sons of Khaos as we all load up our weapons.

A semi-automatic in one hand and a baseball bat swinging in the other, Prez, Bear, and I walk up the center of the trailer park as the other brothers start shooting up the trailers. They don't kill the women running around looking for shelter, but they don't miss any of the Rebels trying to get back into their trailers, surely looking for their own guns.

I know exactly where the main recreational trailer is, but the sight of a half-naked chick running out of what used to be Mackenzie's trailer makes my blood boil. How dare they give it out without a second thought? How dare they replace her?

As I walk up the path, I swing my bat over the bikes and let the satisfaction of watching them fall to the ground seep into every breath I take.

"What the fuck do you think you're doing, you fucking psychopath?" There he is. Isaac fucking Moore, president of the Toxic assholes and number one rapist of my girl. Yeah, I want him. I want him so badly I can taste his fucking blood on my tongue as I dream up all the different ways I can make him bleed.

"Where is she?"

"Who the fuck you talkin' about?" I swing at another bike and watch it fall, the satisfying scratch of metal against gravel like a balm to my stoked ire.

"I'm gonna fucking kill you, motherfucker. That was my racing bike." Like a snake coiled to attack, I turn my head toward the source of the voice and recognize that piece of shit, too.

"Come at me, you little cunt. I wanna see you try." I know what I look like, I don't need the reflection of the trailer's window to remind me, yet there it is. Face angled down, eyes up, and a snarl so profound I barely look human anymore. "Tell me, how many times did you get your virgin ass violated in jail?" We know people who know people and we made sure Brick got a little taste of his own medicine. At the thought of what he did to my Cherry, I bring my Beretta level with his forehead and hear at least a dozen guns cocked and loaded all around me. I don't have a death wish for myself, but holy fucking shit, I do have a death wish for him.

Leaning in, I whisper with the false calm of a fucking psychopath.

"Where." The barrel of my gun taps against his forehead, and his arms rise, worry clearly written in his wide, watery eyes. "Is. She?"

Guns go off to my right and the murmured, "Fuck," from Isaac tells me they lost one of their men.

We caught them all off guard, probably celebrating the release of their evil masters and sporting a blood-alcohol level near death. It wasn't too hard to surround them and dominate them.

The repetitive sound of skin against skin is like music to my ears. Someone is getting the fuck beat out of them and I really fucking wish it were me pummeling these fucks.

"Hey, Psycho, she's not here, man!" Sledge, to my right, hollers from one of the trailers, but my eyes never leave Brick's and my gun doesn't drop an inch.

Problem is, the longer we stay here, the greater the risk.

"Take 'em with us. Jonesy, get the van." Prez's words are like invisible strings lifting the corners of my mouth.

"We're going for a little ride, bitches," Bear calls out, handing his bat to Boner before landing a big-ass paw on Isaac's greasy head of hair, gun barrel pressed firmly at his temple.

One of my hands darts out to Brick's throat, my fingers squeezing hard enough for his airways to be cut off. I'm not suffocating him, the dude's neck is unnaturally thick, but I am restricting the flow of oxygen and that's enough for me.

"Come on, you rapist piece of shit. Let's see how you like shit up your ass. Maybe I'll cut off your dick and let you taste it." Anyone who knows me doesn't have to wonder if I'll make good on my threats. They know I never go back on my promises.

Pushing him forward, I revel in the sight of him falling to the ground and having to crawl first before he can get back up. He doesn't go far because my foot is at the small of his back as I kick him, hard, and watch him trip again.

Just as we're passing, I see Hoops pummeling some asshole who looks vaguely familiar but I'm too far gone to care that it might be Cam, the only guy in this place who's not utter dogshit. Crow's got his gun inside some other guy's mouth and he's begging him to piss him off.

Bear and I hand off our prizes to Boner, Jonesy, and Bash so they can handcuff them to the side of the van—wrists raised well above their heads—and slap some duct tape on their mouths.

Before we all get back on our bikes, three trailers simultaneously explode, the shock knocking us back enough to make us unstable on our bikes.

That's when we all see Sledge and Shade running like they're auditioning for *Die Hard, Trailer Parks Gone Wild*. And they say *I'm* the psycho.

Time to bolt, though, 'cause after that, the cops are going to be all over our scent. Besides, I've got the scum of the Earth to interrogate and the love of my life to rescue.

Revving my bike, Bash and Boner come up to me, hands palms up and shit eating grins on their faces.

"Figured Grinder's gonna be pissed he missed this little party so we got him his favorite treat."

Looking down, I shake my head and roll my eyes.

Fucking teeth, bloody and with the roots still attached to one. Of all the shit we need to do, these two knuckleheads think about gifting Grinder enemy teeth for his growing collection.

"Fucking nasty."

Chapter Twenty-Two
Mackenzie

Moonlight is streaming through the high window, making everything in the room bright and visible, but with an eerie darkness to it all at the same time. I wish it didn't.

Grinder is hanging by his wrists from a hook in the ceiling, his white T-shirt covered in his blood and his SOK cut in pieces by his feet. The bruises on his face appeared soon after a couple of men laid into him with bats, telling him it was payback for Preston—whoever that is. True to form, Grinder laughed through it, spitting blood at them at every opportunity, but it was torture to have to lie here beside Kincaid and watch.

Ropes are wrapped around my wrists, high above my head, restraining me against the bed, and another set are wrapped around my ankles and knees to keep them to-gether. Kincaid is tied up in the same way, so we're both completely immobile, on our backs, unable to do a thing to help Grinder, who seems to be experiencing the brunt of the anger these men have for whatever reason.

I think he's either passed out or asleep right now, because his head is hanging and his swollen eyes are closed. I can still see his chest moving, so I know he's alive. Kincaid has been motionless beside me since we woke up here a few hours after trying to leave yesterday afternoon. All I remember is a sharp pain in my skull before we were here, with Grinder being beat on.

I'm not totally stupid, I know this is all my fault. Thinking things through didn't really cross my mind, though...

Okay, yeah, that was stupid.

If only I'd waited, researched way more instead of trying to be clever and go *directly to the source*. What kind of CEO speaks to randos off the street who turn up at their door to ask questions about pills? I should've tried to get a ticket to the convention. At least then it wouldn't have seemed odd for me to want to know things about it.

Future me is so much more prepared, and I stand by the fact that past me is a dick.

The actual reason these men took us is still a mystery, other than the Preston thing which makes no sense to me. I don't even *know* a Preston. However, the guy that cut up Grinder and Kincaid's cuts really hates the Sons of Khaos. They're probably supporters of the Toxic Rebels, considering we're in Stonebrook.

Shit, they got out of jail. Maybe this has something to do with those fuckers?

"Do you have to think so loudly?"

I guess Kincaid is awake.

"Sorry."

Luckily, the guys that took us haven't touched Kincaid or me yet. I'm not far enough along in my pregnancy to feel my little bean move, but I just know they're okay. I'm calling it my new mommy instinct. Other than knocking us out and tying us up, it's just been a whole lot of cursing in our direction. Grinder's the only one covered in blood and bruises... for now.

"Wakey wakey!" The door slams open and in walks a blonde all-American fuckboy. He's even wearing a fucking pale green sweater across his shoulders, tied in a neat little knot with the sleeves at his collar bone, with a Ralph Lauren polo shirt and beige slacks. What makes me smile, though, are the bruises on his face, the sling holding one arm raised, and the broken, swollen lip that looks real painful. "Oh, look. The big bad biker brought me some bitches to play with." He's got some balls for a beat-up dude.

"Why play with the bitches when you could have all this? Too much for ya, Bougie Boy?"

The loud bang from the door must've drawn Grinder back to the land of the living, because he's now grinning like a maniac, bloody teeth and all, thrusting his pelvis as best he can from his position and through what must be a lot of hurt.

"You're the one that pissed everywhere! Not so tough without your boyfriends." The fuckboy sneers at Grinder, but he doesn't make a move to get closer. Useless fucking cowardly ballbag. "Looks like you're traveling with some club sluts, this time. How do their pussies taste?"

He steps toward the bed, beside Kincaid and opposite the side of the room to where Grinder is tied to the ceiling, and runs his finger down Kincaid's cheek.

"Don't answer that, I'll find out for myself soon eno—oh no you don't." The sharp slap across Kincaid's cheek after she tried to bite his finger rings through the room. Which, in itself, is surreal as fuck with the teal-green patterned wallpaper. It's exactly like someone's bedroom, apart from the hooks on the ceiling that appear to have been there for years.

Two of the bodyguards with bats in their hands step into the room, flanking the blonde asshole and making him look tiny in comparison.

I swear, if he had dark hair and blue eyes, it'd be like looking at my brother; his expression is dark, evil, not a hint of humanity in his gaze, which is now directed toward me.

With his backup in tow, the ugly prick prowls around the bed to me, staying a safe distance away from Grinder.

That doesn't stop Grinder from trying to get to him, though. "Come on, Bougie Boy. Leave the girls alone and come play with a real man." He's pulling on the chain attached to the cuffs on his wrists, blowing kisses at the cowardly asshole.

Bougie Boy is a great nickname.

I think my experience with the Rebels over the last few years has made me immune to this crap. My fear levels are nowhere near as high as I know they should be. Back then, I felt helpless until I came up with my escape plan. Now, I have a lot more to lose, but knowing that is helping my thoughts stay strong. Determination can do a lot for a person.

"You're a pretty one. Not all marked up like the freak beside you. Look at all that thick, blonde hair." Bougie dick grips and sharply pulls my hair. It makes me wince, but other than that, I don't react. I know men like this. They thrive on reactions.

"Oh yeah. Pick on the fucking girls because you're too much of a fucking pussy to come near me. They're not in a position to fight back, so it's easy for you. Is it because your mommy didn't love you enough? You didn't get enough hugs from Daddy? Or was it too many hugs from Daddy, huh? Did you take it like a good little boy? Is your little prick too small to please anyone, so you have t—"

Grinder's rant is cut short by a swift punch to his gut from one of the two men in black. Then he laughs. "Oh, poor baby has to get his hired help to do his dirty work."

"Shut the fuck up!" Bougie Boy drops my head and turns. "I think you'd be better off in another room. I know some people who would very much like to spend some time alone in a room with you." He steps right up to Grinder, which seems like a stupid idea to me, even with his gangster version of the Men in Black beside him.

"Is one of those people you, Bougie Boy? You want some special Grinder time?" Before I have time to blink, Grinder jumps, wraps his legs around him, and squeezes tightly. It's a magical sight as the little prick begins squirming and squealing like the pig he is.

"Get him off me!" There's a struggle, then one of the men in black cracks his bat around Grinder's head, rendering him unconscious and slackening his hold.

Kincaid growls beside me, and I agree with the sentiment. With the damage to Grinder's body so far, I'm worried for him. If he doesn't get medical attention soon… I don't want to think about the consequences of that.

"Take him into another room. Tie him to the bed. I'm gonna call Alastair."

"Yes, Sir." The man with facial hair—which seems to be the only way to differentiate the two henchmen—pulls out a set of keys on his belt, attached by a long, retractable string, and undoes Grinder's cuffs.

The fall to the floor won't have helped whatever condition he's in. I can only hope he's as strong as he makes out and he'll be fine. We'll get out of this. We have to.

I'm not delusional, but I am hopeful.

"Karma must be on my side. You know why, girls?"

It's taking everything in me to hold back the responses I have for this man as Grinder is dragged from the room, and if I were still just me, I wouldn't bother. But I'm not just me anymore. I have a beautiful little passenger on board so I need to curb my anger and try to be smart about this.

It seems Kincaid is taking a similar route, staying just as silent beside me—as if I expected anything less.

"Well, your little boyfriend and his pals came to see me about some frigid bitch. Left me with a few presents. *As you can see.*" The last part is spoken through gritted teeth, barely above a growled whisper, and he lifts the arm that's been hanging in the sling this whole time with a wince. "My dad had to hire security so it doesn't happen again. And, of course, when he visits this little shit-heap town, he needs to know he'll be safe in his own home."

I'm trying really hard to not roll my eyes at this guy's privileged, fuckboy life story.

"Would you believe it, though, when one of the stupid fucks rolls up outside my house for a second time with two needy bitches in tow. My guys saw the filthy logo on those jackets and informed me it was fucking Christmas. So here we are." He's moved around the bed again, and he leans down, his nose almost touching Kincaid's.

She remains still, almost frozen, but there's not an ounce of fear there.

"I bet you're a filthy bitch. What gift do I get from you?"

Kincaid's lips twitch, ever so slightly, right before she spits in his face and headbutts him. He rears back in pain, and in rushes the muscle again, bats high in the air, ready for a fight.

"Chain that fucking freak to the ceiling! The fucking cunt broke my nose again. I'll be back in a few hours. If my father calls, find out when his flight is."

He storms from the room, holding his nose, blood pouring from his palm and dripping over the nice cream carpet.

Goatee and Plain Face make quick work of untying Kincaid from the bed, and like freaking Jet Li, she jumps up, kicks one in the back of the knee and punches the other in the throat. Then, she throws herself off the bed, shoulder-first into Goatee, arms fully wrapped around him, and takes him to the floor. My heart rate picks up speed because I'm so fucking proud of her for this, but I'm also not in a position to help. And I really wanna help because Plain Face grabs her short blue hair and rips her head back, pulling her up by it.

A meaty fist lands hard against her cheek, and I hear a distinct crack before she crumples, passed out from the pain most likely. I've had a broken cheekbone before—thanks, Brick—and it's not pleasant in the slightest.

"She's a feisty one. Think the boss'll let us have a play before Alastair comes over?" Goatee is a lecherous prick.

"We could have a go now, while she's passed out." Ugh, Plain Face. I don't know why I thought he was better than that.

They both make hard work of getting Kincaid in a standing position with her arms above her head, shoving her wrists through the same chains Grinder was attached to.

"They're no fun when they're unconscious, man. I like it when they fight back. Look, hard as a fucking rock." Goatee grabs his crotch, and it's nowhere near as endearing as when Grinder or Boner do the same thing. If anything, I want to vomit.

"You're a pliant little thing, aren't you?" Plain Face looks to me as the click of the cuffs closing sounds through the room. Kincaid now looks like Grinder did earlier, minus the swollen face and blood everywhere. It seems these guys didn't want to damage her too much, even though she attacked them.

Goatee has a little cut on the outer corner of his eyebrow, with a thin line of blood trailing down the side of his face. I want to smile at the damage Kincaid caused, but, again, I won't.

If my time with the Rebels taught me anything, it's patience. There will always be a time to strike, I just need to keep my wits about me so I don't miss it.

I'm in survival mode.

And we *will all* survive this.

Chapter Twenty-Three

Aleko

Twelve hours. That's how long she's been gone. *They*'ve been gone. Not only has my old lady vanished into thin air with our little nugget, no doubt unsafe, but my brother and sister are right along with her. Meanwhile, I find myself in the basement of the compound with the two people I hate most in this world.

The fury that boils inside me is all-consuming.

"Ugh!" The whoosh of air that escapes Isaac's mouth with a grunt is barely satisfying anymore. With the amount of times I've punched his gut, I'm pretty sure there's some internal bleeding in there.

One can only hope.

"You know..." I walk away, one finger caressing the bloody blade I used to carve the word "rapist" into their chests, the letters big enough for the visually impaired to heed the warning. "I could never understand in movies why the bad guys don't just give the information they have and avoid getting the shit beat out of them."

Tsking like this question really eats up at me, I turn to face them again.

"Who says we're the bad guys here?" Brick spits out a glob of blood and grins up at me, the red tint smeared across his crooked teeth. "You're the one who came to our fucking home, shot it up, broke our bikes, and fucking kidnapped us. We don't fucking know what you're talking about, asshole."

I stare at him, head cocked, brows furrowed as I try to read his facial cues. I mean, it's not easy, what with the deep-purple circles around both eyes and the swollen nose from one too many beatdowns. No doubt Isaac's broken knee cap means the end of his riding days. Then again, my plans here don't include him ever walking or crawling out of this basement so it's a moot point.

"They talkin' yet?" Bear runs down the basement stairs to join me after taking a break to eat dinner, a plate for me carefully balanced in one hand.

"Brick here says he's a good guy." Bear snickers at my announcement.

"Imagine a world where rapists aren't the scum of the Earth." Taking the aluminum off the plate, he hands it to me, a fork on top. "Sabrina said you needed the protein to deal with these douchebags."

"She... said?" I quirk a brow and Bear just flips his middle finger at me.

"Did Mac ever tell you she begged for it? I ain't no rapist. The bitches I give my dick to *want* it." You'd think I'd fly into a rage and rip his fucking face off with my bare hands, but I don't. I'm embracing Bear's advice to keep my zen because killing them won't get us answers. Also, this is Mackenzie's kill, not mine. She deserves to sink her pain and anger deep into his flesh and make him suffer for taking what didn't belong to him. "Too bad she's dead; her tight little pussy was unforgettable."

Okay, I lied. I mean, sharing is caring and all that, but there are two of them so killing one won't hurt too badly.

My lips pull back from my teeth like I'm a starving dog and blood is my main course as an agonized sound rips from my chest just as I lunge for this dead man walking.

Bear anticipates my move and I swear to fucking God if he weren't my brother in all the ways but blood, I'd rip his head right off his shoulders.

"Get your head on straight, Psycho. We need answers." I hear his words but my ears are ringing and the intensity in my glare is taking up all of my brain power.

"Your death will come slowly and painfully. I even promise to ignore you when you beg me to off you." My words are lethal, so low and gravelly, I'm not sure he even heard me.

"Look, I get it. You get out of jail and the only thing on your mind is revenge. I mean, it's understandable, right?" Pushing his hands into his pockets, Bear plays the good-cop to my bad-cop, except this criminal version has much more at stake.

"See, that's where you two are fucking pussies. Our first thought was partying and getting our dicks wet. Which you fucking interrupted." I scoff at Isaac's poor idea of an alibi.

"You've been out for a week, you fucking prick. Plenty of time to come up with a plan to snatch up my... *our* members." As the immediate haze of bloodthirst begins to wane off, something Brick said earlier starts nagging at me.

"Hey, c'mere." One of my hands darts out and grabs Bear's bicep, dragging him away into the corner of the basement. "He's still talking about Mackenzie like she's dead. Did I imagine that?" Looking over my shoulder, I glare down at the Toxic fuckers with heads bowed in exhaustion and their bloodied bodies starting to stink up the place.

"Yeah, was wondering when you were going to play catch up." It's his turn to weather the storm of my glare, but it rolls off him like a marble down a hill.

"Fuck!" If these assholes aren't responsible for Mackenzie's disappearance then who the fuck is? Not that it matters since either way, there's no chance in Hell they're getting out of here alive... ever. Unlike the American justice system, in this basement, we are judge and jury. And lucky for me, I'm the literal enforcer for our club.

"Hey, Psycho, Bear forgot your drink."

The unmistakable sound of heels coming down the concrete stairs gets both our attention. What the fuck is she doing here?

"Aww, you got us some pussy on the ready? That's mighty nice of y'all." I barely acknowledge Brick's words because if he thinks talking shit about Rea is going to get to me, he clearly knows nothing about any of us.

"Here you go." Rea holds out her arm and the tall glass of brew makes my mouth water with how fresh it looks. When I look up at her, I flinch at the nasty bruising around both eyes and the angry swelling of her nose. Damn, my Cherry Pie did a number on her. I can't wait to find her so she can tell me all about it.

Mumbling a "thanks", I try to get her attention, not sure what I want to say exactly, but she's staring at the bruised up bodies with something close to fear in her eyes. This is why Khunts aren't supposed to be downstairs. Most of them think of the biker life as being great fucking and all around good times. They know we come with a whole lot of danger but they usually try to ignore that little fact.

"Well, well, if it ain't one of our regulars." At Isaac's declaration, Rea's gaze locks on mine and there's no ignoring the consequences she'll have to face with this new revelation. This Khunt's days with SOK are numbered, but that's Prez's decision. Or Vanessa's, which might be even worse for Rea because Prez's old lady does not do well with betrayal.

"I don't know what they're talking about." See, this is where Brick's admission earlier felt weird. Rea? She's lying through her teeth. It's in the way her pupils are dilated and her eyes shifty where Brick was confident in his words.

"We'll deal with you later. Don't fucking go anywhere, you get me?" She nods and practically runs from me. Well, as much as her stilettos will allow, at least.

In the guise of keeping an eye on Rea, I take a minute to get my thoughts in order. They used the word "regular" which could mean a whole bunch of different things.

Regular at their trailer park? That would make her a traitor, or worse, a rat—no offense to Ninja.

Regular user? That would make her a junkie buying drugs from our enemies. Fuck, is she using the same shit that killed Python?

Regular at the races? Was she secretly hanging out with them? This would also make her a rat.

There is a fourth option: regular in their beds, which, in any other circumstance, I wouldn't give a shit about, but we all know what happens during pillow talk, and when it comes to Rea, orgasms tend to be followed by word vomit.

None of those options sound great; each of them will get her kicked out on her ass on a one way bus to nowhere interesting. I'll fucking make sure of it.

"You thinkin' what I'm thinkin'?" Bear and I have the uncanny ability to get each other. Some say we read each other's minds, which is ridiculous because if he could, in fact, get inside my brain, we probably wouldn't be friends.

"Yeah." Turning on my heel just as Rea closes the door leading to the clubhouse, I lower my head and raise my eyes, a dark, foreboding lift to my lips giving every one of my words a menacing touch.

"Smiley faces. That's you, right? It's why you got pinched. Where do you make them?" The idea of having one more reason to torture these bastards is making me shake with anticipation. Add that to the fact that we still aren't any closer to finding Mackenzie and I swear to fuck, I'm gonna need an outlet very fucking soon.

"Yeah, 'cause we know how to make pills. Don't quit ya day job, asshole, you wouldn't make a good cop." I swing around, grabbing the handle of the bat that was leaning against the table and aiming the full force of my weapon of choice at Isaac's gut.

This time, instead of spewing his words, the Toxic prez empties his stomach of whatever is left, spilling stinking yellow bile all over his lap and shoes.

"Wanna try that again, fucker?" Bear's chuckled words turn into repulsed coughs from the smell of our prisoner's upchuck on the concrete and everything else it unfortunately covered. Prospects are gonna hate cleaning this shit up.

"Jesus Christ, you fucking psycho!" Brick is looking at his prez, concern for him written all over his face as he tries to ask him if he's okay.

"You know, people keep calling me that like it's a bad thing." I turn to Bear, making a big show of my annoyance before turning back and asking them both the same fucking question and expecting a better answer. "Now, is your club distributing these fucking pills all over Rockford?" I mean, I can't get any clearer.

"So what if it's us? Ain't like y'all are fucking choir boys." Isaac looks up at me through his lashes, his chin still lowered against his chest. I bet I ruptured something in there. Good.

"I do love to sing." Grabbing the wooden beam above his head, Bear stretches his huge body out, taking up space and making those fuckers understand that their attitude won't do them any favors.

"Yeah, you do. But not as much as you like to relieve rapists of their limbs. Right?" I turn to Bear like I'm making sure I'm not saying something wrong. It's our favorite skit to play to confuse our captives.

"It's how I got my nickname." With a wink to Isaac, Bear takes a step back and leans against the wall, watching them carefully. "It's fascinating just how easily you can dismember humans when you do it just right."

I have to hold in my laughter because none of this shit is true. Except for the singing, maybe. In the shower.

"So, boys. Tell us about these pills. Where you getting 'em from?" Crossing my arms over my chest, I wait and watch as Brick raises a brow at his president before they both shrug and look back at us.

They look like shit. Broken bodies and bruised egos always help with confessions, though, so it works out for the best.

"Look, we distribute a little here and there. Jake was talking with some bigshot businessman who wanted to get them on the streets and, in return, we got a lot of fucking money for it. I can't remember his name, but Jake went to his place once. On Oleander." I have to clamp down my teeth before I lose my fucking mind at Isaac's answers.

"Beau-something. Beauford or whatever." Bear and I both freeze at Brick's little addendum.

Why do I know that fucking name? But first...

"So, I take it you don't fucking give a shit that those pills are killing kids out there?" I'm not expecting an answer but the question needed to be asked.

"Gotta do whatcha gotta do, man. The club ain't running on good pussy and stale beers." At the mention of pussy, all I can see are their hands on Mackenzie and I lose my shit.

In a matter of seconds, the bat is above my head and swinging down on Brick's hand, then Isaac's, in swift succession, and I revel in the sounds of their cries of pain and confusion. It's gonna be hard doing anything with five broken fingers. But again, they won't be needing them in Hell.

"What the fuck, man! We're talking, what the fuck is your problem?" Brick's shock and agony at his shattered digits line every word he throws at me but, guess what? No fucks here.

"It's the least I can do to pay you back for touching what was mine." I make sure to use the past tense because, for now, they don't need to know she's still alive.

"That—that was Jake's doing, man. We didn't have a choice." Pathetic. Okay, I'm done with this. These fuck-heads don't have my girl and besides going off and handing out dangerous pills to college kids, they're just a waste of space.

But I'll keep them for when my Cherry Pie comes home so she can get some closure.

And she *will* come home or else this whole fucking city is going up in flames.

CHAPTER
TWENTY-FOUR
MACKENZIE

"I owe you an apology for all this, Kincaid. If I hadn't—"

"Don't do that. None of us are fucking angels who think everything through before acting on it. So no, you don't owe me an apology. I shouldn't have let you talk me into leaving the compound with you in tow." Kincaid shrugs as best she can with her arms still above her head. "Does that mean I owe *you* an apology?"

"Not even a little." I sigh, shaking my head lightly. My arms ache after being raised and tied to the bedpost for so long, and my legs are beginning to cramp up from lack of mobility.

I'm not sure how long we've been here at this point, but the sun is rising so it's a new day. Aleko will be going crazy not knowing where we are, the rest of the club too. The thought makes me feel a little sick, knowing the pain he'll be going through because I got bored and wanted to play detective.

Will they be able to figure out where we are and come to save us? I really hope so, because as time goes on, things are looking bleak. Grinder's been gone since last night, or the early hours of this morning, whenever the fuck it was they knocked him out and took him.

"The way out of this is to look for opportunities. Okay, Blondie?"

"For a tall, brooding, Amazonian woman with a resting bitch face that could kill a man, you're pretty optimistic."

"I'm still alive, aren't I?" She huffs a laugh and I smile back. She's not wrong.

"So what kind of opportunities are we looking for? Because I doubt they're going to untie me and let me bake a batch of my famous poisoned cookies. That's pretty much my wheelhouse. Or pretending I'm dead, which, ya know, isn't working out so well right now."

Kincaid's eyes widen a little. Well, one of them, the other is a little swollen after Plain Face punched her before leaving the room earlier.

"We are circling back to the poison cookies at some point, because that sounds like a fun story I need to know more about. As for the opportunities, I don't know yet.

You need to be careful though. Psycho will fucking annihilate me if something happens to you or that baby. Just take my lead if anything kicks off, okay?"

"Yeah, okay." Again, she's not wrong.

Before we can say anything else, the door flies open and we're greeted by Goatee.

"Ay ay, the bitches are awake, Shaun."

Plain Face—Shaun—saunters in behind his buddy, a smirk etched across his annoying face.

"While the boss is away, it's time for us to play. Knew there had to be some perks to this fucking job." Shaun approaches me, taking a chunk of my hair and rolling it through his stubby fingers.

"You want the feisty one or the blonde before Preston wakes up? We've got about six hours before Alastair arrives, too. " Goatee approaches Kincaid from behind, far enough away that she can't use her upper body weight to jump up at him.

"Well, this one does have great tits. Even lying down, they're more than a handful." Shaun laughs and it makes my insides want to crawl out of my skin and throw themselves down the toilet as he grabs one of my breasts and squeezes really hard.

I try not to wince, my past experience making that easier than expected.

"But this one, look at that ass, man. Lots to grab onto while you're fucking it raw."

Shaun's run-down of our features is vomit-inducing, and he continues to squeeze my breast and pinch my nipple. Not a hint of arousal overcomes me and I'm close to trying to black this whole thing out... again. I've survived this shit once, lived it for years, until I was gang-raped. That was my final straw. Trying to get through that happening again... I don't know.

There's already a possibility I'm pregnant with my rapist's baby, I jus—my breaths start coming fast and heavy, making me realize that I'm not as over what happened to me as I thought.

"Oh look, she's getting excited. She likes that. Let me have a go." Goatee circles Kincaid and her death-glare toward me, and I'm about to crack, to show them how much I truly hate this, how much it's breaking me inside. I squeeze my eyes shut, trying to center myself to figure a way out of this fucking mess and control my breathing.

"Do you really wanna fuck with the quiet one, boys? Look at her. There's no fight there." Kincaid snaps her teeth together and winks at them, drawing their full attention back to her. Shaun still has a palm gripping my breast, unmoving now, and Goatee pauses halfway through pushing his zipper down.

"I can give you a real good time. You can even keep me restrained if it makes you feel safer." She's swaying her hips from side to side, pushing out her chest and licking her plump lips. Even with a swollen eye, this woman is stunning.

"I do enjoy a challenge." Goatee scoffs.

"You gonna be a good girl for Daddy?" Shaun finally relents and releases his hold on me, putting his hand to his waist and pulling his gun. He steadily walks over to Kincaid, pointing it at her face, and as soon as he's directly in front of her, body to body, he moves the gun to the side of her head and presses it against her skull.

Vomit climbs up my throat, which I swallow back down, as Shaun forces himself on her, grabbing a handful of her short hair and kissing her. I can't see if she's opened up for him or not because his big bald head is in the way.

I hear her groan and she grinds against him as Goatee watches, pulling out his skinny dick and tugging on it. He's right beside me, his cock eye-level, and there's no way I'm able to hide the disgust on my face. My top lip is curled, my brows scrunched, and tears are trying to fight their way out.

First Grinder, and now Kincaid. I know what they're doing here. They're protecting me. Fucking *me,* the one who got us into this mess, and they're putting their own lives and sanity on the line... *for me and my baby.* I owe them everything for this.

"Release her cuffs from the chain, Iain. I want her on all fours. Keep her hands tied though. I don't trust this dirty bitch." Shaun uses his free hand to reach into the back pocket of his pants and pulls out a condom. His other palm is firmly gripped around the handle of his gun, which is still aimed at Kincaid's head as Goatee—Iain—unclips the cuffs around her wrists from the chain on the ceiling.

Shaun rips open the condom packet with his teeth and haphazardly rolls it onto his waiting cock, which is somehow out already, something I clearly missed with everything going on.

My heart is beating so hard against my chest, I'm afraid it's going to burst. Knowing that Kincaid purposefully drew their attention away from me is the only thing keeping me silent, but I desperately want to demand they stop this. Leave her alone. Crawl in a corner and die. Anything other than what is happening toward the foot of the bed.

A meaty hand, Iain's, grips the back of Kincaid's head, pushing her forward, down to the floor. Next, he pulls a small dagger from the inside pocket of his black jacket, and it's clear his intent is to cut open her pants.

Just as the tip of the dagger is plunging down, Kincaid flips her leg around, taking her body—and Iain's—with it. Iain falls into Shaun, knocking the gun from his hand. The palm wrapped around his cock must've been gripped tightly because the condom flies off as his hands are thrown into the air to try and steady himself. It lands on the bedside table with a splat, and I'm just thankful it's far enough away from my face for it to not be a problem.

Faster than I can blink, Kincaid climbs to her knees and rips the dagger from Iain's grasp, straddling and stabbing him in quick succession in several different places across his body. His side, his chest, his neck... it's brutal, blood spraying all over the prettily-decorated room and cream carpet, but I feel calmer watching this than I did moments ago when the men were in control.

The dagger is still in Iain's throat and I notice Shaun scrambling to get up, reaching for the gun by the wall.

"Behind you!" I shout, but there was no need, because Kincaid's a badass.

Still gripping the dagger with both hands due to the cuffs, she swings her leg up and off Iain and leaps toward Shaun, knocking him back on his ass. There's a loud thud when his head hits the baseboard around the bottom of the wall, and Kincaid doesn't waste a second, stabbing him in all the same places as Iain. More blood sprays up the walls and across the floor, and before my heart can begin beating at a normal pace, both men are dead.

Kincaid doesn't waste any time reveling in the power of what she's just done, but she does grab the wad of keys attached to Iain's hip and quickly works on finding the right one to undo her cuffs. Then she turns to me, in all her bloody glory, and moves to untie the ropes around my wrists and ankles.

"I see what you mean about finding opportunities." I laugh awkwardly, rubbing at my sore wrists as I sit up for the first time in too long. "We need to find Grinder and get the fuck out of here."

"Grab the gun. Let's go." Kincaid nods, determination set across her stern expression.

My legs are unsteady as I stand, and my whole body feels weak from lack of sustenance, but I push through, bending to grab the gun because, out of the three of us, my lack of food and water is the least of our problems.

The door is silent as Kincaid slowly opens it, peering out into the hall before pulling it wide for us both to leave. I think we're inside the Beaufort house, but if the conversation I overheard earlier is anything to go by, he's out of state somewhere. Meaning the fuckboy from before is the son. I also overheard parts of a conversation about a pill shipment, which, if you ask me, is suspicious as fuck considering what's been going on lately. I filed that information away for when we get out of here, because it's literally the only good and useful thing to have happened since we left the compound yesterday.

We make our way down a bright, wide corridor and try the first door to the left from the room we just exited. It's an empty bedroom, so we continue to the next door in the far corner. Kincaid twists the golden handle then pushes, and the stench hits us first. The scent of ammonia fills my nostrils, making me double over and vomit as Kincaid enters.

I'm still heaving when she returns with a soaking wet and bloody Grinder, barely able to keep himself up, even being heavily supported by her. Standing, I wipe my mouth with the back of my hand and quickly move to the other side of Grinder, draping his arm across my shoulders and holding on to his waist.

"Hey, you got blood too." He laughs, noting what is likely blood on my face from Kincaid's performance earlier. "We're triplets." Grinder laughs again, but it's cut short by a cough that sounds like he needs medical attention.

"Come on, funny man." Kincaid gets us moving and we walk toward the stairs at the end of the corridor.

So far, so good, but I'm not voicing that out loud. Tempting fate is not on my to-do list.

The three of us are trying to stay as quiet as possible, the occasional grunt or groan the only sound mixing with our shuffling feet as we try to maneuver the stairs.

A squeal cuts through the silence, making us stop on the penultimate step, Kincaid and I turning to look behind us. There's a woman in a rose-gold bathrobe clutching at her chest and staring at us with wide eyes.

"I-I promise, I didn't see anything. I won't... I... shit, you're trying to leave, aren't you? Did Preston and those two Irish goons his dad hired do this to you?" The woman goes from timid and scared to pissed off and determined, real fast.

I nod. "Yeah, if that's the fuckboy's name. Are you safe here? You can come with us."

She smiles sweetly at the gesture, but shakes her head. "I'm exactly where I need to be. The code to get out of the front door without setting off the alarm system is 7869. Now go, quickly!" She shoos us away, and I'm not waiting for fucking Christmas. Kincaid must have the same thought because we're moving with Grinder between us, down to the bottom step.

I wouldn't have thought to input a code to leave the house, so I'm thankful to the glamorous woman at the top of the stairs for the heads up. Kincaid presses the numbers on the keypad, then a low beep sounds and she opens the front door.

We're on the home stretch, a hobbling trio on the path leading away from the house toward the stupidly low gate at the end. It's easier to walk across the grass and around the gate than trying to navigate the latch with Grinder between us. The area is pretty secluded, a lot of trees and shrubs surrounding the property and roadside. We follow the road toward the truck, which our kidnappers didn't have the foresight to get rid of, the stupid fucks.

I don't think any of us have the keys, seeing as everything from our pockets was taken, and I'm actually looking forward to using the hot-wiring skills I learned from the Internet.

Once we arrive at the truck, Kincaid reaches forward and opens the passenger door. It takes us a few minutes, but we manage to get Grinder inside.

"You're going nowhere!"

Fuck.

Preston—Fuckboy—is running toward us, gun in hand, and the world slows down. I'm halfway around the front of the car, ready to climb in the driver's side, and Kincaid is by the passenger door with zero protection. The gun is pointing directly at her, but she doesn't try to run, instead she flips the dagger to grip the tip and throws it in his direction. At the same time, Preston pulls the trigger and I don't think. I just run.

Pain slices through my thigh as I push Kincaid out of the way, the burn driving me to the ground, grazing my bare elbows and forearms as I have the foresight to try and protect my stomach.

The annoying yelling has stopped and I take a moment to look back at Preston, noting that he's lying in the middle of the road with the dagger firmly planted in his shoulder. With a deep, fortifying breath, I pull Kincaid up, adrenaline flowing through every vein in my body.

I'm numb to the pain after hearing Grinder moaning when he tries to get comfortable, my main focus right in this moment is getting us to the Sons of Khaos compound. Leaning heavily against the hood of the truck, I make my way back around to the driver's side and climb in.

I rip the bottom of my shirt, all the way around so it's a long strip of fabric, and I use it to tie around my bleeding thigh, creating a tourniquet of sorts the best I can.

The doors slam closed and I pull the wires from beneath the steering wheel. Connecting them in the correct way is a little more difficult than it is in my shitty old heap, but I manage it and we're soon driving down the highway toward Rockford.

Kincaid is holding onto Grinder, protecting him against every bump in the road and corner we turn, and me? My hands are shaking, my breathing is irregular, concentrating on the road is difficult, and my thigh is stinging so badly it feels like it's burning me from the inside out.

I barely remember the journey or how long it takes, but I'm screeching through the tall gates of the compound and slamming on the brakes by the garage when I see Crow working on a car outside.

Thank fuck, because I'm not sure how much longer my adrenaline is going to keep me going.

Opening the door, I almost fall out, only to be caught by a very concerned and relieved looking Crow.

"Grinder. Help him."

Chapter Twenty-Five

Aleko

"Tell me more about this Beaufort guy." Everyone here is fucking exhausted, me included, except that my need to find Mackenzie is my fuel and I won't rest until she's safe in my arms. Until they're both safe at home.

"Just fucking kill us, man. We don't know shit." Isaac's mouth is so cut up and swollen that his words are garbled and barely understandable. If he thinks I'm going to have an iota of mercy on him, he's more delusional than I thought.

"Nah, I like to play with my food first." The blood from their cuts starts to dry up and the letters spelling out "rapist" are barely visible so I make sure to go deeper this time. I want the truth of who they are to be visible to anyone who sees them down here.

"You're fucking sick. No wonder Mac fucked you." Brick spits blood onto the floor and before he even finishes his thought, I've got the biggest hammer I can find in my hand. "She liked getting her tight little pussy destroyed by the worst of 'em." Bear doesn't have time to stop me. I don't have time to stop myself, even though I know Brick's goading me, forcing me to end his life so he can escape the pain.

I know all this but my body acts beyond my mind's control.

The sound of bone cracking at the side of Brick's skull is the most satisfying of them all. The force of the hit has his head bouncing left, right, then back to the left before he just slouches forward with his eyes closed. Better than anything, his fucking mouth is closed.

"Fuck, man! Did you kill him? Brick! Brick!" Blood is pouring from the wound and seeping down his neck into his filthy shirt. The shape of the hammer left a perfect indent that brings my heart rate back down and soothes my soul for just a second.

Bear steps up and places two fingers to Brick's jugular before rolling his eyes.

"Quit ya cryin', he's still breathing." I can almost taste the disappointment in my best friend's words. Same, brother. Same.

Until, that is, I remember that I still don't fucking know where she is.

Some of the brothers are out canvassing the town, searching for the truck or for them or for any fucking thing. Everyone knows that the first few hours are critical and it's been over sixteen of them.

She could be... fuck. I can't think of that. I won't think of that because if I do, I'll go on a rampage, and right now, I need to stay as clear-headed as I possibly can.

The slamming of a door upstairs has both Bear and I whipping our heads around and waiting to see who's running down the stairs.

"They're here! We've called the doc but they're here. Come on, brother." Crow's announcement takes a second to sink in before I'm running up those wooden stairs like I've got a blue flame lighting up my ass.

"Why the doc? Who's hurt?" I'm screaming as I'm running but that motherfucker doesn't answer me. "Who the fuck is hurt, Crow?"

When we get outside, the scene in front of me catches me off guard. It's impossible to identify any single emotion coursing through me. Fear and worry burn the hottest in my chest but the anger and the soul-searing need for revenge are a close second.

When my eyes land on my Cherry Pie, she's throwing her head back in pain, crying that she wants to know about Grinder and Kincaid.

"I'm fine! Fuck, ouch! Fuck! Take care of Grinder!"

My legs spring to life without me consciously ordering them, running straight for her and grabbing her out of Hoops's arms.

"I got her, I got her." Oh God, she's alive, she's… "Why are you bleeding, Cherry baby? Where are you hurt?" My eyes are darting everywhere, trying to find the source of the blood, and it doesn't take long to land on the homemade tourniquet wrapped around her thigh. "What happened? Who did this to you?" With every question, my voice gets louder, and with every moment of panic, my legs move faster.

"Hey, handsome!" Fuck, she's losing too much blood, it's making her sound drunk and I'm pretty sure she's two strides away from passing out.

"Hey, baby, I need you to stay awake, okay? Just stay with me, baby. That's a fucking order." The smile that graces her lips and the love that sparks in her beautiful blues almost brings me to my knees, but I'm too busy running up the stairs and looking around the rec room for the first available flat surface.

A pool table will have to do.

"Get me blankets and towels and warm water." The girls around scatter away and I have no doubts that they're doing my bidding.

"Oh my god, what happened?" Vanessa's panicked voice cracks a piece of my armor but I shake it off. Mackenzie needs me alert and strong, not losing my shit.

"I don't know. She's got a tourniquet around her thigh so I'm gue—"

"Bullet. Through and through. Just need to stop…" Mackenzie grits her teeth and squeezes her eyes shut, and I imagine a wave of pain is hitting every one of her nerves.

"Shhh, baby. The doc is on his way." The Khunts come running back in as Vanessa grabs the towels and presses against the entry and exit wounds of Mackenzie's thigh to make sure she loses the least amount of blood possible.

I'm no doctor but it doesn't take a genius to know loss of blood, this much of it, isn't good for the baby.

Mackenzie's hand grabs mine, her nails digging deep into my skin, forcing me to stop what I'm doing and focus on her eyes, mouth, eyes, and back to her mouth.

"The baby. I need an ultrasound. Tell the doc to bring the ultrasound. Got it? We need an ultrasound." She repeats her words like she knows my brain needs the time to register the gravity of the situation.

Nodding, I whip out my phone and search for the doc's number. His voice echoes through the space and my panic hitches up a notch hearing that he's already on the road.

"Yeah?"

"Doc, we need an ultrasound." My eyes never leave Mackenzie's as Vanessa places a small towel in the bowl filled with warm water before wringing it out and placing it on her forehead. My girl just stares back and it feels like she's forcing her eyes open by the sheer will of needing to know it's going to be alright.

"One step ahead of you, Psycho. Be there in four minutes." He hangs up and I throw my phone to my left, hoping it'll land somewhere without breaking.

"He's got it, baby. You're going to be fine. Baby will be fine. We're fine, okay? You just stay awake, okay?" She nods but it's like my words reassure her to the point of relaxing, like she can rest for a minute before he shows up.

Then she goes limp and my entire fucking world comes to a halt.

"Mackenzie!" My eyes dart from my girl to Vanessa, whose face just lost two shades of coloring, and back to Mackenzie before I start slapping her cheek and calling out to her. "Don't you fucking sleep, baby. This is not the time for a nap!"

Snapping back to awake, Mackenzie's unfocused gaze searches around her until she finds me and smiles. "Hey." Fuck, I love her so much it's ripping my heart into a thousand jagged shards.

"Hey to you, baby. You can't do that to me, okay? You need to stay awake for me. We need you." Mackenzie nods, takes a deep breath, then looks to Vanessa.

"Grinder? Kincaid?" Fuck, even in this state, she only thinks of others. I don't deserve this woman but that doesn't mean I'm giving her up. Fuck that and fuck the universe if it thinks I'd even consider it.

"Prez and Crow are with Grinder. Boner and Bear, too. Kincaid is giving Hoops and Bash a hard time wanting to know how you're both doing." Apparently, while I was worried about Mackenzie, Jonesy came and whispered an update to Vanessa.

"Okay. Good. Internal bleed... Grinder. Make sure they check." Just as she tries to inhale, the doc's car comes to a screeching halt outside and it takes him another three minutes before he's running inside. Behind him, there's a commotion and Vanessa's truck passes in front of the open door like a bullet.

"What's going on?" My question is directed to the doc as he's running our way.

"Grinder needs the hospital, probably surgery and I can't do anything from here." Panic makes my blood pump at dangerous speeds, but I have to believe he's in good hands because there's no fucking way I'm leaving Mackenzie's side.

"Hey, Mac, I hear you were a hero out there." My head snaps from the doc to Mackenzie and I swear to fuck if she...

"Pfft." My eyes narrow at her one sound answer.

"What did you do, Cherry?" Keeping my voice calm and even is almost torture.

"She jumped in front of a bullet and saved Kincaid from certain death." Now, I don't know what the normal reaction to this news should be, but I can say, without a doubt, that jerking back and yelling at the love of my life is probably the wrong move.

"You did fucking what?" Anyone else would have recoiled at my tone. Hell, Doc and Vanessa froze for a second with what I'm guessing was fear. But Mackenzie? Oh no, that little brat rolls her eyes and smiles.

"You would have done the same." My mouth hangs open with the shock of her words. She's not even denying it or making excuses.

"Yeah, but I'm not fucking pregnant."

"All right, Psycho. I need you to back away so I can work." My narrowed eyes are on Doc now, promising a whole lot of hurt if he utters those words again.

"I'm not going anywhere." Contrary to earlier, my tone is now low. Calm. Deadly.

"Well, instead of stressing us all out, then maybe... shut the fuck up?" I raise a brow at his sudden growth of big balls and almost laugh as he adds, "Please. I'm just going to check on the baby before I take the tourniquet off."

He's right though. I'm not helping. So I move around and stand behind Mackenzie, my palms on both sides of her face, and lean in to place a soft, lingering, kiss on her forehead. "I love you, baby."

Vanessa assists the doc and we all hold our breaths as she plugs in the machine and lifts Mackenzie's shirt before squirting a dollop of gel on her belly.

"Okay, let's see what's going on." The doc's murmur is soft yet it feels like he's yelling at us.

The wand starts at the base of her belly. Nothing. No sound. No heartbeat. Slowly, with his head turned to the monitor, he moves his hand up, then back down, then across to the other side. Still, nothing.

Holy fuck, I'm going to go on a murdering rampage if our baby doesn't survive this.

Mackenzie's hand flies to grab mine resting against her cheek, squeezing the blood flow to a stop. It's impossible to ignore the tears running down the corners of her eyes and I don't even try to hide the ones building in mine.

Then it happens. It's like a herd of horses running through our rec room, but instead of making us jump with surprise and fear, it elicits a collective whoosh of relief.

"There's baby Kastellanos, back turned and balled up into that little corner." When I look up at the screen, my heart swells into a balloon of pride and love. The ball on the screen is tiny, still, but our baby's there and fighting and... living.

"Hey, Peanut." I squeeze Mackenzie's hand, letting her know we're all going to be okay.

"Cherry and Peanut. Perfect combo." My words are whispers against her mouth and no matter what, I know we'll be okay.

"Okay, time to close up this wound. There's no internal damage from what I can tell, but you do need to rest it and I'll leave you with some spare bandages. They will need changing regularly. I'll have my secretary arrange to send some crutches over for you too. Also, your blood pressure is a little high, but that's to be expected considering the circumstances."

I don't know what the doc does because the entirety of my attention is on my Cherry Pie and every single moment I marvel at the strength of her.

"Hey, got an update for Grinder." I didn't bother closing the door to my suite, knowing the doc and Vanessa would be in and out checking on her vitals. As soon as Mackenzie was stable and the doc had taken care of her leg, we made her comfortable in our bed. Ninja hasn't left her side, curling up around her neck and purring every once in a while like he knows the sound is soothing.

Darlene left her room, despite her fear, and hasn't left her daughter's side for the last six hours. Me? Well, my hand is cramping from being in the same position all this time. The thing is, my Cherry's fingers are curled around mine and there's no fucking way I'm pulling away.

Bear's words shake me from the worry and allow me to think of something else.

"How's he doing?" I ask, looking up at my best friend.

"He's touch and go. Broken bones, I can't even list them all. They had to take out his spleen and fix something with his kidney. He's not awake yet but he's stable according to the docs at the hospital. Kincaid is there, too. She got fixed up but her injuries were minor compared to his." I nod at Bear's update but my fury at the fact that someone hurt my people like this is growing exponentially.

"Retaliation is a given." I say the words because I need to hear them. They reassure me, give me purpose.

"Fucking right." We fist bump and both snap our heads to the side at the sound of Mackenzie's scratchy voice.

"No. You need to be smart about this."

I'm on my feet in half a second, peppering her face and lips and hairline and neck with quick, relieved kisses.

"Hey, baby. How are you feeling?" I'm not even pretending to ignore her words because she needs to think about healing, not about bloodshed.

"Listen to me. We overheard so much." She coughs then sighs, her eyes opening and immediately finding mine. "The guards were from New York, Irish fuckers with no moral compass." Visible shivers run down her body, and for a second my mind goes to the deepest, darkest, recesses of my fears.

"Did they..." I can't even finish that phrase because Mackenzie needs me here, calm and sane, not losing my fucking shit.

"No. No, baby. I'm good, I promise." I smile but it doesn't reach my eyes. I'm still going to maim then kill whoever did this. "But they're moving the pills and there's a shipment happening tonight." Her sigh is loud as her shoulders slump. "But I don't know where."

"We'll figure it out, Mac. I'll go see Prez now." Patting her foot with two fingers, Bear winks at my girl then gives me a head lift, letting me know he'll be in touch.

Mackenzie startles when her eyes land on Darlene, who's been quiet this whole time.

"Mom, are you okay?" Fucking hell, she's the one laid out in a bed and she's worried about everyone but herself.

"Oh, sweetheart, I'm fine. Just worried about you, of course." Tears fall down both their cheeks as the reality of what almost happened hits us all like a two-by-four. "But you're fine and the baby is fine so we need to take the win here." Darlene gets to her feet and gives me a wobbly and watery smile. "I'll go grab us something to eat."

I nod, and although I should be the one to bring us food, I can't deny my need to have a few minutes alone with my Cherry pie.

Alone at last, I sit on the bed, careful not to jostle her too much.

"Hey." I bathe in her whisper.

"Hey."

"I love you." And now I drown willingly in her confession.

"I love you more but, Cherry baby, don't you ever fucking do that again."

"Hmm, no way. Getting a real bullet hurts like a motherfucker."

"Yeah, baby, it really does." The back of my fingers run, whisper-soft, from her temple to her jaw and I'm pretty sure she's asleep before I even finish my sentence.

Darlene won't be leaving her side all night which means it's safe for me to join my brothers to church so we can make sense of all the shit we've learned in the last twelve hours.

One thing is clear, I'm not liking the picture this fucking jigsaw puzzle is painting, considering we've got a rich pharmaceutical fucker trying to pull one over on our entire fucking town.

But that's not what has me chomping at the bit. No, my ire comes from knowing that Beaufort and his cronies almost killed the two most important people in my universe and I can't let that go unpunished.

"Considering the circumstances, there's only one thing to do here."

Everyone nods at my words.

"All in favor?" Prez is the first to raise his hand as he asks the question.

"Aye." The decision is unanimous, collective. It's a death warrant and we're about to deliver it on a bloody platter.

Chapter Twenty-Six

Mackenzie

The last few days have been like torture—at times, quite literally. I've been doing everything the doc said, as well as everything Aleko insists upon, which means I haven't moved from this damn bed unless I need to use the bathroom. All my meals have been brought in for me on a tray and I've been given strict instructions—from Aleko—that I'm not to leave the room because the stairs could be too much for me. Everyone is treating me like I'm breakable, conveniently ignoring any conversation about what happened—other than brief updates on Grinder's condition in the hospital—and I haven't even seen Kincaid since we got back.

It's been a little suffocating, but admittedly understandable.

On the plus side, I get to stare at a bare-chested Aleko waiting on me hand and foot in all his rippling abs glory, day in and day out. Only an idiot would complain about that, yet here I am.

"I just wanna get some fresh air. Get out of this damn room. See if any work needs doing on my bike, ya know?"

Spence looks at me with raised brows, then slides his gaze over to my mom sitting on the armchair Bear brought in from her room. During her visits, she feels more comfortable having familiar things around her. "Okay, I know, I know." Sighing, I roll my eyes, but more so with disappointment at myself. I'm being insensitive by moaning about spending a few days in this room, where Mom spent years in hers before we got her out.

"Sweetheart, it's fine. Have you tried talking to him about what's going on in your head?"

I look anywhere other than in Mom's direction, knowing that the questioning and judgy look she does so well is etched across her features.

"We'll take that as a no, shall we, Darlene? How do you expect things to get better if you won't help yourself?"

"Don't gang up on me, Spence. You're supposed to have my back." I faux-frown, scrunching my brows and pursing my lips.

"I've had your back plenty. And I'd be a shitty best friend if I didn't tell you where you were going wrong as well as all the having your back stuff. So... talk to the man. Tell him all the things. Case closed." Spence flips me off, a smug grin stretching across his face.

"That'd be a lot easier if he was into having a conversation, but with everything going on, he just seems a little distant now. Hesitant to come near me almost." I sigh again, and it feels like my entire life could be summed up with that sound alone. Sighing out of exasperation, exhaustion, confusion, all the *-ion*s.

"You gave him a scare, darlin'. To be honest, you gave us all a scare. Just give him some time, he'll come around." Mom latches another hook with the wool in her hands, crocheting something or other.

It made me smile when I first saw her with it, sitting in the corner of the room yesterday afternoon as I woke up. She used to love to crochet, but I never saw her do it once in all the time she was away.

I suppose she's trying her best to deal with this whole thing. It can't be easy, considering what she's been through.

"I'll do my best." I give a tight-lipped smile, aware that it doesn't reach my eyes, but it rarely does these days.

I have everything I thought I could want; Mom's with me, Jake's dead, Aleko's mine, I'm pregnant—aside from the fact it could belong to someone else—and yet I can't seem to find my happy.

"Ladies." Sledge pokes his head through the open doorway to the suite, grinning from ear to ear. "Spencer, nice to see ya again, mate. Thanks for keepin' us updated on Grinder out of visitin' hours." He nods respectfully at Spence, a flicker of pain making his smile falter, but it's back again within a second. Almost as though I imagined it.

I didn't.

Grinder still being critical at the hospital has been playing on my mind on repeat. I can't bear to think about how his brothers are all feeling about it.

"You're welcome." Spence's response is full of sincerity, and again, I'm so thankful he's my best friend.

"Anyway, Psycho sent me up to prep ya." Sledge's attention focuses on Mom next. "Sabrina is in the kitchen and wanted to know if you're ready to show her how to make that special apple pie you told her about."

It still amazes me how these people are helping Mom, despite the whole stabbing Hoops fiasco. They've accepted her effortlessly, and every moment Sabrina spends with her is priceless. She doesn't need to do it, and she's closer to my age than Mom's, but they have a great blossoming friendship. Spending time with Sabrina in the kitchen or coming to visit me are the only times Mom comes out of her room, and it's progress I won't scoff at.

"Yes, please." Mom's face lights up at the suggestion. "I'd really like that." Pushing up from the armchair, she leans over to kiss my forehead and whispers, "Just talk to him." Then, with a wink, she stands to her full five-foot-five-inches and adds, "I'll come by and see you when we're done, darlin'. Bring you a plate."

Sabrina chooses that moment to appear behind Sledge, her bouncy blonde hair practically glistening under the light from the bulb in the center of the ceiling. She signs something, then Mom translates.

"She said, 'I changed my mind and wanted to come and get you myself.'" Mom turns back to Sabrina. "You just didn't want me to stab anyone while left to my own devices." She signs and speaks at the same time, laughing at her clearly not-too-soon joke.

"Mrs. Wilson! You got jokes." With an impressed glint in his eye, Sledge holds out his fist, waiting for Mom to pound it—which she does with glee before slowly making her way out of the room.

Before she disappears from view, she shouts over her shoulder, "I'll see ya in a bit, darlin'."

"And you, Little Miss Trouble…" I don't know why, but that stings a little. "Ninja is still with Bear in the garage office and Psycho will be here in…" Sledge checks his watch. "Ten minutes. Instructions are to put on clothes you won't miss, aaannnnddd…" He pauses again, holding a finger in the air and leaning out of the doorway to reach for something. "Wear these." Holding up a gorgeous pair of black Doc Martens, one with a pink lace, one with blue, Sledge winks, places them on the floor, and turns his back on the room. "Ten minutes!" he announces once again before he's gone.

"I guess I'm going somewhere in ten minutes?" Won't lie, I'm excited. These four walls are driving me slowly insane—which is ironic considering it literally used to be a psychiatric hospital.

"I guess you are. Your Psycho has summoned you."

"Don't do that, Spence. You know it isn't like that. He's just been worried is all." Standing from the bed, I point to the corner closest to me. "Make yourself useful and hand me those crutches, will ya?"

Jumping from his seat, he sweeps them away from where they're leaning on the wall and helps me position myself on them. Fucking hate these things. I carefully hop over to the dresser and open the top drawer, pulling out a pair of black leggings and a black tank-top because it may be October, but it's still hot as fuck. Part of that could be my hormones, but either way, it's too hot for a full shirt. The pain in my thigh is nothing like it has been, but walking on it isn't a good idea yet, because that pain is definitely real and if I want to be released from this prison, I need it to heal properly.

"Hmm. I know. I just—hang on." The vibrations of his phone are insistent, and he answers as soon as he looks at the screen to see who's calling. "Hey, Steve... With Mac... No, not until tomorrow... Okay. I'll be home soon." He sighs heavily, and he'd be a prime candidate for my sighing club. "I've gotta go, babe."

"You'll be home soon? As in, a together home, his home, your home...?"

"That is gonna take more than ten minutes to go over, so get yourself ready for whatever weird ass date your man has planned and we can catch up tomorrow." Spence winks, standing and shoving his cell in the back pocket of his jeans. "I love you." Pulling me in for a hug, he kisses the top of my head.

"Love you right back."

He ruffles my hair as he moves back. "Tomorrow." With a pointed look, he turns and walks out, closing the door behind him.

After our conversation this afternoon, and all my complaints about Aleko basically holding me prisoner, I can understand Spencer's trepidation. But I also know myself, and I'm aware I'm not processing the last few months—years—of my life. It's fine. I'll be fine. Aleko's just trying to keep me and the baby safe.

I showered this morning, so I change out of the lilac sundress Vanessa lent me—because most of my clothes are suddenly too tight—and into the old clothes I was instructed to wear. Rather than wondering why Aleko asked me to dress in clothes I won't miss, I'm just excited that we're going to spend some time together outside of these four walls.

The door opening makes me jump, just as I'm braiding my hair to one side in hopes we're going somewhere on the motorcycle. *Helmet hair is a pain in the ass.* The leggings and tank-top are convenient for wearing beneath a leather riding suit too, so I'm covered on all angles. I may not be able to ride by myself and am totally wishful thinking here, but with no information to go on, I'm happy living in fantasy land.

"You ready, Cherry? I have a gift for you." Aleko's grin stretches all the way across his face as he grips the door, the white stick of his sucker jutting out between his teeth. The way the cross under his eye crinkles still makes my heart skip a beat.

"Just gotta get these boots on… but do I need to get anything else on first?" I tie the band at the bottom of my braid to hold it in and press myself against Aleko's front. My breasts are fucking amazing right now—thank you, pregnancy—and this tank-top gives him the perfect view of my cleavage from his position.

Closing his eyes, a growl sounds from the back of his throat and he tilts his head to the ceiling, wrapping his arms tentatively around my waist.

"If a bullet doesn't kill me, you will."

"You could just put your cock to good use and fuck me instead of treating me like fine china." I raise both my brows, because I still can't do only one and I'm not giving him the opportunity to give me his sexy smirk. Then I step back, favoring my good leg, one hand on my hip, the other leaning against the dresser for support, and make a point of staring directly at said cock, standing proudly to attention beneath his jeans.

He sighs—and we have another member joining the sighing club—steps toward me, and takes me by surprise when he bends slightly to pick me up, bridal style, crutches completely ignored.

Getting married better not be my gift. Not in these clothes. The boots might be cool though…

Gently setting me on the edge of the bed, Aleko kneels, grabbing the boots and sliding them onto my feet. I say sliding, I mean shoving. He loosely ties the laces into bows before placing a kiss on each of my knees, and as he spreads them apart, my heart leaps into my chest and I'm immediately pliable. The next kiss is softer, more tender, just above my belly button, and he rests his palms either side, where a bump is clearly beginning to form.

It's like a glass of cold water is thrown into my face as he stands, holding a hand out to help me up.

Unimpressed, I glare at him, my chest heaving with anticipation for something that didn't come—literally.

"Baby, you're pregnant, have a hole in your thigh, high blood pressure, instructions from the doc to be on bedrest, and a tendency to disappear on me. So you're fucking lucky we're going *anywhere* right now." Aleko links his fingers behind his head, frustration heavy in the air.

"Well, that made it sound like so much fun. No, thanks. I'll keep my lucky, pregnant ass right here and listen to the doc." I scoot up the bed to the pillows, folding my arms across my chest. I wish I had a book. Now would be a great time to become a reader.

"You're being a brat. Come on."

"You're being a dick. No."

"Thought you liked dick?"

"I do when it's pummeling in and out of me and giving me multiple orgasms. Hell, even *one* orgasm would be great at this point!" My eyes are wide, my tone accusing, because as well as treating me like a delicate flower, he's been depriving me of any and all physical touch more sensual than a hug. The constant cherry flavor of his tongue mixed with the hard ball of his piercing is something I'm craving badly, but nope. Closed-mouth kisses are all I've been blessed with.

"You're ruining your own surprise, you know?" Aleko deflates, sitting beside me on the bed, one knee up on the sheets and his other foot on the floor.

"What is it?" Okay, yeah, now I'm being a brat, but tone is everything, and mine is now lighter, with a smile creeping through. I didn't mean to bring up the lack of intimacy thing, over-protective thing, whatever he wants to call it, and I kinda shot myself in the foot by refusing to go—better than getting shot in the thigh, but ya know.

I really do want to get out of here, if only for a short while. Anything is better than nothing.

"Come with me and you'll see." The playful glint is back in his beautiful blues, as well as that spark of danger I find irresistible. Aleko stands, once more holding out a hand for me to take and go with him.

"Okay. But only because I'm bored in here."

"I'll take it." His grin grows wider as I take his hand, linking my plain fingers with his tattooed ones and gently sliding off the bed. He passes me a crutch once I'm standing, favoring my good leg.

"You really not gonna tell me what it is?" I feel like riding motorcycles is a hard no, absolutely not a possibility after that brief conversation, and I'm disappointed. Although, not at all surprised considering the hole in my leg, but now more intrigued than anything.

"Oh, Cherry. Nope." He takes the sucker from his mouth and pushes it against my lips, encouraging me to open up and take it in.

Of course, I do.

Then he miraculously pulls another from an inside pocket on his SOK cut, pushing the clear wrapper off and screwing it up. The wrapper goes back into his pocket and the sucker into his mouth. Okay, so sharing a sucker better not be the extent of our sexy times this evening. I'm so ready, it's unreal. The two months without him weren't even this torturous.

It's pretty quiet around the place today. We don't pass anyone on our way down the stairs or through the halls as I hobble onward with a crutch on one side and Aleko on my other. But there are brothers outside in the main front courtyard and working in the garages by the entrance, they can be seen through the large windows lining the outer corridors.

I quickly realize we're not even going outside when he lifts me, crutch and all, and we begin down yet another flight of stairs, into what is very probably the basement. Yup… the lighting is dull, there is no carpet or tile on the floor; it seems to be made of concrete.

"Have I pissed you off so much you've decided to finish the job yourself?" I laugh because it could very much be the case.

"Don't joke about dying, Cherry. It's not funny yet." He doesn't stop walking, carrying me to a large metal door at the far end of this corridor.

"Will it ever be funny?"

"No." Aleko pauses in front of the door, places me back on my feet as I adjust my crutch, and turns to face me.

"What kind of gift is kept in a basement and makes you look concerned right before we go inside?"

"The kind that I know will set your heart on fire because, Cherry baby, this is something you've wanted for a long time."

"A custom motorcycle with pink and blue trim, custom lighting, and a full Akrapovic exhaust system?" I grin, knowing this isn't what he's talking about because we'd be upstairs and outside if he was.

"Noted. But no. It's Isaac and Brick."

His admission makes my breath catch in my throat.

"I didn't tell you until now because I didn't want to stress you out until you were ready."

I'm choosing to ignore his comment about not wanting to stress me out.

"So behind that door, Isaac and Brick are just hanging out as my gift?" I know that's not the case, but I'm confused as to why I'm here.

"Saved them for you. Here." He reaches behind him, pulls out a gun from his waistband, and hands it to me before opening the door.

Bewildered and a little excited, I hop over the threshold and into the room. The first thing that hits me is the smell. It's so similar to the basement Jake died in—before Aleko made the SOK prospects clean the house from top to bottom.

There, in the center of the room, sit Isaac and Brick. One of these men—or Goblin, who is already in Hell where he belongs—could possibly be the father of my baby. And while the thought kills a little piece of me, I can't and won't get rid of it. This child will know nothing but love.

Both of them are tied to steel-looking chairs, heads hanging low. Brick's covered in blood, a huge wound on his skull, and I'm not entirely sure he's even still alive.

Isaac's face is a patchwork of welts, bruises, and cuts, as is the rest of what I can see of him, and it's clear they've been here for a while.

"Did you have a little fun without me?" The grin creeping across my lips is the most genuine I've felt for days, and that's a little scary.

"Needed somewhere to take my frustration out while you... while you were missing. Want me to wake them up for you?" Aleko's grin matches mine.

"Is Brick still alive? That head wound looks pretty bad."

"What. The. Fuck?" Oh look, Isaac's awake! "Am I dead? Is this Hell?" He struggles against his bindings, and as much as I've dreamed about this moment, about making it last, dragging it out like I did with Jake, I'm ready to try and put what they did behind me.

I mean, not ready enough to let them live, though.

"You fucking died! Did you come back from the dead for more of my cock?" Isaac turns from angry, shocked, and pissed to disgusting cunt real quickly.

Without a word, because this asshole doesn't deserve anything from me, I lift the gun, remove the safety, and fire. The first shot flies past his ear, making him sneer at me, but it's quickly replaced by fear, pain, and anger, when the next two land in his chest. The fourth goes through his cheek, then I fire three bullets into Brick's head and two more at his cock. Just in case he isn't dead yet.

A heavy weight lifts from my shoulders as I watch the blood pour from their wounds, their chests unmoving and their bodies slumped over.

And like a mic drop, I let the now-empty gun clatter against the floor before hopping into the open arms of my sanctuary. Aleko.

There's no pain for me, no flashes of memories. I just feel empty. Numb.

Happy.

I squeal as Aleko scoops me up, lifting me bridal style and pressing a soft kiss against my lips as the clatter of my crutch sounds through the silent room.

"You did good, Cherry. Now let's go wash off the scum."

"My crutch!" Reaching out as if I could possibly grab it from the floor from this height, I give up as soon as he closes the door behind us.

"I'll send someone to bring it up to you." No doubt a poor prospect will get that ungratifying job.

I think I'm still in some kind of shock as he carries me up the stairs to the main building, then up more stairs to the suites. There are splatters of blood across his cheeks and his forehead, and his knuckles are crimson. It's more visible now that we're not in the dingy lighting of the basement, but it doesn't scare me.

"Thank you." The gift he gave me by handing me that gun is something that can never be equaled, and I can tell he knows why I'm thanking him because he practically preens at the gratitude.

We reach his suite and he unlocks the door and walks us inside, carefully placing me at the foot of the bed.

"Strip." The one word is spoken like a command, which I obey eagerly because my man is hot when he's bossy. I'm favoring my good thigh as I undress, and I roll my eyes as Aleko grabs some plastic wrap and comes toward me.

"Can't get this wet." He nods to my now-bare leg and gets to his knees. My pussy is begging to be touched by him, but his fingers barely brush against my skin as he carefully wraps my bandage.

"You're planning on getting *me* wet though, right?"

He chuckles as he stands, throwing the roll of plastic wrap onto the dresser behind him.

"Always." Pressing his clothed body against mine as he kisses me makes my insides flip, eager for more of this, of him. I squeal again when he lifts me and carries me into the bathroom, where he places me on the countertop beside the basin before turning on the shower.

I want to scream from the rooftop that it's finally happening. Orgasm City, here I come—literally.

He gives me my own private strip show, first sliding off his cut and placing it over the top of the door. Next, he reaches for the back of his neck, fisting his black T-shirt and pulling it up and over his head, revealing the tattooed torso I'm obsessed with.

"Like what you see, Cherry?" Aleko wags his brows as he unzips his jeans and slides them down his legs. The fact he's commando beneath them only makes the urge to get on my knees and worship his cock even stronger.

I nod, biting my bottom lip in what I'm hoping is a seductive way. His gaze darkens and his sexy-as-sin grin stretches across his face. Oh yeah, it was seductive alright.

Fully naked, he stalks the few steps toward me and lifts me again, placing me feet first into the far end of the glass shower cubicle. Grabbing the shower head, he quickly rinses me off before putting it back in the holder and picking up the shower gel. He takes his time washing me, rubbing his hands all over me, being careful to avoid my thigh.

"Much better. I can't stand the thought of how close to them you were in there. It took everything in me not to rip their fucking heads off just for breathing the same air as you." Aleko carefully rinses off the suds from my body, encouraging me to turn around and look to the ceiling so he can do my hair. The whole time, I'm leaning on my good leg to prevent the pain from ruining this moment.

I groan as he pushes his fingers into my scalp, massaging shampoo into my hair before rinsing it out. He repeats the motions with conditioner, then I hear him placing the shower head back in the holster just before his hands snake around to my chest, cupping my breasts and lightly pinching my nipples.

Don't get me wrong, Aleko washing my body and hair was great foreplay, but now we're really talking. I groan, leaning my head back against his chest, and he peppers my neck with his soft lips. Sliding his hand down my stomach, he cups my pussy, one finger expertly finding my clit and applying enough pressure to make me twitch at the contact.

His movements are so soft and gentle as he pushes two fingers inside me, at the same time still massaging one of my breasts with the occasional nipple tweak. An orgasm builds slowly from the pit of my stomach, growing and spreading outward to my arms, my legs, the tips of my toes. It explodes through me as he bites down where my shoulder meets my neck, and I buck against him, feeling his hard cock at my back. After waiting what feels like a lifetime for this latest orgasm, my body is still tingling in waves of pleasure as he holds me close, breathing me in, enjoying this moment with me.

I flinch a little when I accidentally put a little pressure on my injured leg, and with it, all hopes of multiple orgasms tonight go down the drain with the rest of the water as he switches off the shower.

"You need to rest that leg, Cherry. We'll change your dressing in the morning." Stepping out of the shower, he grabs the large deep-gray towel from the rail and holds it open for me. "Come on, let's get you dry."

The firmness of his dick makes me lick my lips as I walk into the towel, allowing him to dry me off.

"Is it my turn to play now?" I reach through the gap and grip his thick length, stroking up and down and loving the way Aleko's eyes almost roll into the back of his head at the contact.

"No, baby. You need to rest."

"All I've done is rest. What I want is for you to fuck me like you mean it. Here, in bed, outside, I really don't care where." I'm pouting, I know, but there's nothing I can do about it because this is what he does to me.

He groans, but stops my hand moving with his own, gripping my wrist and lifting my arm, where he kisses my knuckles. "I love you, and you have no idea how much I want to fuck you, but what *we* want and what *you* need are two different things. Come on." He taps my now-dry ass before lifting me once more, one hand beneath my knees, the other at my waist, and carries me into the bedroom.

After brushing my hair, removing the plastic wrap from my thigh, and rubbing a delicious smelling cherry moisturizer into my skin, we get settled in bed and pull up the sheets because it's chilly this evening. Wrapping myself around him, my injured thigh resting on his, I find comfort, however frustrating it is to be so close to him yet feel so far away.

"Next time you send me to Orgasm City, we go together, and we go hard."

He chuckles, the sound vibrating through his chest as he rumbles, "Soon, Cherry, soon."

Chapter Twenty-Seven

Aleko

"Psycho, let's go! Get yer ass up!" The banging and Bear's yelling right outside our suite door would be enough to piss me off, but the fucking siren going off like we've been thrown back to the fifties and the threat of imminent nuclear attack makes me murderous.

"What the hell is that? Are we being bombed?" Cherry is now wide awake, eyes bulging with concern. To be fair, in all the years I've been here, that sound has only gone off whenever we've tested it and there's no fucking way Prez ordered a test at—reaching out to the bedside table as I swing my legs around in a hurry, I tap my phone and look at the time—three-fifteen in the fucking morning? Not even *he* would be that anal about security.

"Hurry the fuck up, man! Let's go!" Shaking off the sleep from my murky brain, I face Mackenzie and place a palm to the side of her face.

"It'll stop in a second, as soon as we're gone. Sleep, okay?" Under my touch, I can feel her head beginning to shake, probably protesting or on the verge of telling me she wants to go with me.

Ain't happening. Not now, not ever.

In one smooth move, I have my jeans over my hips before buckling my belt and grabbing my shoes and socks. I don't bother putting my boxers on but I do grab my sweatshirt that I threw on the back of the chair last night.

"But what if..." Before she even finishes that phrase, I'm in her face, kissing her lips like she's the most precious thing in my world.

Because that's exactly what she is.

"Go back to sleep. Ninja will keep you both company." I know she wants to protest, she needs to fight me on this, but no fucking way. "I have to go."

Making it impossible for her to dress or run after me—not that she could without suffering the physical consequences—I kiss her so quickly I don't have time to actually taste her and I fucking hate it.

"Psycho, goddammit!" Fucking Bear.

With my hand on the knob, I pull the door open and walk out, giving a quick glance and wink to my girl before shutting and locking it.

No doubt I'll get shit for that, too, but I don't fucking care. Her safety is everything.

"The fuck is happening?" Skipping and jumping I try to pull on my boots, not bothering with the laces just yet, as my sweatshirt bunches at the waist; it's hard keeping up with Bear's strides.

"Rocks Off has been attacked. We've got bodies and some of our girls have been raped." My juggling act comes to a stop. Who the fuck would mess with our strip club?

"What the fuck? Who?" One glare from my best friend and I know I'm holding him back. Bear does not like being late.

"Y'all get the low-down?" Crow joins us in the hall, slamming his door as we walk by and keeping up the pace without missing a beat.

"Someone's coming for us so it's time they find us." Bear has his no-nonsense voice going on, the one he uses when he's about to fuck shit up. Goddamn, I love the sound of that voice. It means I don't have to keep my crazy in check.

It takes us no time to reach the garages, suit up, and get the fuck off the property as a unit. Prez is with us and Hoops stays back to make sure no threats are coming to the compound. Wouldn't be the first time someone tried to distract us so we'd leave our home open to attacks.

We learned our lesson years ago, and with my girl in there, I wouldn't be leaving if it meant she was left alone and vulnerable.

As the Enforcer, I ride with Bear, bringing up the rear of our little party on wheels. All of the prospects stayed back at the compound with a few of our members, on Prez's orders. Bash stands guard at my door while Jonesy is at Vanessa's. A couple of the other members are keeping watch with Hoops around the perimeter of the compound.

The ride to Rocks Off is solemn, no doubt everyone is getting into the zone since whoever decided to attack our club was clearly trying to send us a message, or better yet, wanting to meet us head on.

The whole way there, though, the only thing on my mind is Mackenzie and this situation, this dead sea we're wading through. I'm not a fucking idiot; I know she's pissed off about me locking her up like she's some kind of biker fairy-tale princess locked away in the tower, but what the fuck else am I supposed to do?

In the last six months, I have lost her twice to poor decision-making on her part. Don't get me wrong, I'm not stupid enough to actually tell her that, but it doesn't mean I don't have an opinion about it. One day, she'll look back on this time and realize I was doing everything I could think of to keep her safe... from herself *and* others.

It's not like it's easy on me, either. Jesus fucking Christ, every time she walks out of the bathroom naked as the day she was born, my dick makes my jeans shrink two sizes from its need to fuck. Or when she pushes her newly filled out tits in my face, making my mouth water like a fucking fountain, it kills me to hold myself back.

Me, the one nicknamed Psycho, doing everything I can to stay in control. Any other time, I wouldn't wait for her to tease me, I'd fuck her before she even had time to say "Good morning." Or "Good night." Or "Hello." Or any fucking thing.

So, yeah, maybe I'm pissed off, too, because I have to be the adult and I don't do well with delayed gratification. It's fucking hard, man. Impossible, even. But what's the alternative?

Losing her. Losing *them*. Not a fucking chance. I refuse to take any fucking risks when it comes to her. Those days are over. I'll even change her name to Rapunzel Kastellanos if I fucking have to.

All too soon, we arrive at Rocks Off and, sure enough, the parking lot is full with at least a dozen cars sporting the all-too-familiar orange or blue Empire State license plates.

The sight throws me back to my youth when staying in the background and watching my brother rule his world was enough for me. I was young and cocky but I knew my place. I knew Yiannis, no matter that we shared the same blood, wasn't above cutting off my head if it meant he'd stand taller. The last time I was on New York soil, I'd just shot my brother in the head, refusing any association with his sex trafficking business. Had I been older, had more influence and contacts, I would have killed them all and saved every single one of those victims, but until that moment, I hadn't even known about any of it.

"Psycho, Bear, go in through the back and take out anyone who even looks at you the wrong way. These fuckers get no mercy." We grunt our understanding, the nostalgia that kept me up at night after I left the city completely forgotten. It's time to focus on keeping my brothers safe.

Keeping our heads down, we jog to the back of the club where the lack of music tells us everything we need to know. It's not a wild night gone wrong. This is as close to a hostage situation as we can get.

Once we reach the door, we flank either side and look at each other, using sign language we stole from the cop shows on TV to communicate. Between the nod toward the other side of the door and our fingers in a vee—the universal sign for see—we're basically saying, watch your back and let's go, motherfucker.

Mindful of the creaking hinges, we slink inside and pull the door closed without making too much noise. It's not like those assholes up front are whispering, either. Booming voices full of threats and insults are the only things I can hear, all wrapped in the unmistakable dropping of the *R* and elongated vowels.

Fucking New York Irish. I hated those motherfuckers when I lived there, but knowing they hurt, almost raped, one of our prospects and kidnapped my girl? Well, let's just say that someone's gonna die tonight just so I can feel like this whole show wasn't a waste of my precious time.

"Who the fuck do you think you are coming to my fucking town and hurting my people?" At well over six-five, Prez backs down to no one, and although I can't see him from my angle, I wouldn't be surprised if he had a gun to his forehead and still acted like he was in charge of the situation.

"Your two bitches killed my cousins. That's who I think I am, you hick piece of shit." Now, I consider myself to be a reasonable man—okay, maybe reasonable is a stretch—but I have my limits, and insulting my woman is a hard fucking line that motherfucker just crossed.

"Psy—" Bear doesn't finish his protest before I'm walking out from the back, gun raised and eyes wild with murderous intent, heading straight for that big fucker standing way too fucking close to my president.

"You got a problem with my girl, you talk to me about it, you fucking coward." There are about twenty guys in here and every one of them is now pointing their guns right at me, and every one of my brothers is aiming right back at them. From the corner of my eye, I see Prez shaking his head, no doubt sighing his frustration at me. "What's wrong, Paddy? The Italians kicked your sorry asses all over the streets of New Jersey and now you gotta come down here and play with the rurals?" I'll give him fucking rural. In fact, I'm so fucking pissed off that my own accent has made a come-back.

The guy looks vaguely familiar with his typical blond hair veering on red and light colored eyes that scream Irish descent. It's the birthmark running down the side of his nose and halfway up his cheek that gives him away, though. Back in the day, he was just a grunt doing all of the mob's dirty work. I guess now he's the boss of the grunts. What does that make him? King of the minions?

"Well, if it ain't the crazy one who's got no respect for blood." A few chuckles ring out, but instead of answering,

I cock my head to the side and grin, showing all of my teeth like the fucking lunatic I'm rumored to be. My jaw is tight and my lips are so close to a snarl that I have no doubts I look feral.

"Hate to interrupt your little reunion here, but what the fuck do y'all want?" Sounds like Bear's had enough of niceties.

"Well, shit! The South is finally evolving." The guy who clearly gives off the leader vibe among his flock of sheep nods to Bear and that just fucking pisses me off.

"Aww, man. Just when I thought we were gettin' along, you went and played the race card." Bear and I share a mocking look, shrugging like it's no big deal, and before I even turn back around, I'm walking straight into the guy's personal space and placing the barrel of my gun flush against his forehead—Bear right behind me.

"My Prez asked you a fucking question, O'Toole or O'Brien or O'Connor. Did I get one right?" All guns are cocked and loaded but the Irish clown raises his hand, ordering them to hold their fire.

"All right, all right. Enough blood has been shed tonight." Like they weren't the ones doing the honors. "We're just here to send a message and you know what they say about the messenger?" I'm about two seconds away from shooting it in the fucking brain. "Lay off the Beauforts or else what happened here tonight will just be a tiny sampling of what we'll do to this entire fucking town. You get me?"

Gone is the fake humor and relaxed persona. This guy is all business now, and his job is to spill blood.

Pressing my gun to his forehead, I communicate my distaste for his ultimatum without saying a damn word.

"It don't take a fucking genius to see we outgun you by half but, hey, by all means, start a fucking war." He looks straight at me when he speaks, and it's then I know my comment about Marco Mancini's men razing their numbers definitely hit a nerve. Who knows, maybe this is the extent of it. Unfortunately, without the comfort of our other charters having our backs tonight, he's right. We'd all die in seconds flat.

A year ago, I would have taken my chances. Now, though? Not fucking happening. I've got a Cherry and a Peanut who need me alive and kicking.

Like he doesn't have a care in the world, the prick takes a step back and slowly walks out, taking his fucking fanfare along with him.

No one talks until every one of those cars are gone.

When the crunching tires fade into the night, I turn to Prez, lips pressed against my teeth, and seethe. "If Beaufort is arming himself with the Irish mob, that means he's got shit to hide and it has nothing to do with his son beating up a local girl when she refused to suck his cock." My girl was on to something and that thought only makes my fear of her getting hurt amp up to a fucking million.

"Yeah, looks like that kidnapping wasn't random." We all agree at Prez's words when soft cries echo from down the hall. Fuck, these girls need to be seen by our doc or maybe even go to the hospital.

"What're we gonna do about the bodies? We callin' the deputy or are we gonna clean it up ourselves?" Bear's focus on the dead prompts me to look around and from where I stand, I can see at least three. *Fuck.*

"Until our charters get here, we can't take these assholes on by ourselves." Prez looks at me, then Sledge. "You two get the girls to the hospital. Stay close to the truth, we ain't got nothin' to hide but don't mention the Irish." His hard gaze lands on the girls, one by one, before he delivers the message to our club manager, Candi. "Y'all don't know who they were. Not locals, never seen 'em before."

Smart. It's easier to lie when you're close to the truth.

"Prez, I've got a guy in New York who owes me a favor and he happens to be the only one who can easily stop these assholes." Maybe I could even take a trip up to The City and have a sit down with Mancini so he can help us get this scum out of our state.

"Yeah, do that. Can't hurt. Bear, call Shipman. Same story. We got a call that someone attacked our club but we got here too late to know who it was. As the deputy, she'll make sure there's an investigation and keep our noses clean." Good thing she still thinks we're part of the solution and not the problem in this town, or else she'd be a pain in our asses just like the sheriff.

By the time we get our shit done, the sun is firmly taking up space in the sky and I'm fucking exhausted. Most of the girls had minimal cuts and bruises, but the three who were raped will need a fuckload more time to heal the invisible wounds. The whole time Sledge and I were helping the girls, my mind kept wandering back to Mackenzie, to her suffering, her numbness. How I wished I could wipe her slate clean and take all the pain away. And as we step out of the hospital, there's only one thing I want to do... go home and wrap myself around my Cherry Pie.

It's closer to brunch than it is breakfast when we arrive at the compound, but I grab two plates from the kitchen and throw an appreciative wink at Sabrina when she tries to chastise me for running away with the food.

Anxiety boils low in my gut as I approach the suite, knowing damn well Mackenzie is about to rip me a new one, and contrary to popular belief, a good ramming is only enjoyable when there's a fuckload of lube. I suspect I'm getting it dry as a fucking desert today.

The lock is barely disengaged when the door flies open and a blonde-haired, blue-eyed monster is screaming at me for being such a dick.

Not gonna lie, I'm hoping food will distract her. It seems to work pretty well these days.

"What the fuck was that all about, Aleko? You're locking me in now? Did you ever stop and think that maybe my mother would need me? What if she fell? What if I fucking fell? What if I needed to help Spencer? Did you even think that I. Am. Not. Your. Fucking. Prisoner?"

Deep breath in, slow breath out.

"Babe, Bash was on the other side of the door with the key." I'd pat myself on the back for keeping my calm but I'm not sure how long it'll last. My only move is to make sure the smell of breakfast meets her nostrils before she goes in for round two.

"Is that bacon?" Bingo. I love hormones and pregnancy. Placing the plate on the table, I quickly wash my hands and return to the sitting area.

"Yeah, baby. Come." My hand pats my lap as I fall onto the sofa chair like the weight of the world is pressing right down on me. "Eat."

Eyes darting from me—angry and fueled up for a fight—to the plate of deliciousness, I don't miss the longing written across her lips as she licks them like a fucking panther before it attacks.

When she takes her first step forward on her crutches, I know I've won this battle, but the war is far from over.

"I'm still mad at you but also, I'm hungry." As though on cue, her belly rumbles and my grin is so wide, it cracks away all the bullshit from earlier. She's here, sitting on my lap, one arm around my neck, as I take a piece of bacon and place it at the entrance of her delicious mouth.

"Open up, baby. Let me feed you." Fuck, just saying those words gets me hard but I can't... every time I think about ramming my dick deep inside her tight little pussy, I have nightmares of our baby suffocating and dying. Like me fucking his mother will be the death of him.

Intellectually, I fucking know better. I know sex won't hurt him. Hell, the doctor told us it was fine, great, even.

The idea of being the cause of any harm to her makes my blood burn like gasoline inside my veins.

"Aleko?" I blink at the sound of my name.

"Yeah, beautiful?" Fuck, she's so fucking stunning it blinds me.

"If it's gonna take you two hours to give me bacon and pancakes, then I'm gonna go ahead and feed myself." The serious tone in her voice, like I've personally offended her for zoning out there for a second, has a laugh exploding from my lungs.

"You're cute when you're hangry." I tap the tip of her nose and go in for a deep, soulful kiss where I forget that she's pregnant with my baby. That she's prone to making life-threatening decisions. That there are literal mobsters in our town with their guns aimed at us. I forget it all as my tongue sweeps into her mouth and my fear dissipates with every exhale.

All too soon, she pulls back and narrows her eyes at me.

Sliding my fork along the plate, I scoop up some eggs and bring them to her mouth. "As hungry as I am, I have words that you need to hear. You ever lock me up in here again, I promise you that I will walk right off this property with my middle finger high and proud." Right. As if I'd ever let her do that, but I'm not stupid enough to argue, am I? "So, while you fill my tummy, tell me what happened tonight."

And just like that, a cold shower falls over my head as the anxiety returns and every protective bone in my body goes on high alert.

I tell her everything. The Irish, the Beauforts, and their thirst for revenge because they killed the two guards. Every word I say has her eyes growing wider and wider, and to my surprise, her appetite doesn't even take a hit as she finishes off her plate, licking her lips like a little kitten.

"Guess we need to get the shovels ready, huh? I'm not waiting around for them to ambush me." Narrowing my gaze at her, I speak through clenched teeth.

"You're not fucking going anywhere. I'll deal with those fuckers, you stay and heal."

Chapter Twenty-Eight

Mackenzie

There's officially a bump beneath my—Aleko's—T-shirt, and I'm positive I felt a fluttering after I used the bathroom this morning. For probably the first time since I found out I'm pregnant, it's beginning to feel real, and I'm excited to meet our little Peanut.

My problem, though, is my very frustrating, very overbearing, extremely stubborn Psycho.

I honestly don't know how much longer I can make allowances for his overprotective behavior because it feels like it's slowly crushing my soul. Being locked up here on the compound, told what I can and can't do… it's too close to how I lived under the rule of the Toxic Rebels.

It fucking hurts because I love him with every piece of me, but it's like he's keeping himself at a distance. I suppose I can't blame his lack of trust, all things considered, but it doesn't help. I wish I could throttle past-me.

I'm well aware I'm living in a cage of my own making.

The final street race night of the season is due any time now, and I was so looking forward to an opportunity to get out of here—not that I'd be allowed to ride— but a mass text was sent out a few days ago about the race chief being hospitalized, so it's delayed until he's better. I get it, it wouldn't be right to see out the season without him. He's like a silent wall of complete calm and has zero allegiances to any club or individual racer. That's why he's the perfect race chief.

The thing is, now that I can't actually ride, I'm not even eligible to win the overall second place funds. Although, I'm not sure how that would have gone down with the Rebels all being out of jail now. They were the only ones who knew about me being Cain because I was, after all, racing for their club.

Next season, I'll be racing for myself, for the pure enjoyment of the ride, as soon as this little peanut is out of me and the hole in my leg is healed, of course.

Maybe it's a blessing in disguise that it's been delayed.

The Rebels that are left, though, aren't all bad like their ex-president, Isaac, their ex VP, Jake, their ex Enforcer,

Brick, and their ex secretary, Goblin: four dead men, who deserved nothing less than what they received.

The rest of the club were pretty oblivious, or just flat-out ignorant to what was going on with me. Booker and Cameron, the sergeant at arms and the road captain for the Toxic Rebels, were even kinda my friends. Well, acquaintances. They never participated in my beatings, but while they disagreed with the way Isaac handled the club—and me—they never tried to interfere from fear of literal death. I suppose they could be classed as guilty by association.

Again, all future me problems to deal with.

I carefully get out of bed, grab one of my crutches, and use the bathroom, noting how shit my hair looks in the mirror. It's like a bird has crawled up in there to make a nest. I should've braided it before bed last night while it was still wet, but it was so comforting to be held by Aleko that I just didn't bother to think about it.

It's almost nine o'clock and I'm not sure how long Aleko has been gone or when he woke up this morning, but his side of the bed is cold. Throwing on another dress Vanessa gave me—from a large bag of maternity clothes she had for reasons I didn't ask about—I let the material float down to my ankles and take a moment to appreciate the soft fabric and pretty blossom pattern detailing. Then I hop over to the door, because this mama is hungry and I'm not about to wait.

The handle doesn't budge... because it's fucking locked.

Anger bubbles inside me as I bang on the solid wood with my fist. "Let me out!"

"Sorry, Mac. Church." I recognize the voice, it's Bash, and he doesn't sound sorry at all.

"Unlock the door." I lower my tone, less shouty, hopefully making him more pliable.

The sound of him shuffling around and clearing his throat is all I get in response, so I bang on the door some more, alternating my fists because it's beginning to ache.

My crutch falls to the floor as I continue to bang against the door, then I hear him.

"What the ever-loving fuck?" Ah, there he is. My captor.

I hop back from the door as I hear the click of the lock, just before the knob twists and in walks the most infuriating man in the universe. Some of my anger dissipates when Aleko holds up a plate full of pancakes and bacon—it appears that food is my love language these days, *thanks, baby peanut*—but I'm still pissed that he chose to ignore my request to not lock me the fuck in.

"What's with all the noise, Cherry? I thought something was wrong." The tension in his shoulders falls, his frowning face evening out as he realizes I'm okay.

Even though I'm really not.

"Something *is* wrong, Aleko. Why was the door locked? *Again.*" I rest one elbow against the dresser, my thigh aching a little so I'm trying to keep the weight off, and I place my other hand on my hip, raising my eyebrows in question.

"Considering your leg is clearly hurting right now, I'd say it was a good thing." He's struggling to maintain some semblance of calm if the slight twitch to his jaw is anything to go by, and he puts the plate of food down on the dresser by my arm. "Come on, let's sit down and I'll feed you."

Without warning, he scoops me up and walks me over to the bed, sitting me down before grabbing the plate and bringing it over to the bedside table.

"Aleko, I'm too angry to eat right now." Lies, but I'm on this hill. "Why did you lock me in when I asked you not to?" I clench my teeth, my lips tight together, and I'm trying to contain the goddamn tears that have snuck up from nowhere.

"Eat." There's a fork full of pancake and bacon, dripping in syrup, being held by my mouth, and my stomach rumbles but I'm not giving in. This can't happen again.

It may seem like a miniscule thing, but if we can't trust each other, what is there?

"No. Tell me why. I was asleep. Why would you think locking me in this suite is a good thing?" I push away the food, anger taking precedence because he seems to think brushing this under the proverbial rug is going to work again. It may not seem like the biggest deal in the world, but I need this to not happen again.

He takes a deep breath, putting the fork down on the plate and running a hand through his short hair in frustration.

"You've clearly got something to say, so come on. After I explicitly asked you not to lock me in here again... Why. Did. You. Lock. The. Door?" I'm goading him now, trying to get a response that isn't an attempt at subduing me.

"You really wanna know, Cherry?" He looks up at me from where his head is hanging, his elbows resting on his knees, hands clasped together in prayer.

"Yes. I do."

Huffing a laugh, he shakes his head while inhaling deeply, as if he's trying to contain himself when I'm the fucking angry one here.

"When I asked you to trust me with your life, you took it upon yourself to end it. Wh—"

"What has that got to do with locking me in your fucking suite?"

Aleko squints his eyes at my interruption, and all I can see is pain swirling within the depths. This is my doing. I'm hurting him, but I can't seem to stop. I'm on this train and there are apparently no brakes.

"It has fucking everything to do with it, Mackenzie." Pushing the chair back, he stands, both hands flying to his head when Ninja pokes his little nose out from Aleko's hood. He must have been sleeping. "Sorry, buddy." Ninja climbs down his arm and into his waiting palm just as Jonesy knocks on the already open door, waving some mail in the air.

"Mail's here. There's a letter for Scarlet Green. Sledge said that was you, Mac?"

Aleko and I don't move, him standing at the end of the bed, me sitting on it, both of us seething from our interrupted argument.

"Erm, I'll put it on this table." I can see him moving out of the corner of my eye, but my focus is on my angry man.

"Jonesy, take Ninja to the garages to sit with Bear in the office." Every word is spoken to the prospect, but his penetrating stare is still on me.

"Sure thing." He comes further into the room and holds out his palm, which Ninja eagerly jumps onto because Jonesy has picked up a carrot stick from the table for him. "Want me to close the door on my way out?" He disappears from my line of sight and neither of us answer him. "I'll do it anyway."

There are a few minutes of silence as we continue to stare at each other before I huff and shuffle across the bed to stand and get my mail from the table by the door. It can only be from the doctor's office, since that's the only place that I'm expecting anything from as well as the only place that has my new persona's information. The results scare the fuck out of me and I don't want to look, so I'll just hold the envelope for a while.

"Sit the fuck down. Here." He throws the mail onto the bed next to me before I'm fully standing, all one envelope of it. "Oh, she can do as she's told. Well done."

I glare at him as he slow-claps sarcastically when I remain on the bed.

"What the fuck, Aleko?" The envelope is in my hands and I'm tearing open the top without really paying attention to what I'm doing. Adrenaline is coursing through me, making me shake uncontrollably and causing my vision to blur with unshed tears.

"You died, Mackenzie. The—"

"I apologized for that! I thought we—"

"Stop fucking interrupting me, will ya? You died!" His voice is raised, his hands back behind his head, and he looks to the ceiling. "Then I got you back only to fucking lose you again. You nearly got yourself killed for real because you didn't do what I asked, and you didn't just put yourself in danger. Grinder's in the fucking hospital in a coma, Kincaid, well, she's fine, but you nearly died and so did that little baby growing inside of you. Our baby. Could. Have. Died. Mackenzie." When he lowers his head and meets my gaze, it's like a shot to the heart because he's so angry with me. "I did what I had to do to keep you safe. If you left this room without me and fell down those stairs because you can't hold weight on your leg, you could kill yourself and our baby. If I have to lock the damn door to keep you from doing that, then so be it." He holds his arms out to the sides, palms out, as if to say that's the end of this conversation.

It's not.

"I told you I'd leave if you did it again." What he's saying makes complete sense, and I hate that it's all true. It's eating me up inside how stupid I've been, but it's always with good intentions so he should recognize that.

"You're not going fucking anywhere, Cherry. I'll give Bash the key when I'm in New York. You and our baby will be right here when I come back." Aleko slides out a duffle bag from beneath the bed and opens some dresser drawers, pulling out T-shirts and boxers to put in the bag.

I'm gobsmacked at his audacity. Like, really? Before I reply, the letter in my hand catches my attention, the words at the top smashing my heart to pieces like a sledgehammer. An uncontrollable laugh escapes at the same time as the tears that have been brewing for the last ten minutes. Oh, the fucking irony.

"What's so fucking funny?" He pauses in the middle of shoving the spare gun from his dresser into the bag.

"It's not even your fucking baby." As soon as the words leave my mouth, I'm filled with regret and the tears become so heavy I can barely see. Crumpling up the letter, I throw the ball at him and stand, grabbing my other crutch and hobbling into the bathroom where I slam the door.

I'm worthless to him now.

Silence greets me as my tears stop falling, not a sound from the other side of this wall. He's not even trying to get in, to speak to me, to tell me it's all going to be okay. I've fucked it all.

I swallow my pride, because everything he said is true. No secrets, no lies. That was how we were supposed to begin, and I'm the one who's not been following his one rule. I shouldn't have told him the news like that, but I hate it. Shock, anger, confusion, despair... they're all rolling through my body at the information from that letter and I'm not equipped to handle the high emotions.

I got through my life with the Rebels by having a plan. Now, I have nothing.

No plan, no home, no job, I can't ride, I'm a shit mother before the baby's even born, I probably killed the father...

With a stuttered sigh, I grip my crutch and stand from the toilet seat, opening the bathroom door.

Silence greets me.

The balled up paper is still on the floor, where it landed when I threw it at Aleko. It looks untouched.

Sadness begins to overwhelm me, overtaking the anger that has done me zero favors. I have every right to be mad, but so does he, and I wish I could take back the vitriol I attacked him with.

Maybe he hasn't left yet, just maybe...

The knob of the door won't turn... my stomach twists into a thousand knots and I collapse onto the floor, the stabbing ache from my thigh a welcome pain as I sob into my palms.

I made a promise.

Inhaling another stuttered breath, I rub at my eyes and come to a decision.

Probably another fucking stupid one but, at this point, I've got nothing left to lose.

To be continued in the final book of the Trilogy. Psycho Reign: https://geni.us/PsychoReign

THE BLONDE ONE

This is officially our 11th book as a writing duo, and it's still just as fun and amazing to write with my Brunette now as it was when we began. She's a freakin' queen.

The ending to this particular book caused us some rewrites, and then some more rewrites... mainly because we had an original plan, but the characters just weren't vibing. We are believers that our characters lead us where they want to go, what feels natural for them. They literally become a part of us as we're plotting and writing and we want the best for our creations... even though it may not seem like it at the time. We know we've hit you with some doozies, but trust us ;)

There is always a plan, something we meticulously discuss in great detail, combined with a hell of a lot of research into even the most miniscule things.

So, yeah... trust us. This is only the second book in a trilogy, meaning you'll get your happy ending in book 3 <3

Like with raising children: It takes a village, and we would be nowhere without all the wonderful authors and readers who support us. Our PA, Sam O'Neill, our editor, David Michael, our beta and alpha readers, Hilary, Sarah, Zoe, and also Mercedes who has helped with our North Carolina cop research...honestly, the list could go on endlessly! Just, thank you for giving us this opportunity to share our words and worlds.

THE BRUNETTE ONE

Eleven books in two years feels like it sounds...a lot. At the same time, writing with my Blondie makes it all seem effortless and fun. No words can describe the love and respect I hold for my partner in fictional crime. Don't get me wrong, we put in a lot of work in each and every page we write but writing together makes the process less lonely and colossal.

One thing's for sure, finishing up Psycho Love was a whole dang process because the possibilities were endless but as soon as we stopped and really listened to our character voices, we realized our ending was clear from the start.
I know, I know...

That ending was the epitome of frustrating but I feel like you know us by now and we like to feed you our words like they're chocolate covered candy with a healthy dose of addiction so we can keep you coming back to us.

Luckily for you, in September you'll get your HEA and we promise to make you sigh with contentment. But remember, you can't bask in the pleasure if you've never experienced pain and you can't survive the pain without remembering the satisfaction of pure pleasure.

Like Blondie pointed out, these books aren't just written, they're ripped apart and put back together by an entire team of well-meaning, keen-eyed, honest, and motivated book people.

David, who never misses a teaching moment.

Hilary, who catches our plot holes like a jedi master.

Sarah Jones, whose keen eyes and mind smoothes out all of our kinks (living for that pun!)

Mercedes who made sure our NC policing was accurate without once laughing at our complete lack of knowledge.

Sam O'Neill...what the heck would we do without you?

Lie in a puddle of our tears, that's what.

But you all?

You all are the reason we even exist and write in the first place.

Thank you, from the deepest, darkest, pits of our souls for taking a chance on us, for supporting us, for making us feel like a part of your book lives.

Thank you for picking up our books, for reading them, for reviewing them and hopefully...
For loving them.

Stalk Us

Website & Newsletter: www.author-no-one.com
Facebook: https://geni.us/Facebookauthor
Facebook Group: https://geni.us/FierceReaders
Instagram: https://geni.us/Instagramauthor
Goodreads: https://geni.us/Goodreadsauthor
Bookbub: https://www.bookbub.com/profile/n-o-one
YouTube Channel: N.O One @darkromanceauthor htt
ps://geni.us/YouTubeAuthor
Pinterest: https://geni.us/Pinterestauthor
TikTok: https://geni.us/TikTokauthor
Linktree: https://linktr.ee/n.o.one

MORE BOOKS BY N.O. ONE

Dark Romance

The Escort Series (MF)

The Rich One ~ https://geni.us/TheRichOne

The Kinky One ~ https://geni.us/TheKinkyOne

The Filthy One ~ https://geni.us/TheFithyOne

The Broken One ~ https://geni.us/TheBrokenOne

The Almost One ~ https://geni.us/TheAlmostOne

The Forever One ~ https://geni.us/TheForeverOne

KOK (RH)

Kings of Kink ~ https://geni.us/KingsOfKink

The Reapers Mafia Crew Duet (MF)

One Kill ~ https://geni.us/TheReapers1

One Love ~ https://geni.us/TheReapers2

Sons Of Khaos

The Psycho Trilogy (MF)

Psycho Hate ~ https://geni.us/PsychoHate

Psycho Love ~ https://geni.us/PsychoLove

Psycho Reign ~ https://geni.us/PsychoReign

A Night To Remember Auction - Shared World (MF)

Once Upon A Sale ~ https://geni.us/OnceUponASale

Sons Of Khaos

The Standalones

Bear Hunt (MF) ~ https://geni.us/SOKBearHunt

PSYCHO LOVE

Molly Shelby

Dark Romance

Date with the Devil (MF) ~ https://geni.us/DWTD

Eva LeNoir

Contemporary

The UCC SAGA

Disheveled ~ http://amzn.to/2arpbXp

Disarmed ~ http://amzn.to/2myvxNn

Discarded ~ https://amzn.to/2vWTRPf

UCC Boxset ~ https://amzn.to/3ljvepE

Contemporary Standalone

The Wish ~ https://amzn.to/2FTiKQB

Supernatural

Soul Guardians Series

Reprise ~ https://bit.ly/3cT9nPe

OTHER HUDSON INDIE INK AUTHORS

Paranormal Romance/Urban Fantasy

Stephanie Hudson

Tatum Rayne

Xen Randell

Sorcha Dawn

Georgia Seren Mills

Crime/Action

Blake Hudson

Jack Walker

Contemporary Romance

Gemma Weir

Nikki Ashton

Nicky Priest

Jax Knight

N.O. One